GLOWING
AMBITION

JEFFREY PONS

Published by Returnity Books

Identifiers: 979-8-9923626-1-9 (paperback) | 979-8-9923626-2-6 | (hardcover) | 979-8-9923626-0-2 (ebook)

Cover Design by: Alexandre P
Map Design by: Melissa Nash
Interior Formatting by: Pixel Studio

Published by Returnity Books
Visit us at: returnitybooks.com

CONTENTS

Prologue

Chapter 1: All Hands on Deck

Chapter 2: The Valley

Chapter 3: Lamellae

Chapter 4: The Shipwreck

Chapter 5: A Thirst for Knowledge

Chapter 6: Outcry

Chapter 7: Lignicolous

Chapter 8: The Road to Rapture

Chapter 9: A Calculated Endeavor

Chapter 10: Lorea

Chapter 11: To the River

Chapter 12: A Sneaking Suspicion

Chapter 13: Planting the Seed

Chapter 14: Watch Them Grow

Chapter 15: Limbo

Chapter 16: Watering the Garden

Chapter 17: Trouble on the River

Chapter 18: A Tenacious Sprout

Chapter 19: Tidings

Chapter 20: Brittle Ground

Chapter 21: Dark in a Light Place

Chapter 22: Machinations

Chapter 23: Autumn's Eve

Chapter 24: Fall

Chapter 25: Change

About the Author

The Journey Continues

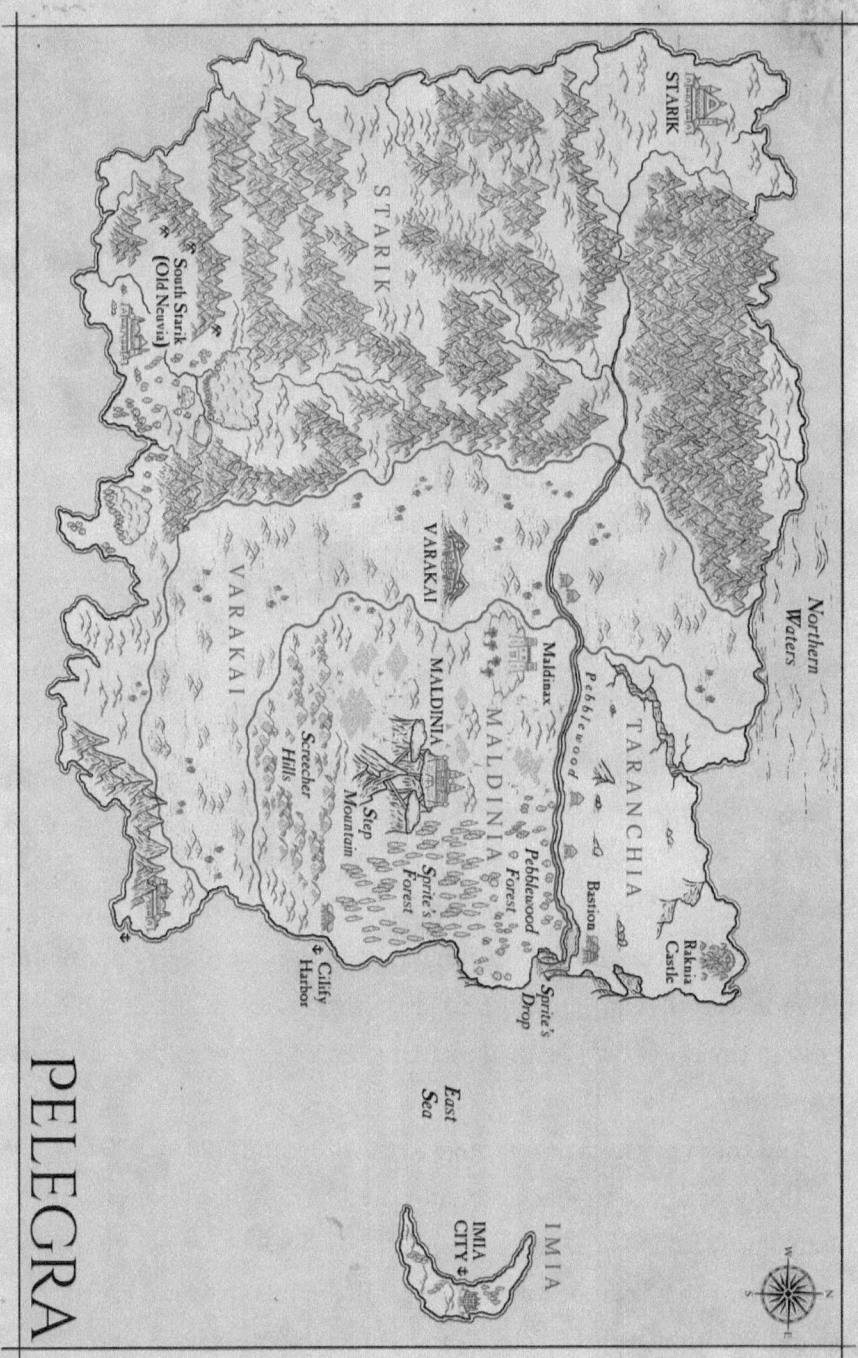

PELEGRA

PROLOGUE

O f all the untold sequences of events, this cluster in particular begins on a dying planet, found within a thriving star system. Of what little that can be said on its last leg, unstable and restless this nameless planet had suffered before its untimely going. A swift shadow left in the wake of a silent fulmination of shards.

An unfortunate fate for the few miserable souls that remained.

Fortunately, not all remained.

Following the key impetus of the planet's ill-fated demise, the collision, fragments of the planet's surface scattered off freely into space. By chance, a number of these orphaned crumbs had found their way into a neighboring ether. One would assume a mighty collision, following a swift yet stuffy ride, would ensure the end of any life dragged along for the endeavor. And yet like a cockroach pressing onward after a clean beheading, so too did the fragments of the lost planet's mycelium network. Spread thin across the neighboring planet of Tethia, the network, in time, not only learned to adapt but coexist with the existing framework.

And the synapse went unobserved for thousands of tides.

That was before a great void had reared its ugly head. Before the Deep Slumber.

Ensuant the dawn of a chance age, inhabitants in a land called Maldinia stumbled their plateaus and vineyards anew. Mere ghosts of their former selves in their chalky impression of a civilized shell, unable to grasp what transpired during the Slumber like the first images on the murky irises of a newborn baby.

They were the souls fortunate to draw breath still. Fifty years older—according to an analysis of trunks found outside Maldinia's altitudinous namesake capital—and no wiser, awoken just in time to witness the bygone fermentation of their loved ones, whilst they lay timeless as minerals embedded.

In their stead lived the Glowers: Night-shining mushrooms with rampant spores like first spring pollen. These mysterious Glowers have since stirred great unrest amongst the peoples of Maldinia, still very much at a loss for a cause of this inexplicable misery of a spell.

In the months that followed, Queen Satina Rook of Maldinia sought to enact a series of ordinances as her peoples recommenced a life beyond. This would include a travel restriction for any who dwell within her acres until a culprit could be found. Accordingly, by law, any places found to possess the Glowers were to be forfeited to the Alchemy Guild for Cleansing.

As for the evicted, a painful if not comforting yearn for the familiar seemed warranted. For others came a sound, a faint sweeping creak of a door opening.

CHAPTER 1

ALL HANDS ON DECK

A skinny-necked council errand boy in an oversized velvet bonnet faced his pointy shoes toward a pavilion tent temporarily occupied by the men of the Nero Company. Following the muggy slog to get into the encampment, the courier permitted himself a moment, reasonably, for a quick tidying, before poking his head inside for an unwelcome *ahem*.

Permitted inside, a rowdy group of men, outfitted in dull gray collarless leather work jackets with shoulder patches of an assortment of colors and stripes, signaled him to the back, to a war table littered with sweaty pressed palms, measuring apparatuses, builders' manuals, and yesterday's news.

At the helm of the war table, well above some flatterer's up stretched neck, a grizzled, red-bearded man answered his busy stare. From his peerless, three-quarter-button silver jacket; to his boxy, war-torn face; to the dwindling particles of rough reddish-graying hair combed ineffectually atop; there was no mistaking it: this was a man who had seen much.

"Good day, Lord Vander," greeted the messenger, his bonnet falling clumsily over his eyes.

The overseer acknowledged him with a grunt. The younger ones—struck nonplussed over a little deference—whispered amongst one another churlishly.

"The queen's council is requesting your presence, my lord. They await a report on the 'well situation.'"

"Right." He looked him over, gliding his thumb up and down the bristles on his chin. "Is that all?" A chilling stare accompanied the messenger as he filed out of the ditch for his next stop.

The overseer unfolded his handkerchief and scanned futilely for a dry spot, before turning to the few faces around the war table. "Where's my lead architect?"

"I haven't seen him in a few days, Marrin," chimed a second builder, in a jacket speckled in metal and wood flakes.

The overseer turned next to a face as wind-slapped as his. A builder with a stunted neck, with a brown hammer stitched upon his shoulder seam. "Selvin?" He began studying the other's solemn expression.

"Didn't even know he was here," he replied. "Barron!" he shouted, answered by a sobering head shake and some rogue laughter.

A thin, long-legged man with a stiff high-standing collar protruding well up his neck exited the far flap with distaste fixed behind a pair of exacting eyes. He had pale white skin, like the rest of the humans of Maldinia, and the Neuvians to whom their forefathers descended, with high-rounded cheekbones and dark brown hair, swept, save for a few rogue strands, to the left. Unlike the brown stripes, to whose ranks the shouting party presided, this one was an architect, soft hands and all, with the skeleton of the company's headquarters stitched upon his left shoulder in red to discern the zenith of his rank.

His posture, once proud and dignified, was withering fast. Indeed, he had seen that look before, that phony air of sympathy, the nervous beard scratching. Meeting the overseer's recessed eyes, he could do little but brace.

"Barron, just the man I was looking for," the overseer started fondly, "*right*, out with it. Look, I know it's not an architect's duty, much less one of my leads, but I am going to need you to pay a little visit to the dam for an assessment. Need someone knowledgeable I can rely on with Devyn and his firsts off-site."

Reticent as ever, he swallowed his repugnance with a crooked smile. "A dam assessment?" he swallowed actually. "Did you ever consider using any second engineers? *Thirds?*"

"I'm afraid there are too few to spare. As you well know the queen needs her war machine back up and running." He shook his head. "I swear, if I hear another, 'wells aren't pumping like they used to,' I'll bloody lose it." He fished a few moments for a laugh, or maybe a smile.

He did not give him the satisfaction of either. Nor a back pat. Not today, nor any day. For today he looked to be one bad errand away from a stabbing spree. He stood there, mumbling, with his eyes fixed to a back now turned. "How's about I fire a ballista at it?"

Beckoned to the map room by the overseer, he and a cartographer with long greasy hair assembled slackly in a bun, gathered around an immersive window into the greater realm. A map; sprawled from one end of the cartographers' makeshift "office" to the other. One that had taken on a color closer to mold during the Passage of Time.

"Look who it is," Barron sighed, sliding a stool beside the cartographer, "Steven Sanguine."

"Never thought I'd see you in here," turned the ranking cartographer, an old friend of his, though more of a stranger today. They nonetheless shared fond grins like they were back at the academy, knee-deep in their old antics.

"Nor you," Barron quipped, leaving the other with an uncomfortable blush.

The overseer smirked. Upon ridding his forehead of sweat, he grunted his way back over to the map. "Now where were we…" As he pressed his swollen finger onto the Lift, his hand trembled. The lead architect noticed, granted, it was sort of hard not to. No doubt the Lift of Residential District Plateau, the most recent but by no means new form of travel in and out of the capital city, was not for the faint of heart. Of course, that is not why the man trembled; not at least according to those who knew him intimately. He trembled because of his stubbornness, for his refusal of treatment.

That brave yet foolish Stare soldier making a run at the former field commander—the same one who dared deliver that fateful axe throw through the tendons in his left shoulder—was still very much dead.

He directed his gaze to his right, to the cusp of the East Valley, pointing and nodding as he traced a path through Sprite's Forest, Leak's Bog, and the Eastern Dam. These once-frequented forest-contiguous locations, amongst several other focal points near and far, had since been marked with inscrutable red markings, courtesy of his old friend.

Barron's feet had since turned sideways, along with his focus. For when considering both the palpable lapse in time since the area's last iteration and the impending admonishment that awaited the overseer in the throne room, his expedited suggestion of route would come of even littler surprise than his original ask.

Following a few precautionary remarks regarding the potential dangers afoot, the overseer hobbled his way back towards the fold, crudely swiping a glob of sweat from somewhere beneath his neckline on his way. By now Steven's eyebrows were half-cocked: a predictable response, Barron thought, following a few recent rumors of vrogelnastia sightings on the horse peddlers' path.

"You are entering uncharted territory now, gentlemen. If I wasn't in such a rush, I would help you find a few extra bodies to accompany you. I leave that up to you now, Barron. You're in charge of this venture. If you must, hire a few escorts. Cheap ones too, yeah?" He reached his hand onto the cartographer's left shoulder, effectively covering the half-century-old ale stain upon the fabric of his green stripe. "Best mark down any Glowers, Steven. I know, I know, believe me, not your responsibility. Unfortunately, these are the queen's orders, and the last thing we need right now is an inquiry," he said, shuttering.

"I'll try to buy us as much time as I possibly can," he whispered to Barron, answered by an apprehensive nod. "We just need to know if the dam is the cause of this water shortage."

"I'll get to the bottom of it, sir. This time." In the common room, he let loose a yawn, expanding his arms wide (in actuality, scoping out for willing help). The good news was he didn't have to clarify his purpose today. He knew the lot of them were already listening.

Yet despite his authority, the residuals at the war table had miraculously lost their appetite for aimless prattle. Not a single one of them had come forth to volunteer their knack or muscle, nor even a little company.

Overwhelmed by the monotony of travel, and the dreaded preparations required for a trek, he stood awkwardly beside the drink stand, hollow as the late spring air. At least judging by the muddy assembly of boots around the last remaining pitcher, yesterday's headline, A CURSE UPON THE WELLS, may as well have been today's. The gnats surely relished in all the sweat.

"Savoring Marrin's pond water?" he eventually spoke to one man, inadvertently causing many men to freeze with their mugs eye-level.

"Mhm," mumbled back the first cartographer, with his cheeks wide.

"Any luck on your end?"

Steven shook his head, wincing as his molar struck a pebble. "Daemon's busy resurveying the South Valley as we speak. How about you? Any spare architects dawdling around?"

"Dawdling," Barron scoffed, lifting the tent flap wide for his old friend.

Hailed by a band of fiending insects outside, a late afternoon sun shied from the cusp of the elapsed dig site. "You mean bridging bridges?" he sighed.

Beyond the moss, on the fallow surface of a plateau, a clay-red hue was cast. A reflection upon its foundation; the *glow*, they called it. The *glow* was especially apparent here, on the holey surface of Loarea Plateau, where healthy grass only seldom grew. "I am actually looking forward to returning to the East Valley again," said Steven, "some fresh air, little inspiration for my art—"

"Here we are, *Post Slumber*, in a new age," interrupted Barron, deaf to all else, "and Marrin's still agreeing to do the realm's grunt work. These are the same bridges, roads, and dams that our company built with our own two hands. This will never not be unbecoming."

"But at least they're paying us, right? I don't see anyone else lining up for work these days."

"And who's fault is that?" he snapped, as though activated by the man's comment. "We should have never agreed to take on this upkeep in the first place. The Foundation Years are over with, yet here we are." The cartographer stumbled upon a break in the main road, causing the other an unexpected laugh.

A year the architect's senior, he was an undoubtedly awkward fellow. He had a big oval-shaped head, and a slight waddle to his walk to compliment his lanky frame. Not to mention blessed with an unflattering belly that fled freely away from an untucked, unwashed tunic. Despite his apparent physical shortcomings, the gaps between the cobbles were quite pronounced, reserved, like the rest of the unused land within Maldinia's production sector, for weeds. And not just weeds but stubs: stringy ones that reeked of wet week's old onion.

"I would really prefer not to be easy prey on our trek," he said to Steven, "tell me, where can we find a few sellswords desperate enough to want to make a trek through Leak's Bog with us?"

"I know a place," he replied, pressing eastward upon the desolate surface of the plateau with a newfound life force behind him. "There's a few we could try."

He raised an eyebrow. "Places? You mean taverns, don't you? Let me guess, somewhere in the West Market, right?"

"You wanted cheap, right?"

"No-no, Marrin wants cheap. Me, I want someone who won't steal from me on the occasional call to nature."

The men quieted as they approached a splintered signpost outside their barred workshop. Notwithstanding the guild's blatant absence, and the stacks of hay bales that now covered the main path leading to the oblong brick factory, they couldn't help but reminisce of its former state. Easier said than done, of course, the once pristine stone pathway and steps, chasing beneath the marble pillars of one grand entryway, now marred in unruly tufts of ivy; and so too its brick façade and roof, and the garden which once wholly surrounded the exterior like a moat.

A lone peacekeeper was keeping watch, daring the late-spring humidity a bit too casually in his steel shell, enforcing the Alchemy Guild's now infamous *Extraction Underway* sign from the tallgrass in which it now crudely stood.

Steven threw his elbows onto the haystack. "Extraction underway? My, and what progress too!" He clapped, answered by a look of quiet contempt. "*Brute.*"

"The Law of Cleansing," he continued, "nowhere did it say my betrothed and I would still be living in the isle of tents, nor working from a buried mine." He sighed. "For all the favors we've done for the queen you would think we would be the first in line."

"Well, Steven, it all started way back when," said Barron, "when the good king named a seasoned sycophant his successor." He shook his head disapprovingly. "Just wait until a certain someone retires—you'll see, things will change. Leastways round here."

"Ah," simpered the cartographer, "still on your quest for overseer I see. I seem to remember you downplaying it as nothing more than a 'logistical nightmare' last time we spoke of it."

"My sentiments about the role haven't changed. As for my father's foolish, shortsighted choice in a successor: I was young then, fresh out of the academy." His lips were still open as if he had something more to say. For Steven knew not that the late overseer's mind was already part way gone by then to the infection. Few did.

Away from the elapsed mines and overgrown factories the altitude only amplified. Valley, canyon, sea, these features were a mere fable from the great vantage of the Market District-Loarea District Connector, where just a faint glimpse of one of its far-reaching stone supports, gone into the impenetrable layer of clouds beneath the capital city, shall send even the hardiest of hearts to plummet.

The wind's burden shooed the two and the rest of its commuters against their nearest ledge.

A spring gale as it turns out was far less daunting than a winter's. Upwards, however, unto the great Market District Plateau up high, every step was as daunting as the last. It should come as no surprise that the carriage lane had been the preferred mode of travel upon the main connectors; though a horse or screecher was indeed mandatory for entry onto its steep and windy two-lane pass.

Eventually, a verdant window broke in the fog, staged like a climbing altar upon the unforgivable green faces of the plateau. Come six hundred steps higher, its escarped surface.

Life in the sky. It was Maldinia's most acclaimed feature. Be it as it may, a life not apt for all of its peoples. Nor an attainable one at that. As for its eleven thousand city-dwellers, it was appealing enough to furnish the labyrinth of the Inner City markets; before that, however, its affluent Outer Circle, to which their feet now firmly embraced; and there was also the place far beneath the cobblestone—the tunnels—where the Tumsib folk had dwelled long since before the Neuvians staked their claim.

Unlike the former, there were cobblestone slabs plopped extensively across Market's surface to mask the grassy plain beneath. This however idyllic and civilized, would not stop the stubborn weeds nor fledgling trees from sprouting through. Steven squinted ahead, where the *glow* rescinded behind a tall castle.

"Is that Darren?" he inquired with eyes wide. "That is Darren!"

Following a swift jab to the gut, he stopped.

"*What*? You saw him too? We need some extra bodies, don't we? Else we'll make for 'easy prey.'"

"So be it then, I shall die with standards."

By omission, he laughed. "It's been fifty-two years since that Gromula Day mishap. Still haven't forgiven him?"

He glared at him, ridding him of his goofy grin. "How could I forget being banned from that Sib's alcove? I'll never forget that awful look he gave me when he found out one of his guests was hanging out of his main balcony. During the grand emissary's speech, no less. You're right, I should really be angry at you and Remus for inviting him in the first place..." It seemed all at once that the green-eyed sights of freshly scythed lawns, citric trees, and shameless topiary were all but gone with the wind. An underpass since exposed below the aforementioned castle, beneath a patch of yearning citrics—clove green in color, the air was no less blessed by their savory sour scent.

Close to the ingress of the West Market, the clang of blacksmith hammers, and the distorted chatter of nobodies with nothing better to do but chatter, was as close as residents might get here to an ambiance. Within the open market, children ran, dipped, and dived amid a playground of storefronts, stalls, and workmen lined up for meals. It was the commonplace of every hungry merchant that ever lived, guilting passers, and without the slightest hint of discretion, into their second-hand jewels and worthless baubles.

Caught up in a hail of desperate plea pitches, the architect forced the back of his head into his collar, shirking plainly from sight. For to know a man, to truly know a man, was to know his aversions. Not the face of control, but the one of chaos. Baseless rules of the sort that served little save for a select few were up there, but beggars were the bane of his existence. And while the merchant's flattering words might've shielded his desperation to some degree, his feigned elation and warm sweats could not. It was a disease, he reviled, which no sum of money could ever cure. Worse than the humiliation of his rejection, however, would be the ire of the Merchant Guild, and it was clear as day whose dues were in arrears.

"There you are," called a familiar voice. "I thought I had lost you."

"If only." He frowned, visibly taxed from the shriek of one of the many unattended children. "I would like to try to do this as efficiently as possible. This isn't a Barron-buys-me-drinks-on-the-company's-crown kind of night. We are here on strict business to find escorts for our quest."

"Is it ever one of those kinds of nights? I can't seem to ever recall."

A subtle grin was swiftly supplanted by a gasp, equal parts fascinated and appalled, witnessing an outstretched line outside a drinking well.

"These people are actually fine sharing these wells? Isn't this how diseases spread?"

"The community wells?" Chuckled Steven. "Suppose for a man whose pail has only ever touched the bottom of his own store could be a stranger to the lowborn practice. What do you think my betrothed and I have had to use these last couple of months? It's just water, Barron."

He furrowed his brow, averting his gaze to the uniformed row of town homes beside him. Distinctive of the Inner City, the three-story town homes were so finely clumped together that they formed one great never-ending wall of wood. An eyesore, he thought it, chasing round and round the surface for miles, drawing inward and coiling, like a snake would, trapped in a tiny wicker basket. At least here the vast majority of them still stood, their red and green facades obscured closer into the realm of brown, with the lime green and black vial of the Alchemy Guild's sign postured shamelessly upon their glowing lawns.

"My daughter's ill!" hollered a woman, empty pail in hand, from the growing center of the water line.

"Marrin wasn't exaggerating. Yep, took me three tries to fill up our pail this morning," remarked Steven, making ground toward a dank-looking establishment with moldy shutters that smacked freely into its weathered siding. "There she is, Sheep's Tavern. Squint hard enough and you might be able to make out a sign." Laughter and heckling had filled the market air as the men approached its anterior gate.

"And what do you suppose we do about it, oh great oneirocritic?" they overheard a heckler say within a mob of onlookers.

Steven suddenly stopped. For it was not every day one might witness an oneirocritic of the Ascendency, nor one with his ankles exposed, preaching freely from the back of an empty bread wagon. A steep fall from the grace these dissectors of dreams had once enjoyed during the early days of the Great Founder's crusade. Today their numbers were too few, reclused, like the rest of Maldinia's fringe Foundation Years' oddities, to the contentious annals of a time long past.

Indiscriminately he spoke to the onlookers as if his words might sway. And pray they may, for he was but a frail geezer to the lot of them. Alone in nothing but a maroon robe, with his unheeded digests and X-shaped staff in his grasp. "Humble yourselves!" he shouted, and quite forcefully too for a man of his later years. "The real Maldinia perished fifty years ago!"

Beneath the doorway came the advent of a banal tune, where the men shared varying degrees of laughter. For the first cartographer, it was rather difficult to take the old man's words seriously with his feet and ankles exposed. For Barron, something just didn't quite sit right about the tavern's mangy mascot, faded into obscurity upon its flaky portico. Though nothing, not the oneirocritic, nor the mob he's roused, nor the time-sheared sheep, nor even the depressing tune being strum upon the harp inside would discourage the two from entering now. Sundown was nigh on their heels.

It was dim-lit and dusty as a dead man's cupboard in a place where patrons crudely stared.

As sullen as their eyes were, these weathered, browbeaten men and women sloshing their discolored ales, milks, and stews, did not discriminate. They stared conspicuously from the bar counter, their splintered tables, benches, and stools; even from the steps, and on, upstairs, where their barefoot brats peered through the gaps in the railings.

"Pity," tutted Barron, seeking a table far enough from the rabble as the space would allow. "Meanwhile our people are forced to live in tents." Although his secondhand outrage was hardly warranted, Steven could not deny this. As much to the dismay of her people, the queen's inclination to furnish "visitors" had only amplified Post Slumber. In most circumstances, it would be seen as a noble act to endow a roof over a visitor's head. Paired with a population in decline, quite an attractive prospect indeed. These visitors, however—northerners mostly—were not the contributing type. Nor were they the sort to return any such favor for their neighbors.

Steven eyed a fat barrel, propped atop the counter top like a museum piece. "What would you like? The usual?"

"Something strong," he said, all the while, scanning for swords.

He dry-heaved as a mug of milk with lumps in it came across his path.

"No milk? Color me surprised."

"Color," he turned to Steven with a sickly grimace, "me surprised."

Out laughed a stranger from a nearby table, squinting peculiarly upon getting a look at the outline of a crow stitched up the side of his collar.

"Two ales it is."

"Make it quick," he turned, awkwardly meeting the stranger's gaze. Now if only avoiding eye contact was infallible.

The first to approach was an older-looking man with a powdered wreath for a beard, fixed upon a head the size of a small anvil. He was no doubt a hard-living man; a commoner, Barron would heavily wager. A former peacekeeper or logger, maybe. The other, a young man of the same hazel eyes and eager expression, had himself a pair of adolescent tree trunks for legs.

The cartographer re-approached, with two ales in hand, awaiting his turn to speak. Luckily for him, the other was itching eagerly for a way out. "Steven, this here is Aer Byron Luca. Next to him is his son, Alanthus. Aer Luca was just telling me how he had recognized my family crest."

"Recognize it? An *Alarie*?" He gawked. "I myself served faithfully an Alarie for many a year. The finest intelligencer the realm has ever known.

Of course, our enemies addressed him by a different name—the 'King in the Shadows.'"

"Father," interrupted his son, correctly sensing the nobleman's polite attentiveness waning. Most unfortunately for him, however, his father did not take the hint. Instead, he shifted his focus to Steven, who gladly entertained the chatty stranger some more.

Barron, at this juncture, was far too preoccupied with his mission to wait for the man's next sip. "You wouldn't happen to be looking for work, would you?" he interrupted.

He stopped and pinched the carpet of silver hairs over his upper lip. "What sort of work did you have in mind?"

"Steven and I require an escort. A protectorate, if you will. We have business in the East Valley."

He stood there, thoughtfully nodding with the illusion of a greater wisdom. "Forgive me, but it's not every day I get to meet a crow. Much less the surviving grandson of the late great Friedrich Alarie himself." A frown materialized. "And while technically I am an ascendant for life, at least in the eyes of the Great Founder, I am afraid I'm not active. I wish I could say it was a heroic end to my service, but no, it's my back and my hip, too."

After brusquely dismissing the two from his splintered stool, he reacquainted himself with his ale, one all too flat like his mood.

Cognizant of the weight of the man's cynicism, the cartographer rotated about in his seat, in search of hope, settling on yet another peek of the thought-provoking shapes traced around the rim of the tavern wench's white chemise. That is, of course, until they had heard the floor creaking beside them.

"Excuse me, m-my lords, if you would, I think I can help you with your predicament," stuttered a froggy voice.

He paid him no mind, scanning Steven's bewildered reaction. "I am *lord* no longer," corrected Steven, meeting Alanthus' gaze. "King Ciguil personally saw to that after my parents left with their friends for the desert."

"I apologize, my lord—*sir*. It's just that I would like to volunteer in my father's stead, as your escort."

Barron couldn't help but gawk at the young man's neck, now up close and personal. It was as long as the half-eaten loaf of bread resting on their table, his fresh red pimples and unhealed scars conjuring up all sorts of regretful memories from a vulnerable time.

The two both looked now to his father who, observing apprehensively from the neighboring table, appeared to have had little say in the young man's impromptu endeavor.

He took a long pause for a sip. "We'll be far too busy with our work to heed our blind spots," Barron muttered, wincing as his brain finally remembered what he had been sipping on. He was answered by an eager head waggle, sparking him to continue. "I expect our route to the dam to be terribly overgrown too."

"They've only just started clearing Conqueror's Road," Steven joined in.

"I could clear a path for you. It would be my honor to." He leaned in a bit closer, causing Barron to slink away. "As much as I enjoy the simulations, I think a bit of real-world experience would do me good. That is if ever I am to begin the trials someday." Somewhat resentful in his manner of tone, he nonetheless opened the floor to his father, where an agreement would be hatched. That is, if by some miracle the aspiring ascendant could fulfill his escort duties to the lead architect's grueling standards.

If he could do so, he would personally speak of the young man's worth to the Ascendency. A poor deal from poor men, he thought. If not, almost endearing.

Even if the young man proved himself lucky enough to be nominated for the trials, it would be an uphill battle to move the likes of the ascendant supreme. Of course, such matters were of no concern to him. Name or not, they were still mere strangers after all—thieves, for all he knew. To Byron's credit, he had the look of a giant, but he was by no means daft. He was at least keen enough to know an endorsement from a nobleman of an old family would prove far more useful to his son than any paltry sum of money.

For an ascendant, the eternal shield of the Great Founder, and to those who've followed in his footsteps, and even those who did not, the honorary title of aer would be worn like a badge of honor. It was a symbol of their strength and commitment to their once-virtuous mission for a different kind of future. As it pertains to its rung upon the ladder of nobility: no aers would go on to inherit large sums of money, nor prodigious castles upon any great hill.

"If you can promise to keep pace and, of course, not defame my credibility if something very unfortunate were to happen to you on our trek, then—" He stopped, overhearing another's gulp (likely the boy's father, who had an inexplicable look of fear on his face).

"You won't regret it!" erupted his son, fixing himself upright and slapping his hand across his chest. "*Aer Alanthus Luca*," he rehearsed aloud, taken in by the strums of an inspiring tune.

The old friends, unable to contain their laughter any longer, swiveled away in their stools.

Rather quickly however did he have his regrets about the interview. A pity; though it was too late for pity, for that ship had sailed following a few cursory logistics, at which point the cartographer thumped his drink onto the table and said, "Welcome aboard!"

The next time he spoke was when the tavern wench had come around to deliver their prairie stews when he had regained his lost voice for a glib "thanks."

Steven carefully met his eyes. "He'll do fine. Don't worry,"

Light in the head, he arose from his seat. "Just…don't be late tomorrow."

It wasn't until he had reached the front gate of Alarie Tower, when he finally quieted his musings for a terse sigh of relief. After all, even on the opposing end of his menacing front archway littered with crows, his home paled nothing like the rest. Perched on the uppermost crest of the Residential District Plateau, on Maximillian Ridge, this fifty-foot tower home of smooth polished stone was paved in the likeness of true nobility. A diamond in a sea of emeralds.

While the same couldn't be said for the vast majority of its citizens, nor even some of his neighbors sadly, his fortress had come out remarkably unscathed from the effects of time. Even the hulking shrubs, flanking the full entirety of his generous acre over the plateau's northern edge, still stood strong, albeit several feet taller. This was just fine, as he did not mind the bump in privacy one bit.

As he trotted up his walkway, his eyes steadied about, meeting its watchers. Melted in iron, stained in rain, a great many of them were scattered about up the hill, somehow never making their presence too well known. An ordinarily welcome sight of his little black friends tonight, however, would be tarnished by an anomaly.

He could hardly believe it, but there it was, staring back at him, the dreaded Glower, poking its cap and the tiniest sliver of its chewy, translucent stalk out from the burial mound of his family's childhood feline friend, Preston. Premature in stature, he knew a detail like this mattered little to the alchemists.

"So much fuss over a little mushroom," he exhaled, hovering over the stubby mushroom like a hunter upon his poor old injured prey. "Unfortunately for you, little guy, I would much rather lie here in the ground beside Preston, than give up my ancestral home for a tent." Following three firm tugs, its stringy hyphae exposed, and far more soil than he would have liked. Quite miraculously its stalk and cap still glowed.

Intrigued, he procured himself a fire, and a generous chalice of Frostberry wine, and relocated to his den. There the infamous glowing mushroom would be finely examined before its slow descent into ash.

CHAPTER 2

THE VALLEY

"Seventy-nine years of age," he said aloud, meeting the distorted reflection of his mother's nut brown eyes within the wrinkles of his bedchamber freshening barrel, "and only a single forehead crevice deeper. Nay, I say."

He dipped a glass bone into the water, and showed it through his hair, patiently waiting for the front ends to curl and harden—evidently alongside the moon-rinsed blades of his lawn, as he moved at the pace of a penal drudge long orphaned from the bite of a lash. In a closet fit for a king, he settled on the grimmest, darkest undershirt in his collection, one with a collar taller than the rest, surpassing that of even his ear lobes. He slipped on next a pair of close-fitting grey slacks and some mint black side-laced leather boots, like it was any other day at work. "Believe that's everything," he announced, making his way outside to a clouded sun.

All in all, he looked tidy as ever for someone without a horse. Dangling beneath his company jacket was a weighty letter opener with a beguiling bloodstone socket at its hilt. A fine piece of work, like Alarie Tower of his father's creation, in whose will he had also been left, worth a nobleman's weight in teeth. Seldom it's seen combat, it was naturally sharp as ever, following him around like the eyes that ever stared.

En route to his gate, a terrible sense of dread crept over him, far worse than the feeling of forgetting something important far from home. It is precisely why he scanned about the entirety of his hilltop for dormant Glowers, until there were no tufts or rocks or shrubs left to overturn. Yet still even now, after relieving this itch of his, he desired not to leave the comfort of his home.

His worries dwindled somewhat, spotting a glimpse of his escort playing in the road beyond his hedge wall.

The young man came prepared today like a failed soldier turned militiaman: donned in a ratty brown cloak over a sweater of rusty chains, in pants with holes, and a secondhand helm that wobbled to and fro as he pranced about with his short sword swinging for his neighbors to see.

Blissfully unaware of the unsolicited attention he had since attracted, he moseyed on, slashing the air on the apparent losing end in a fight with a far better-skilled foe. Yet even more unexpected than the firm word of a stranger, Barron just realized, was the cartographer's punctuality. He couldn't help himself, slinking over, and placing his palm to his forehead in response.

"I know, I know, believe me," the mapmaker scoffed, peeling his back off the man's signpost, revealing the letters "Alarie" beneath yet another set of leery eyes. "Guess I wasn't the only one who couldn't wait to get off that forsaken isle of tents. But look who's late now." With a stout breeze to keep at bay, the trio set off for the Lift.

It was a lengthy walk southeast from the north-most ridge of Residential, but at the very least the commoners would have the distinct privilege of gazing at the unparalleled suites perched upon his row without the fear of cross-examination from one of his neighbors.

"This is where my mother grew up," the architect pointed out, crossing a lordly brick manor infested with wildflowers.

An alchemist, garbed in bulky leather hazard gear and a beaked mask, watched them suspiciously as they crossed, casting a bushel of rooted Glowers into the bed of his wagon, before returning to his work.

"Have you met the new neighbors?" joked Steven.

Nowhere is safe, he feared. "It's not funny. I swear, if I come home to one of those signs, I will burn their decrepit base of operations to the ground."

"Won't take much now, will it? I just don't get it. We were in that compound for fifty whole years surrounded by those things, and nothing, least not for us younger folk."

Fatefully confirming the attention of another beaked figure further down the ridge, Steven moaned. "Get me off this rock."

The others could do little but laugh, for the Alchemy Guild had stolen quite enough of their morning already.

At the very end of the nobleman's row, the path continued on beside an unscalable crag. From what little they could see from the hills beneath it, the *glow* was shy but the wind and fog were surely not.

For miles they ventured, along past the sundry rows of homes of Residential, in a place where the distinction between status, by right, was lost within the fog; in the diminishing spaces between the next, and the next, concluded eventually, far out of visible sight, in Lower Residential, where status was as foreign of a concept as a bath.

Passing the limits of a well-acquainted sign, the cartographer came to a sudden halt. It was like he had seen a ghost.

The row which he once called home, was now a row wholly obstructed by hay bales. "Nearly two months it's been since they came knocking, and what does the Guild have to show for it? Nothing, nothing at all. First my house, now the whole row?"

"You must've had a lot of them, huh?" inquired Alanthus.

He took a moment, frantically pacing about. "Mostly out back, some in the cellar. Nothing I couldn't handle myself. Savannah still seems convinced my neighbor tipped off the alchemists. I don't know, maybe she's right, that old hag always did have it out for me."

"Well look at where that's got her now," chimed the architect.

Alanthus nodded, though it was obvious he had not been listening. He couldn't keep his eyes off a path, since revealed within the fog beneath them.

"How about you, Alanthus? Where were you and your family located before, *well.*"

"Laird Street, Market District, sir. It's been a little over a month since we received our notice. Apparently, clay wasn't enough to stop the Glowers from sprouting through the floors." His eyes shimmered as if they were bordering on the edge of tears. Somehow though, and for whatever reason neither of them could guess, the escort managed to maintain his air of optimism—a smile even. "My mother and sister nearly fainted when we discovered where we would be living. Oh well, I suppose the old tournament grounds aren't all that bad. Plenty room for my father and I to train—"

"We're making good time," interrupted Barron, glancing at a signpost slanted in the moss below.

"Where's the outer wall?" Alanthus immediately advanced, joining the men on a road eastward, down a slippery slope flanked by wet rolling hills. "I was hoping I'd be able to see if by now. I can't see much of anything from here. What's it like, the Lift?" Unsettled by the more amenable of the two's abrupt silence, he scanned the slope from whence he came, only to find a few unfamiliar faces with axes in hand.

"Keep up, Alanthus," revealed Barron from a blind spot in his father's hand-me-down helm.

He pulled off the old thing, revealing a fresh shave on every side of his head (save for the top, where a thin cluster of curly red hair still remained). "Right, yes. Sorry, my lord."

Far above still the sunken edge of the outer wall, sharp and sturdy the wind blew, collecting a slew of dew in its path, regaining momentum, and yet again, some more moisture down the slides. A recipe for a fateful happenstance, if not traversable for a distance. Residential was one of a kind in that sense. While its neck wasn't half as daunting as its siblings', one wrong step was all it would take to send someone and their belongings for a long roll.

The dew had since melted some as the men veered off the pathway into a market wedged on a flat part between two knolls. A horse emporium it was, not long ago, evidenced today by a cluster of overgrown stables and empty stalls. Today, not even a third of the stands had been manned.

Within the market flat, a sharp, floral scent filled the young man's senses, and so also a few stares. This apparently was all it would take for his smile to regain its full form. He reached his hand out to wave, in doing so sending his sweaty helm fumbling from his grip.

And yet despite his clumsy first impression, he managed to get a second look from one of the young girls who piqued his interest.

"Might I remind you of your mission?" said a voice sarcastically from somewhere outside an elixir stall.

"My mission. Of course, my lord." He placed his helm back on his head and stood up with his back straight. A crisp pop emitted from beneath Barron's grip, sending his back even straighter.

He chuckled, pulling a narrow glass vial from his mouth. "Did you want one too?"

The young man shook his head. It was obvious he hadn't a clue as to what it was. "It's a pema elixir or liquid endurance," he explained. "Never had one before, have you?"

"Pema? Like from a pema root?"

Barron waggled his hand apprehensively. "Let's just say there's a reason why the Alchemy Guild doesn't make known their recipes. Soldiers would often chug these concoctions before a battle. Come to eventually realize they weren't actually soldiers, nor were there any actual battles to charge into."

The young man scratched his head.

"Let me guess, no luck at the stables?!"

"A merchant laughed in my face," Steven approached, undoing the top off of his fizzy concoction. "Told me I'd have better luck wrangling Gromula.'"

"Just my luck," he threw his hands up. "At this point, I would even settle for a mule."

"You can say that again."

Taken back by a brownish dribble sliding messily out of his associate's mouth, the man shivered and spun the other way. "Let's go, we're losing daylight."

Their path came to a sudden end in a courtyard manned by the queen's soldiers, across ramparts obscured in the fog. In the shadow of the outer wall—where a functioning ballista tower seemed as rare as a smile—the men filed into a messy line of outbound loggers. "Where is it? Where's the Lift?" pressed Alanthus nervously.

"You've never ridden it before?" turned Barron, his left eyebrow arched.

The lift operator briefly acknowledged the three, before rejoining the loggers' conversation.

He shook his head rather regretfully. "I've never actually been outside of the city before."

Steven stood there, discernibly in search of something nice to say. "Plenty of subject matter for a nice water painting. If you're into that sort of thing." A horrible grinding screech reverberated from the hole underneath the wall. Louder it grew upon its rusty rails, shaking the whole courtyard beneath them.

"Is that it?"

"Sure is," said Steven.

The young man swallowed, scanning the newfound object and its passengers—capital loggers, hands slivered and calloused, in clothing stained of bright colored sweat. Barron, unlike Alanthus, avoided analyzing the platform in its current state. Especially so when considering how dreadfully it blended in against the stone, its flimsy wood frame, and rusty railings for perceived safety. He believed whichever Nero engineer it was that had designed the contraption must've been on a sadistic streak, for the fate of its commuters hung in the clammy hands of a lone lift operator.

Alanthus waltzed on ahead for a look through the forward embrasures. Unfortunately for him, the fog cared little for his interest in peeking at the East Valley's scenery; the same went for the lift operator who, despite the platform's newfound availability, chattered on some more with the loggers.

Noticing the injustice afoot, the ranking footman, overseeing a ballista tower repair up high, cleared his throat. His subordinates, staring curiously from their windy posts, gave one another comical looks.

It didn't take till marching down the steps when the lift operator had finally come to his senses. "You three can go on ahead," he whistled, peering over at the officer for approval, before giving the group of outbound loggers a contrite look.

"Quite the heavy cargo, is it not?" questioned Barron.

"No more than the last. If it makes you feel any better, if I croak, Sir Horntree over 'ere will crank you lot the rest of the way." His irreverent words were met with cold stares from both Alanthus and the officer in question.

"You blind, Matias? That there is an Alarie—a crow!" the officer rebuked. "Show a little respect."

"Aye, you're probably right." He shrugged, giving the lever a firm shove. "Off you go now."

At once the rusty gears began to churn, and off the screeching platform went.

Right before the courtyard slabs disappeared from his sight, the architect parted a cordial nod Sir Horntree's way. Though for all he knew the lift operator may just have been his everyday jaded self. And who could blame him? Kin to a renowned family, yes, however, he was undoubtedly unknown to the realm on the whole. In contrast, his father Varus served as overseer of the Nero Company for just short of two decades. By his age, he was an instrumental figurehead of the Construct Era, at the forefront of the infrastructure flare in Residential during his tenure as lead architect.

"They're massive," Alanthus gasped, leaning over the railing for a vague peak of a faraway forest.

The logger beside him chuckled. "Those are karnip trees," he said, "hard to tell now with the mess beneath us, but Sprite's Forest once extended from the cliffside up to Conqueror's Road."

"And what happened to it?"

"Industry happened," replied the logger, his feet facing the nobleman and his colleague.

"Of course, the fire didn't help any," mumbled Barron, his typical floaty eye contact tossed away for a cold stare. Cold enough to avert the other's attention back onto Alanthus.

"You know, we could use a big lad like you down there."

"I reckon we'd be out of a job," joined another logger.

Humbly he shrugged, however for this he knew the loggers told no lie: he towered over all but one—an enormous, tri-colored Tumsib male with small anchors for arms.

"Welcome to the valley," nudged Steven.

Barron peered at the vista apprehensively. For it wouldn't take much else, outside of a fell swoop of the hairy jungles beneath their platform, to confirm how terribly overgrown the East Valley had become since his last visit. A civilized land, it was, once upon a time, renowned for its purebred horses, now one with a newfangled forest of weeds.

Following a rumble and a thump, the lot of them, unfirm on a mossy hill in the shadow of Residential, were now one with the jungle.

"Look sharp for vrogels!" shouted a gravelly voice. He figured it ought to have been the Tumsib's, based upon the sheer force of gravity alone, since frightening little critters back into their furry dens. And yet as the loggers chuckled amongst one another churlishly, he knew the joke was surely on them. Far outmatched, it was a race against the mounting sun to pick up where the last group left off: hacking and slashing a foothold exhaustive enough to defend and, hopefully in due time, extend.

"Vrogels? There are vrogelnastia in these woods?" inquired the young man over the sound of fading laughter.

"About that," Barron said, alluding to Steven.

"Technically there were never any woods here," murmured Steven, eagerly unfolding a map.

"Don't listen to them," advanced Barron, "with the number of resources we've poured into this cleanup, or whatever it is the queen's handlers have decided to call this shoddy exertion, the whole realm should've been cleared weeks ago, every last bit of it." He sighed. "No. But rest assured our fine capital work-hands will continue with their scam, echoing grand tales of mythical creatures drawn upon the cavern walls of our long-forgotten deceased. All for just a few more resources."

They utilized what little the capital loggers had cleared off the old horse peddlers' path, their steps leading them far from the Lift, far from the pain their ears had yet to endure.

Watching the way ahead, like any good escort should be expected to do, the two followed Alanthus beneath a dangling branch, all the while doing their best to avoid the surrounding tall grass of many a burr.

The stumps were already tapering away, and so too the scent of their freshly hacked remains, though the fledgling trees still remained; new ones that had found refuge on the abandoned pathway through the old country. "Suppose even if I was lucky enough to have scrounged us up a few steeds, they wouldn't be of much use out here anyway," commented Steven.

"You're right," Barron retorted, "they would be of much better use on the main road."

"You're sure about that?" In a haste his eyes have seldom seen out of his old friend, Steven rushed up ahead. "Look at this!" He crawled beneath the underbelly of a fallen oak tree, where some thirty peach-colored bulbs grew profusely. "These are fungi...First thought they were flowers."

"I wouldn't touch 'em," Barron whispered, halting both Steven and Alanthus from the action.

"Why not, my lord?"

"For all the random imperfections in nature, its many blessed creatures aren't just pretty for no reason. A rose, for example, has thorns," he explained, "always there is something more. Something sinister, I reckon."

"I'm not sure if I would use the word 'sinister' to describe a rose; however, you might have a point." Steven himself shied away from making contact with the pretty-looking mushrooms. Up ahead, he watched Alanthus bend his full weight onto his back feet. He then swung, and with a mighty whoosh an obstructive branch went twirling off the path, lost somewhere in the tall grass.

Barron wiped splinters meticulously off the front of his work jacket. "Reckless."

"My lord?"

"Surely your target will see that coming from a mile away…" He was now wiser as he vented, falling several bodies behind the wild man's shadow. And a good thing he did too, as deaf to all else, Alanthus performed yet another uppercut, this time on a patch of crucifers, sending bright colored juices spurting all over himself and the cartographer's wares, and a putrid smell.

"That's quite enough!" snapped the cartographer, finding a new-found stain on his map. "Don't want to dull your blade now."

Just like that, he had found his catalyst to keep going. "Steven," wheezed Barron, "what's wrong? Your face has gone red." Steadily, they did just that, until about noon, at which point Sprite's Forest drew close enough over their sunburned heads for a much-needed breather.

"Why is the ground so brittle here? Is this from the arson too?"

"Just wait till we get inside."

In the immersive shade of the Sprites' cherished ashen gray trees, Alanthus followed his gaze up the first trunk in sight, until his neck had finally had enough. He sniffed the bark. "It smells like the ocean."

"I would ideally like to wrap up at the dam before sundown!" Barron shouted, stirring silence in the songs in the boughs above. "And how would you know what the ocean smells like?" mumbled Barron, before releasing a wet, winded cough.

"Yes, yes, just jotting some notes!" replied Steven. In actuality, he was foraging for a last-minute meal.

Alanthus caressed his hand up yet another salty piece of bark. "They're wicked tall, taller than any tree I've ever seen. And beautiful. So why chop them down?"

"Because this is karnip. It's sturdier than brick and cozier than any stone. House your kids and their kids, and their kids' kids—*Steven*!" he yelled, causing yet another echo in the enclosure.

"I'm coming, I'm coming!" The cartographer feigned, flicking a tick off an over-ripened stainberry.

In the thick of the Forest, an ethereal glow was ubiquitous. Glowers. Some were over six feet tall. In the dwellings of the karnips' meaty roots, on its bark, and in the fox holes, too. He wondered how it would look at night, of course not nearly enough for him to wait around to see.

Alanthus, upon sheathing his oily blade, stooped below one such spring of Glowers beneath the base of an old karnip tree. In its shade, its extended family had found a nice bit of solace in the recess of the sun.

"Be careful, you don't want to end up like Blind Eye," jested Barron.

"Who did you say went blind, my lord?" half-attentively replied Alanthus.

"Never mind."

"My father says the Glowers are to blame for the Slumber."

He rolled his eyes. "Well, then it must be true."

In the third glade on their eastward trajectory, the men unshouldered their bags. Their stomachs, sore from growling, could go no further. That is with the exception of Alanthus, who wandered off aimlessly in the woods some more.

It took Barron a whole four minutes to find a rock free enough of slithering insects and moss to finally settle. Settle was sort of an overstatement, however, for his facial expression described someone who had been sitting on a door knob.

Beyond the clearing, Alanthus shouted: "Where are all the Sprites, my lord? This is Sprite's Forest after all, is it not?"

"Does this kid ever stop?" Reaching his hand into his bag, he sifted through his collection of jerkies, settling on the first to meet his grasp. Steven meanwhile started looping a leather object around his head, fiddling with its straps.

It was a contraption shaped like a horseshoe, but this was no shoe of any kind. It was an *optae*. And outside of the few unfortunate volunteers within its inventor's inner circle, the Nero Company prototype had seen littler movement than a mountain. And for good reason too. With his hair pulled back tight, in the light bright red rashes revealed on the surface of his temples.

As for its stated purpose, it was quite simple, arguably valiant: to bring aid upon those with defective eyesight. The creator's thought process was as such: If you need to squint in order to see, then you may as well equip a device to squint for you.

"Barbaric," Barron shuttered, "you couldn't bribe me a thousand gold crowns to wear one of them. Why Devyn still employs Remus is beyond me."

He tightened the contraption, sending his eyes sideways. "If I had that kind of money lying around, then perhaps I would be in line for a miracle worker."

He almost spit his food out after getting a closer look at his comically squinted face. "Alanthus!" he shouted, holding back a laugh between bites, "Steven is chafing! Do let us know if you happen upon any vement in there!"

"I do admit the chafing hasn't gotten any better. Remind me to ask Remus about that."

"Didn't your parents offer to find you a healer if you resettled out west with them? Before they, well, you know…"

He sighed dejectedly. "Don't get me wrong, it's great and all in Varakai, but why would anyone want to give *this* up to live in the desert?"

Besides the whole Slumber setback, and your parents dying in their sleep? He refrained from the very thought. "Why? Why else? Varakai's an autonomic, self-governing nation free from the ever-swaying hand of corruptive—"

"This ought to be the bog down here!" interrupted the escort.

CHAPTER 3

LAMELLAE

Their vision went dim as a dungeon downhill, where a second awning, twisted, unrestrained, exposed in and out of a lazy fog.

An afternoon of firsts of an already one too many.

This was quite unlike the Leak's Bog of his memory. The ground here was fragile, and sinking fast, far too fast for but the mightiest of karnips' anchors to consider, and most certainly too soft for a weighted carriage or horse.

Already he had cursed his choice of footwear, the sheen on his boots soured by a film of soot, pollen, and mud.

"Was this the bog you saw from the ridge?" Steven asked over the synchronized trill of ten thousand crickets.

"Well, no, not exactly. I, uh, didn't see anything," he stammered. "I did hear your typical bog-like sounds, however. I figured it'd be a bog, is it not?"

Barron smacked a biter with his bag and scoffed. "Do any of you actually know what a bog is? I for one sure don't, but I did always hate cutting through here."

"You and me both."

Obstructed by a wall of reeds, the men heaved two handfuls aside, abrasively enough for a light tear upon their fingertips.

"I can't see a thing." Like a moonlight twinkle upon a midnight lake, gluttonous cypress trees lay bare in the tiny poke holes in the awning, slanted upon stilted mounds of grass, encased by stagnant pools of water, and the occasional running stream. Jutting out of their adaptive foundations were their hairy roots, where fungi and arachnids vied for a coveted spot above the murky waters.

The cartographer unfolded his latest iteration of a topographical map of Maldinia, pacing to and from the deviant tangle. "Leak's Bog might need a new name." Whether it be a swamp, a marsh, or a bog, none could say for certain, though the simple fact remained: unforeseeable was its end.

"What a nightmare." Steven juxtaposed his unaltered map with the other, contemplating an area of interest thirty leagues west of Cilify Harbor, beneath a mountain range sprawled across the full entirety of the southern border labeled *Screecher Hills*.

"Not a chance. Way too far south," joined Barron over his shoulder. "This is it, or what's left of it."

Steven inhaled. "The good news is we are still on the shortest path to the dam. The bad news is I'll need a few extra minutes to resurvey this mess."

"A wolf's pace, Steven. A wolf's pace." Barron and Alanthus ambled off to nowhere, hopping from one half-sunken piece of wood to another, only to turn right back around at an unscalable crag. In the process, Barron had fallen away to another time, an earlier time, when the sun had shone through the canopy when he was but a humble two-stripe architect with the all too familiar family name.

Heeding a woman's call, a group of children of the same piggy nostrils and auburn hair glided through the berry bog, laughing and shouting and shoving their way across a makeshift bridge of crudely tied-together planks. They leaped one after another onto firm ground and whizzed past him, weaving through a last row of ripened cranberries, sending robins scattering, before piling into their farmhouse behind their mother.

He was back, his attention seized by an inadvertent plop in the water. "Alanthus." The young man turned at attention, yet not before subtly discarding the other rock from behind his back. "I have a gift for you."

He watched Barron swing a farmer's scythe in a decisive, upward motion, sending a cluster of reeds now headless and now soaring, to their untimely graves. "Now you'll never have to dull your father's old blade again."

He gripped it with both hands and over his head like a war hammer. "It's perfect. Thank you, my lord."

"No," retorted Barron, fully aware of the hairline crack at its snath, "thank *you*." He whistled, directing the young man's attention onto the wall of reeds.

As Alanthus folded the farmer's tool over the wall, the other let loose a melancholic sigh. "No bridge, no nothing. Just some big old roots." He clicked his tongue. "Oh, how I loathe water. Well, Steven." He turned. "We're off."

Following the nobleman's lead, Alanthus extended his massive boot onto the slithering tail of a woody serpent and danced around for a few worrisome moments before finding his footing.

"I'm coming, I'm coming!"

Utilizing the occasional window to the outside world, the trio hopped and plopped and hacked and veered, taking breaks on the occasional rock sound enough to whip out their bladders for a quick swig and, naturally, release. Further east the air grew languorous. It was just thick enough to allow oneself to get pick-pocketed, and without the slightest possibility of identifying one's assailant. Thankfully there were more than a few Glowers scattered about the hairy bog to prevent their path from veering astray, discernible enough to use as mental markers, however not for use as a guide.

A pungent smell since joined, pervasive as the maddening nibbles of the biters upon their skin. One might easily have mistaken this putrid smell for sulfur (and yes, that was a given as well), but this smell was not from any sulfur, it was visible, a mucky yellow color, interwoven within the smog itself, and very much unfazed by their flailing limbs.

"Save some scythe work for our venture back home, we need you in fighting shape," commanded the man, noticing the escort's once consistent tempo slowing. He had on armor suitable for a small skirmish, not at all ideal for a bog slog—hither and thither it jingled and sloshed like muddy nails in a rusty bucket.

"Steven, let's see you take point now." Just then he heard a thump and a splash.

"...I guess I just lost my step." *An understatement*, Barron thought; he looked to have been in a drunken stupor as Alanthus carelessly tossed aside his scythe to assist the poor man out from the nasty mere. His face was as pale as his fingers were wrinkled. His bun was matted and halfway out. There was decomposed plant matter in the little gap between his bushy-brown eyebrows, and water all over his jacket and optae.

"It's a sign, Steven," said Barron, studying the human-shaped hole left in the sheen. "Leave that awful contraption in the water where it belongs."

"What is that rising from the surface, my lord?" the young man asked, pointing into the water. "They look like little bubbles. Could that be where the smog is coming from?"

"It would appear so," Barron concurred, "come, let's go. I want to make it home for my after-supper wine." He pulled his cloak over his head, then proceeded eastward at a wicked pace, leaving the others panting to catch up.

"Do you think it's poisonous?!" shouted Alanthus, his froggy voice muffled within his hooded head.

"Very likely," Barron facetiously replied, sending the young man hustling to catch up. "Rumor has it the Alchemy Guild would use this bog to test their latest prototypes. They'd pay this bogger and that to look the other away, so don't be surprised if we stumble upon any three-headed frogs along the way."

A pool and a half behind them, Steven shouted their names.

Unfortunately for him, his deflated voice would not be enough to cause much of any alarm in the ghoulish bog. Unbeknownst to him several leeches had found a suitable host as he entered their spongy domain; slipping freely in through the openings at the bottom of his breeches for an afternoon bite.

Barron, though wearisome his legs, powered through the pain, swimming and climbing atop rocks, roots, and hilly mounds of moss diminished. But his pace was progressively slowing. In the next dim-lit lagoon, he climbed atop one such roomy isle of moss diminished for a swig.

Trickle-fed by an inlet somewhere unseen ahead, the mound of grass was home to the ruins of an outhouse, and a forked elm tree with roots as old as the bog. He slumped his back against one of its many sinewy strains, surveying what little he could of the way ahead.

There was light foreseeable, but not an end, just cracks in a thinning canopy.

"What am I doing here?" existentially he uttered.

"My lord, may I ask you a question?"

"Yes, but quickly. We still have much ground to cover."

"I am sure you are tired of hearing about this, but my father tells me that your grandfather was named King Maximillian II's heir not once, but twice."

"That's right."

"And he turned it down on both occasions. *Why?*"

He met a glimmer in the young man's eyes and inhaled. "My grandfather used to say he 'hadn't the stomach for it.' Of course, you and I both know that's not true. You don't just happen upon the top by chance. As a runt, I figured he meant the food was bad. But no, the truth is actually quite dull. I believe he felt guilty. Guilty he was too busy spying on the king's enemies to watch his children come of age. Here with me, he had another chance; an opportunity, perhaps, to right his wrongs."

Taken back by a disturbance in the waters, though too timid to interrupt his employer, the escort began flinging his head and throwing his eyes toward the opposite end of the tree.

"…had he accepted the crown, likely someone more apt to assess the dam would be in my place today—"

"*My lord.*"

"*What?*"

"Look." Amidst a thick film of leaves, a stifled light gleamed upon a freakishly large pair of yellow eyes, lidless, unblinking. "Do you think it's a—"

"No." Barron removed his hood and unsheathed his ruddy blade, holding it stiff by his side.

"I think it's gone now." Alanthus waltzed to the edge before speaking again, "Where's Steven? I think I lost Steven, my lord."

"Steven lost Steven," said the man. "*Shh.* Do you feel that?"

The young man slinked back over to him, swallowing. "The mound's moving."

"Listen." He heard a noise.

Not so much a voice, but close; like a wolf with a bone caught in its throat.

Womp! spoke the water.

A dream, he thought, motionless, cozied by a thin strand of light.

Leaves no sooner fell from the canopy, permitting two or three more slivers of light. Alanthus flung off his hood and bent his unwieldy legs. His hand-me-down helm, meanwhile, may as well have woken the dead. It rattled around like pots and pans on a bumpy carriage ride, scraping the tops of his ears.

WOMP!

About the only thing they could make out, sopping wet, on their rears, was a wrinkly figure frowning, with its chewy legs bent like a readied grasshopper. An amphibian of sorts, though nothing like he'd ever seen. It was thicker than the outhouse beside them, with a head the length of a watermelon.

His escort slumped to his knees, surveying the oily wrinkles on its fat face. "What do you reckon it is?"

"How would I know?" There seemed very little for him to report on the doings behind its gaping yellow eyes, anyway, but he did feel something: a warm, fuzzy feeling that aroused the hairs on his arms and legs. The creature was emanating steam.

It started dipping its head forward, revealing great big sores on its neck and back, along with a bipedal figure with long, gritty hair and an olive-green complexion. A she, he wagered, dismounted, based on a familiar placement of swamp covering, corded across her chest and between her skinny legs. A female shied long away from the light. There was some beauty to be found here nonetheless, as he scanned about her lissome frame and human-like features for intent. Beauty enough to envisage a quiet life together somewhere in the remote valley.

Her focus remained fixed upon the two men as she pulled forth a carved cylinder swinging from her neck. With a great, big puff of her cheeks, she blew. Oddly enough, neither heard a sound. Leastways not from her instrument. In the waters, however, several more mongrels of the swamp emerged: a few males slightly taller than her, but still no taller than a half-sprite, clad in sharp tanned hide with spears in hand. Another leaped atop the isle, saddled on the back of another womp-beast, while a few more inched their heads above the roots—one holding a peculiar-looking barbed shovel.

The humans watched her as she retreated to the other side of the forked elm.

"Did you see it, sir?" whispered Alanthus.

"See what?"

"She has little flaps behind her ears. Do you think they're gills?"

He sighed, scanning for his ray now evanesced. "Steven's really itching for a reaming, isn't he?"

"I could go back and look for him, my lord."

"No." He knew it was too soon for that; the mongrel scouts had yet to lower their weapons. Though beyond that, he had no intention of enabling the laggard.

In due time the female scout returned with a sack in lug. One in which she had placed into Barron's hand like a gift.

He humored her, reaching inside of the sack. "A portrait," he said, forcing a smile. "Was half expecting a rock."

Although its frame was warped dearly and the glass was covered in grime, he was able to discern a few faces. A family of them. "These are Humans: H-U-M-A-N-S. Humans. And a new sampler too. Alchemists must've been here recently." His eyes were followed by the lot of them as he parted his sopping-wet bangs from his vision.

"I don't think they meant 'em as gifts, my lord."

"I really truly don't care. I have a dam to assess." He turned to the mongrels behind them, whose faces hungered for more.

With a heavy sigh, he continued. "Boggers used to live here. They tended this land. This portrait probably belonged to one of the families." As he spoke, he could hear the rustle of whispers: a cue, he surmised, to continue. "Don't let the absence of the great trees fool you, they're still here, way up high over these lesser tones. We call this place Leak's Bog. Way back when, before the Eastern Dam was built, there was a lake here."

"Leak's Lake?" asked Alanthus.

He looked up, grinning after sighting the look of bewilderment on the mongrels' faces.

"Might I suggest another approach, my lord?"

"Go on."

The lad set on, first scouring about through the remnants of the old outhouse.

He then wandered to the far side of the mound, where he assessed the sturdiness of its lower fringe. The architect took the opportunity to scan for an escape route; until at last the others were all gathered around the far edge for a show.

"What'd you find?"

"Looks like a door-frame," he said, taking a breath before dropping down onto what he likely thought to be firm ground, only to submerge himself up to his crotch in peat. "It's a root!" he struggled, "just a root!"

Barron observed the struggle with a maleficent smile when suddenly the group's aura turned to stone. Their necks and heads were cocked westward, in high alert. The humans, half wondering if they had insulted their hosts, ceased their foolish charade.

"Esna," was all that she had said to the man as she rubbed her womp-beast's head and mounted up. She and her friends went catapulting into darkness, severing the moss in their companions' cumbersome wake.

"Something's wrong," said Barron, gazing at the last of the mongrels on foot.

"What if it's Steven, my lord? Maybe he's in trouble."

He jerked his mouth from side to side, aiding the muddy man back atop the isle. *If I delay, Marrin himself will be forced to show.* He shook his head. *No. The dam's obviously been breached. Yes. Selvin's crew will require specs and a sketch.* He rolled his neck in a full circle and sighed. "Fine. Whatever. Let's just make it quick." The two did a far better job at keeping dry this time, as they backtracked their way tactfully through the bog for their missing friend.

"Up here," Barron signaled, gripping a saggy cypress tree at the peak of a ten-foot-tall mound.

He could see very little in the fog past its branches, save for a great open mere, wrought long ago by a fallen comet, and the faint twinkle upon its sheen. As for the sounds, he swore he could hear a struggle. It was only a matter of time before his escort would notice.

"Do you hear that?"

"Yes. *Shh.*"

Alanthus crept below, leaning his full weight on a furry root.

"Don't make a sound. I think it's the Swampgrels. They're tussling with something. With what I don't know."

"Don't you think we should help, my lord? What if it's Steven?"

He was answered by a yelp, frightening the young man cold. As he emerged up top, he had found something on the man's back. "There's something on your back, my lord!"

"Yes, now get it off me…"

Panting, Alanthus unsheathed his sword. "It's like a giant gelatinous slug. Must've leaped from the canopy." Lardy puss seeped onto his blade as he slowly pressed the tip of it into the creature's side. Even injured, its bloated head seethed for organic material to sink its venom into.

After stabbing it again, the fiending blob lifted its mouth from off the man's shoulder and let loose a nasty cry. With one last stab in the back of its head, the deformity seized its call. Gone was the burden from his back.

"Now you know where its head is." As he wiped goop off his now blemished work jacket, he spotted another on the bough above—this one the size of a swollen rat upon the banquet of a bloodied battlefield. Before his escort had even realized, the creature had fallen clean onto his dagger—a quiet kill, followed by an egregious splash.

Unbeknownst to the two men, the whole swamp had soon come alive. Out from the holes and up through the roots they climbed, eventually engulfing the mound by the dozen.

He had only merely managed to evade one's mouth before leaping into the questionable safety of the lagoon beneath them. Alanthus himself closed his eyes and followed, falling ungracefully beneath the surface of the water for a few moments before finding a footing.

By now the creatures' mouths were as wide open as when they had followed them off the ledge, making strides towards the two men like snakes on water.

"Aid!" shouted Barron, deep down hoping one of the Swampgrels would heed his helpless cry. "Over here!" called out Alanthus, managing to redirect a handful of creatures his way.

Following a momentary stint of denial, Barron singled out a pair with precision. Another was approaching fast, and so he shrugged water off his face and dove desperately for a floating branch. They were now crossing into the dominion of yet another mound, narrow at its base with a wide crown of moss atop it, where a frightening pig-sized shadow appeared, along with its children, out from the nooks on both its ends.

He could find little solace in Alanthus's grunts, as the young man struggled to plow the monstrosities away with his father's old kite shield. Barron lined up on his rear, holding out his branch like a cowcatcher, helplessly pushing away the godless creatures as much as its weight would allow.

They could do little now but hold, on their tiptoes and feet, as the creatures launched eagerly a final assault. That's when their pig-sized foe had reared its ugly head, making quick work of their questionable formation following a great splash.

He shoved his branch into the creature's mouth, and shouted, "This way, Alanthus!" before making a sloppy attempt at an escape.

"I can't touch here!" cried Alanthus.

A massive pillar of water just then came curling over his head, effectively nullifying the last bit of light through the tangle. It was the female scout, marking the pig-sized monster with one quick flick of her friend's tongue.

With the smaller ones now off for a ride, it was the big one's turn— sent so very swiftly through the air that it popped like a bubble against the side of the same mound from whence it came, ejecting bile, bones and undigested clothing freely into the water.

"…Is it?"

He said nothing, but he knew it was him: mummified in a six-foot-long sack of wet leaves with the Nero prototype half hanging off his head.

They stood and watched from afar as the Swampgrels hummed around a crackling fire; below their feet, the motionless sack of wet leaves. Their elder—at least what Barron figured to be one—approached it, while his kin moved respectfully out of his way. He pulled out a chiseled bone from behind his back—strangely enough, not from any pocket or bag of his, but an immensely wrinkled section of his lower back.

The escort had begun moving his hand over his weapon, sizing the potential threat. This he sensed, instinctively placing his palm over the young man's hand, giving him the wait-and-see. He had little choice now but to trust.

The elder peeled back the swamp dressings, confirming both their suspicions.

"Steven!"

His escort lurched forward, yanked back immediately to his side. The poor guy's face was a ghostly white, though his chest still fluttered ever-so-slightly. His legs were gangrene, overtaken by puffy red leeches. One by one the elder began peeling them off his skin, setting them into the fire, as the rest of the scouts maintained their croaky hymn. The two men looked on in horror, frantically searching their own legs for the parasites. After meeting the flames the leeches curled and collapsed beneath the fags, eventually forming one big puddle of discolored blood, until at last there was naught left but the sickly marks left on his legs.

Peculiarly enough, the humming did not yet stop.

The elder started plowing his chisel up the surface of a womp-beast's chest, popping a few boils on its way. His hands were now covered in its phosphorescent puss. Beside the fire, he presented the human with his hands out dripping. Barron looked him long in the eyes before parting a nod.

After the elder applied the strange solution to the unconscious man's wounds, they wrapped his legs back up snugly and propped him by the fire. There they sat beside him, wishing, waiting for his eventual return. As for their hosts, they had since returned to staring.

The long-haired scout singled him out, scooching onto the log right beside him. She of course was not privy to the concept of shuttered body language, and so she extended her arm out, pointing to a freckle on his frigid hand.

"Go ahead, touch it if you want. Just don't get any of that puss on me."

"You fancy yourself a deity now?" uttered a deflated voice, swept quickly in a fit of coughing.

"Steven!" up jumped Alanthus.

The man held his head in pain. "What did I miss?" He chuckled.

"You fainted, sir," said Alanthus. "These folks helped rip leeches off you. They were about yay big—" He motioned. "Glad to have you back."

"Glad to be back," he said, making quick work of his bladder.

"Yes, hooray," said Barron sarcastically, climbing to his feet and sighing. "Now we can finally go."

CHAPTER 4

THE SHIPWRECK

For miles, the old friends said very little to one another. Even as the sunlight eluded the lattice of leaves, the nobleman's lips remained pursed, his eyes fixed below to where his boots sank clear in the mud. This was far more productive in his book than arguing. Still, he couldn't help but stew. Not only was Marrin's route flawed from the get-go but Steven's little accident had cost him several hours of daylight.

An easy reminder as to why he and his colleague had drifted apart all those years ago. This, however unfortunate, would not change the fact that his knack was yet in need.

Amidst deeper waters, their heavied legs strode up the back of an island, home to a lonely, abandoned cabin.

"Do you think you'll actually be able to make it back tonight? If I haven't made myself clear before, I don't intend on stopping. Not 'til this face has felt the warmth of my hearth and the chill of my chalice."

"I'm not sure—Alanthus! Have you ever carried a grown man before?" jested the cartographer.

"It's funny. It's very funny. You know what's even funnier? The sun is at its peak and we haven't even made it to the dam yet."

Steven looked now to the looming horizon, where the great trees burgeoned above the mist. "I'd say we are getting pretty close. Although seeing as our flooding problem hasn't gotten any better, I'd wager you have your work cut out for you today."

"Me? Oh no, Steven, you're mistaken."

"I can't imagine living out here," panned the escort, "all by yourself, surrounded by all this water."

"It wasn't like this before. I assure you that," said Steven, "loggers used to live out here, once upon a time. Look, over there, you can still see that one's roof. And over there"—his attention was seized by a floating box of wood in the waters ahead—"that house is a boat now."

"Hopefully none of them were around when all this flooding happened."

"Yes, yes, fascinating. If only you had your easel, Steven." He joined them at the water's edge, where he cupped his hand over his sunburned head and sighed. "Might want to throw your optae back on, because that there is a macro wagon, not a house. Right over there is its wheel."

"My lord, I don't think my feet can touch beyond here."

"Just move your arms," demonstrated the man, "and kick your legs."

"He's wearing armor," scoffed Steven. "He'll surely sink."

"Guess there's only one way to find out." He placed his bag on his head and sank into the water.

"Don't mind him. He's got his eyes on the prize! Here, give me your shield and your bag. I can float them behind me if that helps."

He trembled. "That current seems awfully fast for someone who has never swam a day in his life. I just know I'll sink."

"We can always come back for you once we've wrapped up at the dam. I'm afraid, however, with all this flooding, this could take some time."

"Let's go!" reprimanded the man. "We're losing daylight."

"For my part, I won't fault you for turning back."

He parted a cordial nod. "Wait, that's it!"

"Hm?"

"My thanks, sir!" turned the escort, setting off towards the cabin door. "I shan't be long behind!"

It didn't take much long before the spillway's push had grown violent. Once their legs stopped touching, this problem of theirs only seemed to worsen. With every last burning stroke of their arms, more and more sunlight had slipped from their grasp. "Follow the sound of my voice, Alanthus!" shouted the cartographer, joining Barron atop a sunken stone fixture.

"Can you guess what that is?" By now he could hear little beyond the sound of his own voice, and see little more than the treetops over-head. The channel was a full-on river, capturing grades on both ends and on, up to the great trees' ankles.

"Considering the levees are now underwater, I'd say that's our aqueduct."

"Correct."

"Right behind you!" shouted Alanthus. Floated upon a door with his arms and legs outspread, the escort's persistence drew smiles.

Upon confirming the dam's toe intact, he glanced unsuccessfully down the rest of its face, and above, where the stone slabs climbed quickly past a slanted N, out of sight. "You owe me a sketch, Steven; a good one at that."

It wasn't until reaching its crest, on the upstream face of its western end, that the source of all their troubles, thus far, had revealed. There was a hole there about the length of an oar. Not huge, but apparently enough to modify the immediate ecosystem. He hung his legs over the backside, where he laid out his schematics and started drafting a damage report.

Eastern Dam Panel 2b

Status: Breached

Cause of Damage:

"Tell me if you see anything lodged down there, Alanthus!" he shouted, an echo repeating this very command.

"I don't see anything lodged, my lord." He marched down the stairs parallel to the hole, some eighty feet below, to a river pathway clasped by the great trees. "Just over here, off to the side of the hole, there's another damaged slab, sir! A thick scratch; this one doesn't look to be leaking through."

He sighed, setting his sights on the other. "STEVEN!"

———

He gazed nosily over the cartographer's shoulder who, with little convincing, had already begun constructing quite the intricate drawing of the damaged slabs. Though it was not to say he was off easy just yet, for the evening was undoubtedly near, and the bugs were out biting in full force. But not too near, as it was still quite temperate despite the sun's newfound shyness, especially up the river on the far side of the dam where the breeze was as mild as the mist was thin.

Barron approached an anomaly upon the lower pathway he now patrolled: a plank of wood knotted in twine. "Did either of you notice this here?"

"I'm starting to think that it was a ship that hit the dam." The young man pointed his finger towards 2b, dragging it diagonally from the spurting hole. "Do you see it, my lord? Do you see the outline?"

Feeling another sun rash forming, he waltzed closer into the comfort of the wall, away from the river twinkling in reds. "Maybe it wasn't a wagon wheel after all..."

———

"Hm?" turned Alanthus. "I'll be right back, my lord," he said, turning away towards the woods.

Barron studied the damaged wall some more. "The sun should be going down soon. Wrap it up," he said to Steven.

"I'm almost finished."

"It's a dam, Steven, not a canvas."

"You wanted a good drawing, didn't you?"

"Yes, but not *too* good. I don't want Marrin thinking I had help."

"My lord! I think you'll want to see this!" shouted Alanthus from the woods.

Steven lifted his head, grinning. "Go on then, *my lord*. Then we can go…That is if you still feel like walking back to the city tonight."

Jokingly jolting his body towards the water, he followed the other's voice into the woods, to the precipice of a flood gulley. Below past roots exposed, the escort alluded to an object amidst a thick layer of shriveled leaves. "Do you see it, my lord?"

"See what?" He harassed the hairs on his chin with the tip of his thumb, squinting. "That's what you wanted to show me? A broken mast?"

"Not that, my lord, I'm referring to *that*," he extended his hand, "does that look like a map to you on its underside?"

Intrigued, the man descended into the ravine. There Barron carefully extracted the piece of parchment with his blade. "It is a map. Quite long has it been since it's seen any light." He started blowing on it, disseminating leaf fragments and pollen. "The labels are still intact, if not slightly outdated."

"How do you figure?"

"Look here," he tapped on it.

"856," read Alanthus aloud. "Foundation Years; *oh*. What are these etchings up here, scribbled across the top?"

"I'm not sure."

"And why is the capital circled?"

"Perhaps we can ask its owner." He looked up and down the gulley like a lost tourist, causing the young man to grin.

Smiles slowly formed as the cartographer accoutered his optae. "*So? What is it?*" eagerly inquired Barron. "Can you read it? Can you read the symbols?"

"I can't decipher what it says, but I do know what language these symbols up here are scribbled in." Steven's words reeled the two men in close. "I'll give you a hint: they were here long before us Neuvians came."

"The Tumsib?" replied Alanthus.

"Earlier..."

"Sprites?"

"Pyrithian." Barron shook his head. "We'd have an easier time finding a canyon-dweller, much less finding someone who can decipher it. You're sure it's Pyrithian?"

The escort scratched his sweaty head. "Didn't the last of them go extinct well over a century ago?"

"My point exactly," said Barron.

Cool was the valley air and pink the clouds as the trio made their way back over the Eastern Dam, all the while conferring their colorful theories of the map's origin. A simple yet aimless means to elude the long stretch ahead.

"Are you coming, my lord?" asked Alanthus, the other a ghost in the channel's mist.

"Why don't we try the main road this time!" shouted Steven.

He said nothing. His eyes were down, fixed intently upon the unfolded map's contents. "Sure, yes, great." The locations he knew of were all there. In the same familiar spots too, but the Pyrithian etchings across the top, he wondered.

"I would have thought you would want to cut through the swamp again," he said, reapproaching.

"My observations of that route are complete. I just need to consolidate my findings. Honestly," continued the cartographer, "Daemon and I are convinced the only real reason we're doing this resurvey job is to somehow aid the alchemists in their search for Glowers. Think of it, why else would Marrin stress marking them down? Why would he care?"

A sly grin was creased upon the man's face. "Hersey! Marrin would never agree to such favors for our syndicate overlords. Not unless of course the queen herself asked him personally. Oh, wait." At the very base of the dam, on the last platform of the flooded spillway, the men winced in anticipation in the face of a turbulent stream. This time around when they had met the waters, they knew they would have to be wiser—without shoes, that is, for the long slog ahead would not be so generous in the way of light. They ended up leaving them in the careful hands of the young escort and his makeshift woody raft.

But first, they turned a last time, facing the company's stamp upon the Eastern Dam's belly. A pretty picture, if not for the gushing water's mist obstructing it.

"I'm just surprised it's still standing. Surely a flaw that significant would have eventually toppled the whole structure."

"Well, Stevie, this is no ordinary dam now, is it? That there is the work of our Malyptah, the greatest architect the realm has ever known. Besides, I suspect the dam was breached during the Slumber."

Perfectly it had seemed clear now to him their only glaring advantage of their route through the flooded spillway, as they flapped their arms and legs (and door) away from the realm of the Eastern Dam, around the sunken aqueduct and the last of the levees toward dry land: the pervasive grime had at last whittled away from his jacket.

As for his colleague, he now looked cleaner than ever, even more so than when they had first departed; healthy as well, his face since returned to its alabaster hue. "…I suppose a ship could have detached from the harbor and drifted into the riverway," considered Steven, "as for the stop gate, I don't know how it'd be possible to get through one intact."

"I wouldn't exactly call that ship intact. But regardless of how it got here…if that hole was created before the Slumber, we would have been made aware. I seem to remember a time not long ago when our bannermen frequented this quadrant of the woods." After ringing out their clothing they refilled their bladders and set off onto the patrol-men's path through the woods, southward, where the faint semblance of a minced stone pathway could be found amid the forest floor.

"OW!" they watched Alanthus jump, his face aghast like that of a scared child's. "What was *that*?"

"That would be a helix whip," chuckled Steven. "Left unchecked, this invasive weed will easily suffocate the entire realm. For now, they'll only lash out at you if you step on 'em."

The weeds had become far too loud not to notice, spreading their roots unshyly across the pathway and on, up the great trees' bark. The young man made a game out of finding the crispiest, most voluptuous helix whips as targets for his boots. A short-lived game, that is, following yet another spanking thrash to his ankles, sending both himself and a family of nearby deer wide-eyed.

Following a good laugh, Barron's mind wandered back to the hoary map, and the cryptic symbols scribbled on its rim. "Do you think it's a treasure map?" he whispered aloud.

"It very well could be," said the mapmaker, "but what treasure? A few bloodstone jewels and veins?"

"Maybe someone knows something we don't, who knows. What if these are coordinates? I can't believe that I am saying this," he said, a funny glimmer in his eyes, "but I think we should head back to the dam for the night. Some rest might do us some good. What do you say?"

They halted in place, allowing the birds and crickets a turn.

Steven pulled his feather from his mouth and tapped it on his iterated map. "I wholeheartedly would have agreed with you back there," he said, "yet here we are, almost halfway back to the main road by now."

"Where's your sense of adventure? Besides, you've injured your leg. Yes—yes, and we had to stay the night in order to tend to your wounds." He had a queer look, enough to cause the mapmaker a good chuckle.

He looked now up the path from whence they came. "So very thoughtful of you," he said. Barron wasn't dim, he knew he knew something was awry. His sarcasm was a shield—a man who is desperately trying to distinguish himself from the other leads would most certainly not dally. Nevertheless, the prospect of some sleep apparently outweighed his desire for an argument.

"Why don't we set up camp here, then? Good access to running water, nice cozy canopy to keep a fire warm—"

"No, no, no. Not here, we're far too exposed. Plus, I need more information. More clues. Anything. Alanthus?"

Steven rolled his eyes.

"Either or is an upgrade over the tent, my lord."

"Exactly," he said. "But first the two of you must promise me something. You mustn't speak a word of this map, or the shipwreck to anyone. Not to your betrothed, not to Marrin, not your parents…no one."

"You have my word, my lord."

"Come on, Steven, if what I say is true, your bride-to-be will be more than understanding."

"What do you need another treasure for anyway?" scoffed Steven. "You're second in command at the only design and build company in all of Maldinia. Your dagger is worth more than my home—"

"Do you think Beau Nero asked himself that after a long, hard day's work?" he interrupted, "what about Lord Stainberry, Lord Frostberry? Lord Vanic?!"

"Okay, okay," exhaled Steven, "you win."

On the surface he looked several shades deranged as he stomped the river pathway, throwing chunks of splintered wood and rope indiscriminately into the awakened woods. And it's true, he was discernibly cantankerous as if he had been actively trying to cause his stomach knots, but he was by no means deranged. Just busy. Though he wasn't the only one busy. By now the flames of Alanthus's fire had reached well over Steven's head, luring biters from deep within the forest for a brief and unforgettable rapture.

"I thank you for entertaining my curiosity," coughed Barron, joining the men around the ungodly fire.

Despite coming up short of additional clues to the seamen's purpose, the men had found him in quite a decent mood as he sat there warming his hands.

Little did they know, the pathway and woods had been wiped clean of any indication of a shipwreck. This, however reassuring to him, would not stop his eyes from wandering the woods near and far. Thankfully, for his sanity, there were Glowers enough to go around to entertain his angsts: chubby and elastic their stalks, they were everywhere the moon's gaze was not.

They warmed their soggy boots and feet by the flames, filling their deprived bellies with what little rations they had brought along (or foraged), saving little, some none, for the journey back.

"How are your legs faring?" asked Alanthus.

"Oddly, they've never felt so good."

"Whatever they rubbed on you, that womp juice, it should be bottled," chimed the architect, wincing uncomfortably as his bony rear met a root. "Thought for a second they were going to amputate them."

"What do you think will happen to them?" inquired Alanthus.

"Once the water levels return to normal? I suppose they will have to resettle elsewhere. Back to wherever they're from, I guess."

"And where would that be?" pondered the cartographer.

"You're the map expert, you tell us. *Oh*, and that reminds me, Alanthus…my associate and I have a matter we'd like to discuss with you."

"We do?" mumbled Steven.

"Yes." He glared at the man. "We do."

Upon leaning the last of the broken mast upon the raging fire, Alanthus sat.

"Even though you technically fall under our jurisdiction, it was you who had found the map," he started, forcing himself to meet his eyes. "With that being said, it wouldn't be appropriate for us to just commandeer it from you—"

"It's yours, my lord," uncharacteristically interjected the escort. "I don't desire it."

A great sigh of relief followed.

"So, what do you desire, then?" averted the cartographer, "to be an ascendant?"

"Yes, that's right."

Barron forced a smile. "Well, so long as you keep your end of the bargain, I shall do whatever it takes in my power to ensure that your qualities are stressed to the Ascendency."

CHAPTER 5

A THIRST FOR KNOWLEDGE

There was a brash light peering down upon their camp when he had come alive to a familiar sound; whooshing water, padded by the enclosure, and by the battered wall in which it fled.

The morning had come, and his once tame head of hair relaxed entirely into bangs. His eyes, desiccated from their long exposure to the unbridled flames, could hardly be opened. As he re-acclimated himself to his senses, it was clear that the young man had taken it upon himself to tend their fire throughout the night. It would at least explain their now empty kindling cache, the shriveled bags beneath his eyes, and the clumps of scattered ash encircling their still-running fire. But it would not explain the smile on the young man's face.

Quite an unnatural sight so early in the morn, Barron thought.

"I apologize if I woke you, I was just about to go try my hand at fishing. The canal's—"

"You two can forage on our way back home." He couldn't stop thinking about it: a beautiful chest with thick girdles and a narrow slot for a key. The way it *clicked* when it opened. Even in his dreams, it was quite weighty.

Steven's boots were just beyond the edge of his feet when he stirred awake to the sound of his stomach. His utter lackadaisicalness had allowed the pair to warp and curl overnight.

If it wasn't obvious before, it was now: Steven would not be ready any time soon. This he knew well as he watched him struggle to fit his feet inside of his hole-ridden boots, and without a care in the world either. As such he set off back towards the lonely island for a "little swim," or so he insisted. In truth, he had found himself an even better purpose; ridding the world of the ship's wheel.

When the trio had finally departed, they had seen a shimmering morning dew dissipate into a garish afternoon. They found little comfort on the road eastwards, the Merchant Road, where the helix whips still actively guarded their steps.

A glimpse of a crumbled sentry tower found due south of the Merchant Road, caused the men to stop. A sad sight presently, for it seemed yet another casualty of the Deep Slumber, to which some abominable, meddlesome thorns have since claimed. "Come to think of it, Daemon did mention something about some thorns in his last letter," Steven jotted, "nothing like he's ever seen before. Unlike the Glowers they've evidently found solace in the Screecher Hills."

"What your colleague fails to realize is their potential! Quite an effective stopgap wall, if you ask me," replied Barron.

"I want to thank you again, my lord, for returning the door," approached the escort. Steven's eyebrows perked up. "Abandoned or not, it felt odd borrowing it without anyone's permission. I'm just glad you were able to find me a branch fat enough to hold my weight."

"You never did strike me as a thief. Of course, that's not up for me to decide..."

The escort's smile wilted into a frown.

"Oh, don't worry, what happens in the valley stays in the valley," he turned, answered with an uneasy nod.

By mid-sunlight, their legs had turned to mush, but at last progress was palpable. Like the fog upon Step Mountain afar, a vestige of civilization had struck them high in the wind.

"Never thought I'd be happy to see the queen's colors again."

"What's that smell?" asked Alanthus.

"That my friend is wet paint." The cartographer exhaled. "We've made it to the Crossroads." Steven and Alanthus utilized their break to explore the outpost in repair. Barron all the while shied away in the shadow of a freshly minted watch tower, avoiding the many glares off the arbalists' shiny brims. The East Valley had ceased its turn, with their journey on the Merchant Road at an end, but there was one such keepsake from his trek that he could not yet evade. Even now, in the cross-hairs of the realm's finest crossbowmen, he had an insatiable itch to pull it out, unfold it, and give it a good look.

"There you are," approached Steven.

"Would you believe we're still sporting this nonsense?" he averted, alluding to the wet banner chasing up the side of a newly constructed watch tower. The Maldinian flag stood tall, perched high upon the foreground of a fertile backdrop. The Great Three, at the minimum, were present, arranged, like the original, with Loarea on the left, Residential on the right, and Market District looming ever-so-slightly on their rear. But that color, he couldn't shake it. "I thought it was a joke the first time I saw it, but now even old Ciguil would be rolling in his grave. *Violet*," he added, "what on Tethia does violet have to do with plateaus?"

"Clearly she's never witnessed the *glow* in all its glory," replied Steven.

Down below at the ford of the river Crossroads they meandered, where they topped off their bladders, and the mapmaker penned something across the way.

In the tall grass penal drudges, closely supervised, legs shackled, were attempting cleanup on an outhouse strangled by the barbed asphyxiators. The same ones that yet graced their path. Their dull farmer's tools paled against the thorns' meaty anchors, though, in rapid succession, they stood little chance at clinging on. Something of a similar tale northbound up Conqueror's Road. To the east, on the outskirts of Sprite's Forest, where for the longest time nothing had ever grown, heaps of penal drudges wriggled wheeled carts, over-encumbered, through a newfound jungle of Glowers and weeds.

The taint that was left following the Deserters' Arson of 851 F.Y. was still plain to see, but the dirt beneath it was on a miraculous start to something new.

Ere long the sun had vanished behind a long shadow. That's when machinations had begun churning, of all places, on the Great Founder's climb up Step Mountain the Unconquerable. A contingency plan had been concocted by him alone, dreaded in the event of one's overlooking. A plan that would require a certain linguistic knowledge that only a few alive could claim, Pyrithian. Finding the right book was a start. But first, several hundred dizzying layers later, the men were hailed by a stout wind and a clamor of combat drills.

Amidst old, jaded drill instructors, and their fumbling, bumbling cadets in training, they held, allowing themselves a brief moment to rehydrate with what little water they had left remaining from the river Crossroads. They sipped and watched the impressionable young cadets wave their training swords against target dummies and one another. That was until a group of penal drudges came by, drawing all eyes as they tugged along an enormous ballista tower on wheels.

They set it down over the southern edge before collapsing like corpses.

"Home at last," stretched Barron, setting off into a wet fog. The others followed behind, crossing beneath a sinister front gate wrought by crude effigies, and a top-heavy rampart manned by the queen's finest arbalists.

"I've never seen it from this angle before," Alanthus panned the cloudy sky in awe, his eyes wandering to a red mass at the summit of an ascending stone bridge. "Wish I could see the plateaus through this fog." Even within the clouds, surrounded by the nothingness that lay below them, Barron noticed the fissures in Conqueror's Bridge. Deep-seated fissures, which no amount of resin could halt; ones in which he bore no desire in reporting, nor perchance overseeing, which would continue well beyond the proximity of the main gate, all the way up onto the back of the red mass, on a busy cobblestone road polluted by the thwacks of arbalists' bolts. "So, this is it? The Armory District Mesa?" asked the young man.

"It sure is," humored Steven.

"Tut, tut, tut," jeered the man, drawing deflated stares from the armor polishers in the prison yard. "If I ever find myself in such a depraved state, I shall gladly welcome a lightning bolt to end my miserable suffering."

"Be careful what you wish for. The war machine gladly welcomes abled bodies," said Steven. "Speaking of abled bodies," he alluded to a group of fellow gray jackets across the road, builders, thatching the roof on a few scrappy-looking barracks.

Barron returned his attention to the prison yard, scoffing indiscriminately at the many a pouty face. "You see, that's the whole point, I won't be able—I'll be dead."

At the northern face of the mesa, the road thronged at the great stone pavilion of the Hub. There the young man's contract had come to a sudden end amongst maps and plaques and statues of old.

Straight-faced, the architect met his eyes. "I will see to it the Ascendency receives a written attestation of your courage and initiative on this venture."

There was dirt and sweat visible on the young man's head as he removed his helm and parted his best attempt at a bow. "I thank you both very much for this opportunity," he bowed again, his armor clinking and clunking as he sped his way up the central connector towards Market District. "What an adventure!" The two shared a laugh as they entered upon the left-hand connector to Loarea.

"Finally, some peace and quiet," said Barron over the edge of the world.

"Let me know if you need help finding that treasure," said Steven, his flippant words causing the other to tense.

By now the architect had the look of a man whose hands were caught red in the act; cuffed in rope, with but the littlest chance of escaping. Of course, he was dreading the obligation. But as much it pained him, he knew the repercussions of keeping his old friend in the dark were too risky to ignore.

He set his sights on the eastern skies, to the veil of a torpid cloud.

More had evidently since joined, considering how muddy the ditch had grown as he filled his team in on the situation at the Eastern Dam. As for the many questions that had followed its sharing, pleading ignorance for a task that should never have been assigned to him in the first place came somewhat naturally.

The rain continued through the night, and into the afternoon that followed, flooding the buried mines with just enough water to require the construction of moats. To make matters worse he had found himself in a quandary: a leak had sprung in his private flap, leaving him with little choice but to join the rabble. The passing chatter was the worst of it, though the ordeal proved not a complete waste of his time. For a tidbit of information had been shared by an underling of his; a tidbit of information that would save him an unnecessary slog to the Isle of Knowledge: Viamar Library had been closed on account of a nasty leak.

Begrudgingly his quest to learn the ancient language would have to wait.

There was a break in the storm the next day, and the ditches were emptying. In line for a busy food stall in the West Market, a beggar approached the architect in a desperate attempt to sucker him out of his hard-earned crowns. After disregarding his existence entirely, he watched the same beggar ambush another unsuspecting gray jacket in line.

"Scram!" finally noticed the merchant's wife, beneath a sign that read "POLETREE."

"You all right there, Barron?" commented Steven, "you look a little bit disturbed."

"No, I am not all right. Why must these vagabonds insist upon the same old 'injured horse, pregnant wife' nonsense? I haven't seen a horse since before the Lull, have you?"

Judging by the few nonplussed looks from the other gray jackets in line, he wouldn't be surprised if it was the first time a few of them had heard his voice.

"Which did you mean?" popped out the dirtied face of a builder, "a horse, or a pregnant wife?"

He frowned. "Neither, come to think of it."

Upon a secluded bench in the Central Market Plaza, a figure approached him mid-bite, blotting out an already-blotted sun.

Assuming it was another beggar, he continued chewing. *Ironic*, he thought it: A trade hub once renowned for its busy auction houses and bloodstone jewelers, was now a beggar trap in which the Great Founder's statue must forever suffer to witness. "Barron Alarie," uttered the stranger, a female voice, whose face was lost in a shadow overhead, veiling all save for a few dangling strands of her honey-blonde hair.

He knew that hair. That voice. That pinkish pale complexion. "Myleyn Thornrose," he replied, meeting her cerulean-blue eyes, "surely it's been a while."

She smiled, exposing a dimple in the bottom left corner of her left cheek. "The last time I saw you was in preparation. What would that be? Fifty-five years-fifty-six maybe?"

"Do you remember when the two of us were nearly expelled for cheating?" He felt his heartbeat fluttering in the space between each word.

"It's a good thing Lord Encore was in a good mood that day," she said. "What have you got there?"

"Poultry," he said, sitting upright. "At least that's what I think they meant…" He stared her up and down awkwardly. "My, you were but a girl last time I saw you. Now look at you, all grown up."

"Barron, we're the same age." She laughed.

His focus was stolen by nearby chatter—vagrants, loitering outside the only storefront in sight without boards covering their windows. "What are you doing walking alone through the Inner City?" he found his eyes lingering some more on the storefront, an elixir emporium, with strange characters congregating around the heat lamp on its curb. "I am beginning to think it's not so safe for a lady to do so anymore."

"I travel quite a lot." She tucked the fleeting ends of her hair behind her ears. "I'm a high society etiquette teacher."

He could no longer ignore the signs: the pang and the patter on the mossy rooftops, the metallic smell weighing down the air, the forewarning chill chasing down his back. "Allow me to walk you back to your residence. Is that where you were headed to?"

"I was actually on my way to the Viamar Library. Would you…care to join me?"

She was answered by a longing stare. Then a smile. "I thought the library was closed."

"What's so funny? Is there something on my face?"

"No, nothing. You're perfect. I mean, I suppose I could find myself a nice book for such a gloomy evening as this one. Shall we?"

Thunder shook the very fabric of the rock beneath them as they set forth from the Central Market Plaza, away beyond the crying statue of the Great Founder, disappearing into alleyways gone from the sun, trickled in slow-burning lampposts, amidst shifting lanes of droving droplets and weary storm drains, wide and lockless.

At the very end of an underpass, the light shone, uninhibited by the cathedral gables and the wall of rooftops. This however promising would not save the man from slipping over a break in the road, nor Myleyn from bursting out into an adorable fit of laughter.

There was a steady plume of smoke cut swiftly in the rain as the two linked arms and scurried their way off the Outer Circle.

Even as he approached the first islet on the Isle of Knowledge, the Viamar Library, his reservations did not yet fade. More aptly they had been placed on hold, following a great whiff of a million pages decaying: for just one look at the skinny little bridge with cracks at their rear, away the main body of once it was fully attached, flanked by the nothingness that lay below them, shall induce shivers. But not anymore; not at least as they entered through a rusty archway through a yard of scraggy trees.

"Good evening, gentlemen," said Myleyn to a pair of passing peacekeepers, "do try not to catch a cold in this unruly weather."

Even outside, as he scanned the shoddily patched sections of the library's rooftop, he could infer the locations of the rumored "leaks"; and hear the scattered plops of water meeting the overworked rain buckets inside. "You must really be itching for a book," he said, honking his way up a questionable set of stairs of a split-level tower of lesser wood and brick.

"Not exactly. We lost a couple of our own to the Slumber, sadly, alongside their collection of training material. I am to train their replacements. Are you familiar with the Vement sisters?" By now her shin-length floral dress was nigh see-through, and her hair crept unshyly down her forehead.

He opened the door to a cozy waft of air, smirking as his eyes grazed a rain bucket. "I was right."

"Huh?"

"Nothing. Not really. Lord Vement was a friend of my father's, however."

"Well then, I'll have to introduce you to the girls some time. I am going to find the librarian, Barron. I shan't be long."

"Take your time, I don't intend on returning to work today. Not unless by some miracle our workshop is miraculously reopened."

Losing track of one's time proved quite easy here, in his old study place of preparation. Seconds quickly turned to minutes, like in the old days, sifting aimlessly through timeworn volumes, tombs and scrolls.

And yet promise for the one was fickle. That was until he bumped into a lopsided display on floor three, *History and Artifacts*. Where, on the other end of a glass window, a mask wrought of pure white bone lay. An "Ancient Pyrithian Hunting Mask," it read.

A cruel joke, he thought it. The eye slots were smooshed, taking on an unnaturally rectangular shape. It was cracked in a few more places than one as if a rock had fallen from the skies upon the poor old hunter's head.

But that was irrelevant now. Just beside the display, the One stared back at him: *A Proper Guide to Pyrithian*, by Lord Lester Encore. A product of his former headmaster, it was the only known linguist guide to the ancient language; and quite possibly his best and only chance at deciphering the mysterious symbols upon his map (with relative discretion, that is).

"There you are. I thought you had left." She started grasping at the tattered binders of the book stack beside her leg, revealing a rose locket between her breasts. "I found something that might interest you." She handed him a book with the letters *Malyptah* embossed upon its cover.

"Aha. Regrind Malyptah. A good find. He was once a Nero architect, you know. One of the greats. Next time find one I haven't read." The feverish languor struck a boiling point at the librarian's counter where, only feet from its source, an old woman sat alone with her head down and her lunch cold.

"Is she dead?"

She gasped, playfully nudging him. "Pardon, my lady. We'd like to borrow a few books if you wouldn't mind."

It took a few seconds before her eyes finally perked open. "Oh, yes, yes, of course. Do please note your selections. And names if you will," she said. "Nothing like a nice fire to warm your bones."

"Alarie," shrieked the woman, her shoulder, neck, and chin poised like she was fifty years younger. "My dear boy. Any relation to Lord Friedrich Alarie?"

He forced a smile. "My grandfather."

She squinted her eyes, scanning his facial features with a deep fondness. "I believe there is no denying that. I am old enough to remember when your grandfather was king."

"Right," he side-eyed Myleyn, not nearly enough in the mood to alter an old lady's memories. He moved from the hearth's aim, maintaining his composure ever so politely out the door.

Outside the rain slowed some, allowing for a more leisurely stroll on the main body. Offering his escort services, he minded not. After all, for the first time since conceiving his contingency plan, he had found a glimmer of hope for success: inside his bag was his copy of *A Proper Guide to Pyrithian*. One such translation guide he could not wait to unravel.

Their paths converged at a charming, two-story cottage with an extraordinary view, if not nebulous, of the streetlamps on the rows of the corpus below. Lost in a sea of tawny karnip manors, hers was the lively one with the white shutters.

"If you are wondering what that noise is, those would be my temporary guests," she remarked. "I have allowed my newest trainees to stay here until their home has been cleared."

He met her at the front door. "Perhaps we can get together again soon, Barron?" she turned, a shy glimmer in her eyes. "Somewhere not the library next time, perhaps." They both smiled.

"Have you ever been to the Floating Lily?"

It was this simple yet effective routine he had adopted in the last week of spring: obliging his day-to-day duties as lead architect and company lead, then, quite immediately after, returning home for his Pyrithian language studies. Often, he would even forget to eat as he was far too preoccupied with learning a new alphabet to care.

On an uncomfortably humid start to a summer season, the realm saw yet another bout of rain. Vintners, farmers, and gardeners rejoice. With the surplus of rain came an excess of unabashed alone time. Although escaping one's obligations didn't stand much of a chance for him either way.

Month six also saw the recruitment of his old friend to aid in unraveling the enigma. Steven's help, thus far, had actually proved quite useful, even if it meant the slightest possibility of sharing his chance reward. However, based on his choosy focus, he was not sold that the mapmaker would see this treasure hunt through to the end. In fact, he was quite confident that once the rain finally stopped, so too would his help. Overall, that was just fine as he didn't mind the second pair of eyes.

Within the course of the next few days, the two had meticulously absorbed the entire Pyrithian alphabet. Even a few words.

Ruh, or more commonly known in its Proper form of *no,* was his personal favorite, as not only was it easy to remember but it was also quite amusing to say.

With the *glow's* eventual return, it was quite time for a break from his Pyrithian studies. Deserved even more so after seeing his once hobby now weaseling its way into his real job. He was not one to let a good thing get away…It is for this exact reason that he had surprised Myleyn with a bushel of fresh pekni flowers, plucked crudely from her newly evicted neighbor's lawn, along with an invitation for supper at the most desired eatery in all the North Valley.

Sharing a ride into the North Valley in the back of a packed macro wagon was by no means ideal, nor cozy, however it would most certainly beat braving Loarea Tunnel by foot to and fro after dark. Myleyn didn't seem to care, despite her hair being thrown around more than a willow tree in a summer squall. She was as much a child of the valley as he. (That is, of course, like the overwhelming majority of noble offspring, exclusively during winter.)

Even before entering the domain of the North Valley, he could visualize the vivid green rich setting; the golden fenceposts fending the hectares of hilltop estates and their harvests. The best smell too: wet fertilizer after a long day's rain.

It was dark by the time they had left the Loarea Tunnel in their rear, too dark to see the flowers, but not nearly dark enough to deny his whole vision. He could at least say he embraced the sour smell of yellowing citric trees like it were daytime, bordered upon the old brick road to Maldinax. Though it was clear that this was a far more overgrown, less tidy version of one's vision.

Indeed, the rolling hills of old stone manors in the background of his vision were all accounted for. The same went for the rivers and the brooks snaking through their backyards. Even the lingering songs were present at night, gifted from what little birds were left in the boughs above. But not the weeds. For the weeds, it would likely take the city's bloated supply of penal drudges six years to rid them from just the North Valley alone—or a few weeks with a good fire.

Tonight's supper was being held at the Quincunx of Maldinax, in the sacred plunge pool of the four rivers, where the moonlight twinkles heavy as stars upon shallow falls, where well-to-do patrons have the distinct privilege of indulging upon on their favorite savory fish, wines, and pies from valley to sea, all from the comfort of their very own floating lily.

"…Again, I do apologize for the bumpy ride," said Barron, dressed dapperly in a woolen overcoat, with a standing collar half the length of his arm. "I suppose it is a glimmer of hope we should see a couple of horses in these trying times. Our men have been scouring the Pebblewood River long and hard for our missing steeds ever since the Awakening."

"Let me know if they find any." "My father says he will trade just about anything for one," she said, before turning to a vague reflection of herself in the pond beneath their floating pedestal. "I just hope I look satisfactory tonight."

He leaned forward, musing, a mischievous grin plastered on his drunken face. She was the most beautiful girl there. "I would like for you to meet my mother someday. I think she would find it amusing to meet one of the women my father insisted that I court with long, long ago."

She scratched her head. By now her face was as ruby as his. "So, am I privy to any of these other suitors?"

He set his chalice down and grinned. "Oh Myleyn, we may be one of the littlest realms in all of Pelegra, but our land is ripe with secrets. *Shall we?*" Two long sickles were extended when the fettered, crater-touched lily—along with its two guests, their table, empty plates, chalices, and chairs—descended to the ground like the steady wobble and weave of a falling snowflake.

On land they stumbled like drunkards out of their chairs, their lily returning safely into place all of twelve feet high over the sacred waters of the Quincunx waters. As they found their footing, Myleyn's corset nearly busted at the seams, sending the two into some ugly laughter. That alone, he felt, was worth the hefty bill and bumpy ride.

On break the following afternoon, Barron and Steven's hard work had finally borne fruit. Following a rigorous all-day long study, the two had finally translated the cryptic symbols stretched across the map's border. In Proper it read: "An anchor for a vessel, so one may grow." Next to the bewildering honeycomb were a few more letters, numbers, and symbols: 52*41' 11" N|111*30'23 E.

"That can't be right," said Steven, staring intently at his atlas.

"What?"

"The coordinates," he clarified, "the location's in Loarea District, just a short distance behind our workshop. Nothing but weeds and adders back there."

"Guess we won't know until we start digging."

"Yes, but how deep? I see no indication of depth here. Unless, maybe, it's on the surface."

"Doubtful."

Confirming once more their coordinates, the two sank into the back of his leather sofa.

"Maybe there's something more to this riddle," sat up Barron, "what do you suppose this 'anchor' is?"

"Might be referring to the ship's anchor," said the mapmaker. "At any rate, I don't know what that has to do with Loarea District."

"Possibly another clue or a key of some sort." Barron started stroking the prickly hairs on his chin. "Well, if there *was* an anchor it likely sank with the rest of its hull. Either way, we can't go just go digging around the dam now, nor Loarea for that matter. We'd be questioned silly." Upon pushing the map closer to his candle, he tapped. "What is this here, beside our coordinates? Do those look like more symbols to you?"

Steven leaned in closer, pressing up to his synthetically squinted eyes. "Too faded to tell."

"Knowing our luck, that's probably our depth." He banged the table deflatingly and leaned his head back. "Let's revisit this matter when you get back from your expedition. And please, not a word of any of this to Daemon."

"You know me, I won't say a word."

"Well, no, I don't know. Speaking of talking, I received a letter from Alanthus yesterevening. He's been selected to undergo the trials. The old boy may yet just be an ascendant," he scoffed, shoving his front door open to a calm summer breeze.

"So, I guess this means Daemon and I will have to fend for ourselves this time around?" On the opposite end of his front gate, the cartographer clenched the iron bars with a pouty frown. "Just promise me if you do end up finding that treasure, set aside a few shiny ones for Savannah?"

"Two blind, unarmed cartographers alone in the untamed valley," he started, locking his front gate, "what could possibly go wrong?" Following a clean sweep through his yard, his body was quite ready for some rest. As for his mind, restless in riddles, he had himself a chest full of elixirs in his closet designed exclusively for such conundrums in mind.

CHAPTER 6

OUTCRY

Weightless with naught but the clothes on his back, he was back, on his back, in the waters of the flooded spillway, peering upwards in the mist through the hole in 2b, where his eyes could not help but to wander. That was when the sunlight had gone; when rubble and water began to erupt like lava from the gap. A reflective object appeared. Closer and closer it teetered over the edge, before falling toward him, awakening him in a puddle of sweat of his own making.

His work week commenced with a scare, witnessing a mess of gray jackets staggered in the ditch. Amidst the lips' shade and onward up the mossy hill were heaps of gray jackets: red stripes, brown stripes, yellow and green; the fat ones shying away inside, where they peered out awkwardly from the entrance flap and air slits as if to avoid the inevitable slip and fall down the hill in front of their fellow workmen.

"How lovely," he muttered aloud, "the whole team can witness my tardiness in all its glory." He wondered first whether it was the heat, seeing as how dreadfully heavy the air had grown since the rain had finally decided to cease. But that would not explain the peacekeepers, nor the young woman in the dark green bell-sleeve gown huddled beside Marrin and Selvin.

"Bite your tongue," he said through his teeth, cocking a crooked smile as he climbed his way down towards them.

The sun skirted low behind the Cloud Spice Company factory, giving him a better view of the stranger in the green dress. She was a young female, only a few gray hairs older than himself. She had stark white skin, like he, with medium-brown hair, braided jarringly tight in traditional Maldinian fashion with two plateau-shaped loops on both ends of her ears, and a last, hiding behind her head. Closer down the hill, it had finally occurred to him whose green eyes that powdered face belonged to. It was the queen's regent, Falun Knish: The only council member with as much root powder and tree sap on her face as the queen who dared not wear purple.

"Barron, come! This here's the queen's regent, Lady Knish. She's come to personally invite us to a declamation this afternoon," explained Marrin, rousing little in the way of fervor.

"The realm is in your debt, Lord Alarie," she smiled, "thanks to your efforts the wells are pumping once more like normal."

It was a simple compliment which most would not think twice of. And yet he would be the first to distinguish a careful act from a genuine one. And careful it was indeed. But that's not to say he didn't enjoy hearing it any less, especially so in front of the lead builder.

She signaled over her guardsmen. "We shall see your men come noon today, Lord Vander."

"Why is everyone outside, Marrin?" he turned to him.

The overseer sighed. "Thought today was our lucky day…"

The sun was not even yet at full mast when the ditch was swept in the clammer of far-off horns.

The threescore gray jackets not currently on assignment were led by Marrin, Selvin, and Barron, sticking firmly to the back of the queen's courtyard, in distant view of the Market's head. Although unlikely, it was not far-fetched for him to believe that the overseer's choice was intentional; at least when considering the convenient access and the fair bit of shade found within the shadow of the late King Maximillian Plateau I's statue.

"In peril, we ride!" read a builder sarcastically aloud off the Old King's plinth. Its patina was staling, and yet the Old King's crossbow paled fierce as ever against the open sky.

"Barron!" he heard a voice call out his name.

There were dizzying sparks cast upon the diminishing open spaces of the courtyard's cobbles, as he approached an unkempt man with sandy-blond hair. Not nearly bright enough not to notice the other crossbows just like it, however. Quite like the Old King's, the arbalists too held their crossbows: firm like the Old King's, and yet skinny like a skeleton's outstretched arm. Today their presence was felt by all, menacing the gaps in the labyrinths of hedge walls and flower gardens, continuing up above, onto the Crown Butte: the stubborn boil upon the northernmost edge of Market District Plateau, and the ruling place of Maldinia.

It had occurred to him as he made his way to his old friend, dwelling upon his newly deciphered coordinates, that the tintinnabulation and horns had all but come to an end. There was a vibration underfoot when petals had begun to rain upon the courtyard. Their eyes now shifted to the Crown Butte stairs, fell unto the queen's ascendants, armed to the teeth in their emblematic telleum teal armor, their X-shaped helms allowing little for guesswork. They were a strong lot as stalwart as a castle's walls, but few, too few, quite like the telleum ore they bore of Neuvian lore. And with the last of them assembled, the upper stratum of Market District fell eerily silent. Their nervous chatter wiped clean in a fell swoop of crashing shields, scanned the petal-touched podium over the edge of the above butte.

"Let's see what she'll denounce this time," mumbled the man aloud, noticing a profoundly red glimmer over the tip of the escarped rise.

Out from her dueling gardens came Queen Satina Rook, a sheltered pale woman with a long neck and sad eyes, garbed in an ill-fitting purple dress with gold pattern lining.

And not a clap could be heard.

Typical of her infrequent public addresses, her silvery-blonde hair was braided in an elaborate bun with tiny pins pricked into its many folds. Perched loosely atop it was the bloodstone crown of King Utazeb Pontis: a magnanimous gold headrest with a band of pure bloodstone ore. She came shadowed by the ascendant supreme, Aer Paulvin Elder-more, his telleum pauldrons climbing up and down his shoulders like a mountain range; and another, to whose presence was felt though not yet revealed.

A nervous smile suddenly formed on her powdered face, witnessing the many scattered looks in their eyes.

She leaned forward into a cowel—a cone-shaped device used to amplify the breadth of one's voice, a product of the Nero Company— where she carefully regurgitated a pre-prepared statement regarding the recent easing of disbarment on several homes and storefronts through-out the city which, although promising to hear, was but a drop in the bucket. Next, an assurance for yet another Gromula Day celebration. And still not a clap was heard.

Barron himself tuned out the woman, chattering instead with his fellow workman. After all, it was like he had been listening to a double of her late husband and predecessor, King Ciguil Rook. Disparately void of charisma, she at least made an occasional attempt to lift her crown onto her uninspired masses, if not for a few brief moments. "...without further ado, I present to you Lord Vanic Dacmaster, master alchemist at the Alchemy Guild, to share a report on his team's recent progress on the Cleansing effort." She extended a hand behind her to a stoic man in a dark trench coat. Stiff-backed, the Alchemy Guild's second-in-command walked slowly to the rhythm of his own beat, his hands held dubiously behind his back.

Although he was no council member of hers, many whispered that the man with the silver-streaked ponytail and acid burn had the queen's ear. As he came upon the masses, an inexplicable sense of malaise weighed upon the courtyard. Barron knelt into the workman's ear beside him, an unkempt man with sandy-blond hair, and whispered, "Remus, is it just me, or does the queen look a few years younger than you last remember?"

"Maybe," replied the man, "kind of hard to tell with all that powder."

"Did you sleep in your uniform last night?" He laughed.

The tinkerer wiggled his hand. "Technically never slept."

"...Eleven thousand Glowers!" repeated the queen, since returned to the comfort of her podium. "A most impressive if not concerning revelation." She cleared her throat. "Which, I am afraid, is all the more reason for us to remain forthwith and vigilant in this fight to reclaim our kingdom from the Glowers." She lowered her head, causing the light to spring off her crown like a weapon. "Now, for the matter in which I have summoned you all today...I have received word that our beloved, General Konnix, has fallen gravely ill and has passed away in his home overnight." Her words were received with a mix of gasps and gossip.

"I don't understand," turned Marrin to Selvin, "since when was the general sick?"

"Upon further investigation, the Alchemy Guild has found the man's home to be infested with Glowers," she added, lowering her head even lower. "I plead we keep General Konnix and his family in our memory, however, this is all the more reason why the Cleansings should continue, until either a Slumber culprit is determined or every last mushroom is rooted out."

Her words were met with venom, which she naively attempted to cull with affirmations alone.

Rooted out, peculiarly Barron repeated to himself over a lively commotion.

"My heart is with you all, but do not weep, as your future is bright! Your continued cooperation during this troubling chapter will ensure you and your children a safer, more prosperous tomorrow."

"When will it end?!" they cried.

"I'm not sleeping in a tent another night!" jeered another.

The outrage soon spread like a plague from one end of the court-yard to the other, causing her skin to shed more than a moth's wings under the hot sun. Peacekeepers started shoving their way through the more congested inlets, blocking off dead-ends, while removing as many disruptors as physically able. And able they were, especially the Tumsib peacekeepers, some so very tall that their heads poked nigh over the hedge walls—a sound of agony followed as they dragged some three agitators at a time by their hair and limbs.

"I am sure many of you are eager to return to your homes and shops, however, it is my role as your queen to protect my flock from all threats foreign and domestic."

Considerably outnumbered, a dispatch of ascendants broke off from the formation to engage. Citizens with a bit more sense took this as their queue to scarper.

"Let's get the men back to camp." Marrin signaled, almost blowing several of their ears out with a deafening whistle.

"Right," replied the man, sneering past a beating as they continued westward upon the Outer Circle for the Loarea bridge.

"How could they just accuse the former general of irresponsibly harboring Glowers?" vented Barron to Remus over the plod of muffled chatter and busy footsteps down the blustery slope. "It's blasphemy, those things were everywhere when we awoke. Some the size of a lamp-post. If they really are as dangerous as they say, you would think they would have gotten him long ago—try maybe during the Slumber."

Later he perseverated on the queen's words from the lofty roost of his bedroom balcony, sipping on his dessert wine from the comfort of his chair, soaking in the last of the *glow*, a faint tremor interrupted his train of thought. It was similar to the one produced by the ascendants just hours earlier, but not identical. This one was subtle. Then again, what would be considered subtle on a ten-mile run atop a three thousand-foot tall plateau in the sky? —the army marching off to war? The climatic return of the realm's horses? An otherwise quiet evening in the secluded comfort of his home was now officially soured by an anomaly.

His thoughts betrayed him, sending him rushing downstairs in a hurry in nothing but his night robe to confirm the security of his front gate. Pebbles poked and prodded the soft layer of skin beneath his feet as he scampered down his walkway, but he pressed on. In confirming the security of his front gate, he was acquainted with yet another tremor. This time around it shimmied the hedge wall just slightly. But more than enough to notice with no wind about. It was getting closer, more per-sonal as if the very ground beneath him was opening. He wondered if it was a dream as his gate began rattling.

His cheekbones were cold, and his ears started to ring. Startling him enough not to notice the carriage rolling on by. He feared the worst, lighting the sconces as he hustled his way up the many flights of his spiral stairs to the top of his tower.

In his attic, amidst the graveyard of his mother and father's old supper wears, he shined his lantern on the ceiling, revealing a barrel-sized hatch. Following a few firm tugs, he held his breath and ascended a ladder through a narrow passageway. Just as his face started turning blue, the next broke free, sending bats scattering off the merlons in a hurry.

"Two baths it is," he coughed, rising with blackened hands. Tucking his torso through an embrasure, he scanned quietly from the vantage of his roof for a source.

He was ready this time. But nothing since availed, save for a passing carriage and the few dwindling wicks in the street lanterns below.

That's when his paranoia began festering, for the prospect of the alchemists' coming was far too much for him to bear.

Thankfully, there were elixirs for that. And for now, the tremors had stopped.

CHAPTER 7

LIGNICOLOUS

He felt a nice long soak in the tub was merited before setting off that following workweek.

This was no different than any bath, however, today's felt different to him. Deserving, almost.

Fear of the alchemists' coming had taken seed, and yet for the first time in a long time, he actually was looking forward to leaving the privacy of his home. This was not a raise or a promotion that had caused this renewed pep in his step, as he moseyed on down Maximillian Ridge towards the Market District-Residential District Connector, but a test, a test of his innovation, one which would serve as the numbing agent from the monotony of the bridge repair he had been forcefully assigned to oversee in the lead engineer's absence.

Closer into the shadow of the looming behemoth, his route had become congested with a swarm of tattered children, shouting and laughing their way up the ridge in their holey hand-me-downs.

He drove straight through the middle of their reckless game. The little girls, now absconding, taunted the boys from afar. Expecting a good reaming or flogging, the boys nervously avoided eye contact with the nobleman, aiming instead at his faultless leather boots.

"I take it you boys must be from Lower?" Without much of any push at all, the smallest of the group burst out into a confession: "Yes, yes, my lord. We were just playing is all. We didn't mean to disturb you, none." The boy immediately fell back in line behind a young Tumsib, just a few inches shorter than himself, though no less timid than the next boy. Barron thought it amusing, looking upon a Sib child almost as tall as he, with a skin complexion not totally inhuman. Of course, through time and sun, that subtle gravel-gray undertone of his would alter in every which way of the rainbow (and alter it would, for this pup was lowborn).

"I see. Well, then I won't say a word of it to your parents," replied the man, answered by a swift sigh of relief. "*However*," he added, drawing their attention once more. "I do ask of you each a small favor." In perfect cadence, the boys wiggled their heads. "I am concerned for our brethren, is all. There was a troubling disturbance afoot a few days back. You boys wouldn't have anything to do with it, would you?"

They shook their heads.

"Great. Then I ask you this: if any of you hear anything suspicious down in your…installment, or anywhere else for that matter, you find me at the news board down yonder. Information I deem useful and, of course, not a far-fetched tale, I'll even toss one of these your way." He flicked a silver crown into the smooth clasp of his hand, sending the lot of them gleaming. "And yes, given time I will find out who has lied to me. Don't test my patience. That is all."

WANTED: LUMINA MUSHROOMS, read today's news board, after nearly passing it with his optimism intact.

The reward: a whopping two gold crowns.

"No wonder those signs are surging everywhere," he overheard one of his neighbors say to another.

Gold crowns? For a mushroom? He scoffed, continuing up the connector in disbelief.

With not a cloud in sight, the late morning grew hot as sin, and humid as a windowless cabin.

The truth of the matter was he really hadn't a clue as to the ins and outs behind the bridge repair he had been assigned to oversee today. All he knew was what the overseer told him, that Lord DuSprite and his firsts were still spread thin, and that he was to report to the Academy of the Conqueror Connector for a patchwork of a fissure "no wider than a bird's feather."

His bitterness aside for being tasked with such a waste-of-talent chore, he had put his ingenuity to good use, improving upon the existing tread-wheel pulley system for scaling tasks. Requiring a base and an operator on opposing ends, his innovation possessed the ability to not only extend and retract but to shift from side to side. This, in theory, will allow a single builder to perform death flirtatious tasks, and without the burden of its predecessor's top heaviness. A risk undoubtedly, but necessary, as the existing pulley system may just as easily deepen the extent of the crack.

Here marked the first time it would be used out of a test environment.

This would at least explain the half-petrified look on his face as he approached his team of builders for an overview of his invention. Luckily for him, choosing a volunteer to test this new contraption of his had come quite easy. As a few builders attempted a seal on the surface of the bridge with karnip resin, Second Builder Darren was carefully lowered into the fog towards the belly of the bridge.

"Keep your weight centered!" shouted Barron to his least favorite builder, who began forcefully rocking the floating platform into a full sway.

"This is fun!" shouted the balding builder, on a dangerous ride in the clouds.

"His grave," Barron whispered to his now snickering colleagues.

"Little lower," said Darren, "okay—good!"

Barron threw a balled fist in the air, sending First Builder Xarlen to tighten his end of the rope. Meanwhile, on the other end of the abyss, on the second and last islet of the Isle of Knowledge, the Academy of the Conqueror, First Builder Krieg confirmed the signal, tightening his half.

A few hours passed before the all-clear signal was raised by Darren. "Just in time for lunch," Barron exhaled, rolling his treasure map up, and exiting his portable tent. Poor timing it proved, however, as a great gust of wind came sweeping in from the sea, yanking a helping of wet fog across the work site. The platform was swaying. He started rushing up the connector towards the menacing academy, waving his hand in a pulling motion. "Pull him in, Krieg! Pull him in!" he shouted desperately.

"I am!" bellowed Krieg, "I am getting resistance from the other end I think!"

"O, don't tell me that," he swallowed, rushing back to the former islet.

Following a winded sprint, his message was duly received—the rope began to loosen, allowing Krieg to reel the dizzied builder into safety. "My apologies, Darren," smirked the architect as the builder hovered into view. "Can't see a thing in this fog."

"Apologize for what? This thing works like a charm!" he laughed. "Lord DuSprite better get home quick or he'll be out of a job."

"Get this place cleaned up," he said to anyone listening. "I have some administrative work that needs doing." After collecting his belongings, he set off for the Outer Circle, where a nasally voice caught his attention.

"Steven…Back so soon from your expedition? Don't tell me the entire West Valley has been resurveyed already—"

"No, no, we ran out of rations," frowned the mapmaker.

"You never learn, do you?"

He shrugged. "You should see the place, it's almost as feral as the East Valley."

"That reminds me," said Barron, "I need to speak with you in private. It's about, well, you know." They found a quiet alleyway where he said: "a root."

"A root? What do you mean a root?"

"*Shh.* Not so loud. The riddle, Steven. The riddle. Not a ship's anchor, but a root. At least I think."

The other scratched his head, lifting his bushy eyebrows up and down. "And how did you come to this conclusion?"

"Long story, but maybe just maybe this means we won't have to do as much digging as we once thought."

"What if the treasure *is* a root? Have you thought of that?"

"In Loarea?"

"Good point. So, what are we waiting for? Should we do a little digging later?"

"Not until the alchemists have finished cleansing the workshop and the lawmen clear; lest we draw unnecessary attention to ourselves. Oh, by the way, do you know what our tax crowns are now being used for?"

"The Glowers," he spoke prematurely.

"Luminas, you mean?"

He frowned. "I can't be the only one who thinks 'Lumina' sounds a hair too pleasant for an alleged murdering mushroom." As the two departed the alleyway, Barron pondered as to whether Darren's almost-accident would warrant an incident report. In the end, he settled on an alternative. For one thing, overshadowing his innovation's success in any way just seemed an awful shame to him.

Sheep's Tavern had their hands full with a rowdy bunch of builders that night. Financed by the reluctant foreman, a little thanks seemed not at all unwelcomed by the brown stripes in his employ. A generous gift for his closed pockets, for not one of the builders seemed to mind the warm, discolored ale one bit. Following a few rounds, a few more colors of the Nero color palette had miraculously found their way to that same West Market tavern and table. Quite a miracle indeed. Of course, it didn't take much mind for him to guess whose big mouth it was that had blabbed—the second builder was drunk before they even got there.

"I don't mean to pry, but is it true that you have been courting *the* Myleyn Thornrose?" inquired Steven's betrothed, Savannah, who knelt forward with some bright red ends spilled over her freckled face.

He grimaced upon noticing a thin yellow film on the front of the girl's teeth (an otherwise informative sign screaming LOWBORN). "Yes." In the two years he had known her, he had always thought the girl sweet, if not a bit odd. Even now, the way she knelt forward on her stool like an adolescent, unknowingly exposing her breaches for all to see, he couldn't help but smirk, wondering what it was his acquaintance had seen in the girl all those years ago.

"Did any of you hear some strange noises underfoot lately?" queried Barron.

Steven and Remus shook their heads.

"Could you describe these noises, sir foreman?" joked Darren over the sound of his own laughter.

"Either old Grom's been on the move or the Alchemy Guild's working overtime."

Darren's jaw dropped, noticing a trio of Tree Sprites climb atop the resident harper's stage, blessed, like the rest of their woodland kin, with silky yellow hair and warm eggshell complexion.

"Sprites!" Darren obnoxiously said, sending the rest of the party diving behind their hands in secondhand embarrassment. Granted he was only partially correct: the tallest of the three, the one now tuning the harp, was indeed a Half Sprite—or Half Human, if you were to steal a look from her identification. Though even with her title as Tallest Sprite in Sheep's Tavern, she was only but a wee thing; five feet two inches at the very most.

After observing a disturbed gaze from one of them, Darren blushed.

"I am going to get some air," mumbled Barron to anyone listening.

Upon paying his crew's tab, he shuffled stealthily out through a herd of inbound academy students, into a temperate windless evening. Though it wasn't the air that had brought him hither. More like the cushy prospect of a stealthy retreat back to his home for some quiet.

Unfortunately for him, his silent exit would not go unnoticed.

"There you are!" shouted Steven, "off to go digging without me?"

His eyes nearly bulged out of his head, scanning the open plaza to see if anyone heard.

He was mid-lecture when he saw another familiar face inbound. "Change the subject. Fast." He sighed, folding his arms. "What do you want, Remus?"

"*Hic.* Where are you guys going?" asked the tinkerer, swaying in place with a half-empty mug of ale in hand.

"The better question is where are you going? Off to make some adjustments to your optae?"

"He's not paying for our drinks, Remus, I already asked."

Unknowingly, the two kept him company on his stroll back home. It was a nice night for a walk after all, if not a hair bit quiet for an evening stroll through the Inner City so very early.

"That's no candle," ominously whispered Steven, pausing in front of a sad-looking home covered in ivy, with a mighty glow leaking from the boards over the upstairs windows. "This is a nice home. The alchemists didn't even care to fasten any of the boards down. Scoundrels."

"Half these homes wouldn't even still be standing if it weren't for my father," said Barron.

"These are some of the lucky ones in comparison. I swear, one of these days I'm just going to cave and move into my parent's old home. I'm tired of living in a tent in squalor."

"I hear they've been dealing with a fungi situation of their own in Varakai," remarked Remus.

"You heard right," replied Steven.

"You never told them about Savannah, did you, before they—" Barron bit his tongue and tossed a stick into a graveyard towards some enormous man-sized moths, fighting one another for a coveted spot beneath the few mausoleum flames.

Steven avoided the subject altogether as they emerged from darkness onto the northeast bend of the Outer Circle. "Gromula Day can't come any sooner."

"Here's hoping one of our servants can find me a couple of horses in time for the festivities next week..." Something felt awry to him after the trio finally parted ways. This feeling of his only worsened as he descended into the gray abyss of the Market District-Residential District Connector. A funny feeling was stewing well within his core. Enough to send him rushing back the other way.

His intuition, as it would turn out, was merited. There were active shadows on the first and second floors of Myleyn's neighbor's house. His heart began to flump. It was the Alchemy Guild. He had not doubted it one bit. Inside, behind closed curtains, there were egregious banging sounds, like metal on wood.

He leaped off the road, out of the light's way, peering curiously from behind her neighbor's shrub. That's when he observed a hooded figure with a beaked face covering, a lantern in one hand, a rope in the other, passing through the shadows.

"Can't he see the sign?" mumbled a peacekeeper, unhooking his club as he approached the suspicious onlooker. "You there! What are you doing in the bushes?"

"I heard a noise," advanced the man, "is everything okay in there? A bit late for carpentry, I should think."

The guard approached closer, scanning the figure sewn up the side of his collar with his lantern drawn. He cleared his throat. "Alchemy Guild business, keep 'er moving."

Heeding his advice, they watched him carefully as he proceeded to the home with white shutters. But something was awry. It was dim as the night sky inside her home, save for a single light in the window beside her front door, and far too quiet. A quiet on par with even the vacant homes.

Before he could even knock, the front door creaked open, along with a pair of familiar blue eyes. "*It's you.*" Myleyn emerged in nothing but her nightgown, staring about. Startled, she grabbed the man by his jacket and tugged him into her foyer. "Barron, what are you doing here? You don't know how happy I am to see you." She hugged him, before sliding two brass chains into place. "The girls and I heard something coming from next door."

He nodded, examining the smothered fire in her living room hearth from afar. He then looked to her sofa, where two young girls, no older than a quarter century, stared back. Eyes wide like owls, and hair dark as night, they studied his mouth as it moved, nervously waiting for any hint of hopeful news. But he just stood there, nodding.

"Well? Did they say anything to you?"

"'Alchemy Guild business,'" parroted Barron, removing his arms from his jacket, "'keep 'er moving.'"

"Huh? Barron, you reek of musty ale." She grabbed his hand, "I want you to meet Andrea and Esca Vement." Curled under a wool blanket, he could discern little beneath it but the shapes of their hips, oval and slender. Of course, he knew who they were. Esca Vement was on his father's shortlist of potential suitors. Myleyn knew not.

"Ah. Heiresses of the great Vement family's ointment empire," he jested, "I will say I was a bit surprised when Myleyn told me you were staying here. I should think noblewomen of your stature would much prefer staying with your parents in the valley where it is safe."

"Safer," replied Esca, "and yes, we could have. Alas, without a horse we'd be out of a job fast."

He smiled, though the prospect of a quick visit was waning fast. Somehow, he felt sitting would only capitulate a night of armchair-listening. This is precisely why he remained standing, poking at Myleyn's lopsided fire with a prod.

"Well? What did you see out there?" pressed Myleyn.

"Alchemists, they're tearing up your neighbor's home," he said. "What I don't understand is why. This is not your everyday run-of-the-mill softwood, it's karnip. How is a mushroom growing through such material?"

"They managed to get through ours too," chimed Andrea.

He paced about, twirling her fire prod like a spear. "There's something else they aren't telling us about these Glowers. They're offering two gold crowns now for information—*information*. This makes no sense."

"They're trying to get rid of them fast, of course," said Myleyn, "they've been on a real tear this week."

Esca scooched upright, shirking her sister off her shoulder, and a small puddle of her tears. "I was on my way to Residential earlier this week for a lesson, when I saw them entering Lord Stilwell's cottage, garbed in their exposure gear and masks, tugging along a leviathan moth. They evicted him mid-breakfast." Her sister gave her a quiet pinch, causing her to squawk.

"A leviathan moth? They're not going to condemn my house, are they?"

"Should we go out ask them?" Barron sarcastically replied.

After observing the petrified look on Andrea's face, she gave him a glare. "It's not funny, Barron."

"Well how would I know? They don't have any reason to, do they?"

"No, not in the slightest. My father and brother were here just the other day. Didn't spot a single one. Not in my yard, not anywhere."

"Well." He climbed to his feet and stretched his arms up over his head, yawning. "It's getting late. I better get going." He extended his hand into his jacket pocket.

A relief. His map was safe.

"Is there any way you could stay the night? I think we'd all feel a bit safer if you were here." Her words pierced him from behind like the cold touch of a blade. While it may not have been her intention, Myleyn surely succeeded in putting him on the spot. He stood there for a good nine seconds, studying their half-hopeful looks, before finally opening his mouth to speak. "Well, I should be going. Need to check my lawn for Glowers."

"Didn't you tell me that Prescott was watching your home for Luminas?"

"That word has never left my mouth."

"I can make us a spread." As these words left her mouth, he very slowly backed away from her door, inhaling. "What kind of spread are we talking about?"

She smiled, exposing her bright white pearls.

Later that night, he had little trouble falling asleep. Remaining asleep, however—overhearing imaginative noises seemed but a common place for the worried girl. Indeed, on not one but four separate occasions she sent him up and down her stairs in nothing but his breeches, peeking out her windows and doors (or so she thought), into the early hours.

By the time the alchemists had wrapped up next door, the sun was almost nearly out. Himself he awakened just shy of noon to a mouthwatering spread of his dreams: sizzling hog sausages, fresh stainberry jam on warm toast, and runny eggs. All that seemed missing now was his "Milk," she said, handing him a tepid mug.

He studied the burden on her face as she departed back into her kitchen, that underlying anger. That same fear and anger was reciprocated. He could do little but distract her. It's what she would do for him. "So, who's ready for another Gromula-less holiday?" he queried the table.

Andrea sighed, breaking out into a passionate debacle with herself as to which outfit she will wear to the coming celebration. Barron and Esca meanwhile delved into Gromula Day lore. Most peculiar to him was how tame the girl's rendition of the plateau-dwellers' espoused holiday was. Of course, not peculiar enough to ruin anyone's appetite with his own.

CHAPTER 8

THE ROAD TO RAPTURE

"To Maldinax!" shouted Darren jocosely, startling a staggered flock of footed peasants off the side of Loarea Road.

"Out of our way!" he resumed, retracting his head inside a cushy cabin for a droughty sip of red wine.

A plucky peasant with a buzzard belly raised a balled fist, visibly angered by the man's dido. Just as quickly did his mug turn into a grin, catching a glimpse of the vivacious entourage inside the black, top-heavy, two-horse shay.

It was Gromula Day, after all, a day for feasting and fun (and based upon their startling pace alone, both inside and out, a couple of early morning headaches too). Courtesy of their host, dressed dapperly in a grim getup, the young festival-goer's companions would have the distinct privilege of witnessing the sacrifice today in style in a cloud of dust of their own making. Although undoubtedly a later start than their host had originally intended, he and his guests should thank the old man in the overcoat and top hat, Prescott, and his newly wrangled but by no means new steeds, Quinn and Raine, for their quick recovery of pace. This was the Alarie family's chauffeur after all, who had been driving for the family so very long that he was even starting to look like one.

"Marrin doesn't care for flattery," whispered Barron to his date.

"Forgive me, but what is his wife's name again? Starts with a C, right?"

"Camille," replied the man, "Don't forget it. He won't."

Steven's date began fanning her face with the sleeves of her borrowed white dress. "Let me help you, dear." Myleyn scooched over, aiding the girl in rolling the same white sleeves of the same white dress she had worn fifty years to the day. Doing their best not to suffocate from the heat was far a more pressing task, however, with not a cloud in sight. Then there was the poignant intersection of aromas that joined as they crossed the vacant Cloud Spice Company factory. This however headache-inducing the smell would not stop Darren from approaching the hole in the wall, nor from shouting nonsense onto yet another group of characters making their noble pilgrimage by foot.

Barron sat sullenly for some time as the cart coasted westwards upon the thoroughfare, glaring at Darren, and the other guilty parties involved. Sadly, not even a half-century would mend Remus and Steven's insufferable gift of gab. It was a disease they had all shared, spread perhaps from the same community wells they all shared. And yet, as much it pained him, he would have to play nice. Particularly so following the vocal praise he had received earlier that week for a successful repair of the Academy of Conqueror Connector. No way would he risk turning down this unwanted guest of his with a loud mouth, only to be lambasted by the overseer for a bitter rumor of his carelessness. That was not to say he would just roll over like a rug. Quite the contrary, actually. Following an impressive sip of wine, he treated himself to another, then, flipping stiff his eight-inch collar, he rose from his velvet bench.

They watched him as he carefully knelt his way over to this unwanted guest of his from behind and, forcing the window down onto the back of the man's neck, reseated.

Full gallop, Prescott fixed himself upright, pressing his top hat over his thinning head of hair. "Get!" he shouted, aiming the only horses in sight towards a hole in the ground just shy of the outer wall.

"I'd start covering your drinks now," warned Barron, pressing his palm over a lordly chalice.

Remus rolled his eyes. "He exaggerates..."

It seemed at once that the warmth of the sun had vanished when the carriage had become one with the hollow rock—winding, jolting, bouncing, level after level, cavity after cavity, with only but a few flames on the walls to light the way.

"I thought you said the Vement twins are going to be joining us at the sacrifice today," said Steven.

"Why do you ask this?" whispered his date suspiciously.

Myleyn fanned her powdered face with a dose of cool air. "They are. We may want to consider joining them atop Endurian. That is of course if we have enough energy left after our pre-celebration to make the hike."

"Good luck with that," scoffed Remus, "if the sun doesn't beat us, the crowds surely will."

"The girls just so happen to be in the company of Duncan Plumscint."

The few of them gave one another looks.

It was clear they had all heard the tales of the great Plumscint family of Maldinax, the famous smugglers who amassed their great fortune in the early days of Taranchia's founding. Although the Four Families, the ardent thorns in the Great Founder's side—the Raknias, the Palasores, the Trawls, and the Clovasseurs—were all but gone from his memory, never to challenge his rule again, some of the stories—rumors—most certainly endured.

"…Andrea claims he has had a spot reserved on Endurian for several days now. Perks of being the chief administrator's son, I guess."

"I'd be more impressed if he got an alcove," chirped Barron, eyeing the second builder bitterly.

"At the dawn of a new age? Good one. I'd be surprised if even if the queen was able to afford an alcove this year," remarked Steven. "Could you imagine the tale, though? Historic."

"Oh, shut it, Steven," Barron said. "How did your friends become acquainted with the chief administrator's son, anyway?"

Myleyn turned to him. "Andrea and he are courting. I suppose the only good that has come of this forsaken Cleansing is that the three of us have become quite close. A bit too close perhaps."

Without warning, Prescott tightened the reins, sending red wine flying from both Remus and Darren's chalices. (As it pertained to the unsuspecting torch lighter, rising nimbly from the shale back onto his feet over the sound of fading laughter, he could almost be considered lucky; or rather, not as unlucky to be wearing white on such a day.)

Several hundred long layers later, a violent glare appeared at the end of a long stretch of tunnel, smoothened like butter over the ages by the rolling trundles. If only the crows guarding the gables of his rooftop were alive to see, as now would be the time to squint.

After resuming beyond a checkpoint, they observed swarms of weary festival-goers eastbound on a road through a poppy field. A source of contention for many, as the queen and her predecessors would have it, but there would be no shortcuts available for her peoples today through the immediate canyon, nor any day for that matter, a few fallen rocks and some dead noble children later, but this was their holiday, as much as it wasn't theirs, and few such things would hamper a day off from work.

Beyond the shadow of the monstrous seed of magma, a stream of languorous heat returned through the windows, carrying with it some floral, fruity notes.

Several ounces of wine heavier, an unpruned mountain revealed over a bridge of soaring cyprinids. "That's Vina Mountain, isn't it Stevie?" turned Savannah.

Steven hugged her from behind. "It sure is."

With a glance at the red and green pennants, hovering slovenly over the confines of the valley oasis, the festival-goers rushed their heads out of the only two windows in his cabin. The buoyant sounds of whistling bolts and smashing, crashing plates were just loud enough to awaken Myleyn from her impromptu lull. As she fanned her swollen face with the tips of her fingers, Darren, followed by Steven and Savannah, began a chant out into the open air: "Prescott! Prescott! Prescott!"

Several bystanders joined in on the chant, singing the driver's name like it was one of their old friends. Even their host couldn't help but smile, taken in by the lively sounds and welcoming smells. After all some penultimate celebration before a sacrifice was not at all unwelcomed, even if it meant having to share it with an unsavory brute.

Thus far from what he's observed of the northern vassal, he was confident the chief administrator, Lenox Plumscint, had done a number on Maldinax's coffers, as he had in years past. An otherwise prudent man, the Gromula Day pre-celebration party would ironically likely forever be his legacy. The ramparts of his south gate were decked brazenly in red and green petals today, as they should, where the few fortunate enough in luck or pocket attempt to squeeze their carriages through the horde of inbound festival-goers.

Rather futilely, however.

"Why don't we walk?" Remus said, fidgeting in his seat while eyeing the door.

"Prescott, we're not getting anywhere any time soon; find yourself a shady spot by the east gate," relayed Barron.

"You're certain, sir?" asked the old man.

"Yes, but do try to keep the old girl clean!"

"I don't think I can hold it any longer," groaned the tinkerer.

"Shush, Remus," snapped Steven, "we all have to go."

Outside the group of friends were swept quickly in the kerfuffle. "Evidently Lenox left no room in the budget for ushers," remarked Barron, "typical." As they inched their way gradually into the town square, already did his date stick out like a sore thumb; her hair straight down over a bright green dress, rings of gold and silver poking out from her sleeves. Not at all unusual for a lady of an old family. However, the atmosphere was slightly different here in the melting pot of the North Valley, where females in strapless dresses danced seductively atop upstretched platforms, luring passing bodies with every hip thrust, curtsy, and smile.

Darren and Steven seemed all the more struck by the sight of an elusive Tumsib female than anything else, guiding light off her rose-gold tinted legs and shiny head onto unsuspecting passers.

"We're going to go tidy up!" shouted one of the girls, lost helplessly unto deaf ears.

"A melee!" averted Darren to a giant metal dome, aggroed by the sparks of clashing blades.

Inside the dome, a characteristically light-armored Sea Sprite, garbed in the same rocks and sands their coves defend, danced gracefully around his poniard-wielding human opponent, despite possessing only a sliver of his height. Unlike the Tree Sprites, with wings thin and long, the Sea Sprites' wings were stubby, fine enough for short flights, though powerful enough to plow ripples in the waves before assailing their unsuspecting sea prey.

A piercingly loud impact shattered off the human's shield, sending shards of sea glass flying. "What are the rules of these melees again?" winced Barron, as another sea bomb came crashing down upon the human's shield.

"You've never seen a melee before?" scoffed Darren, far too preoccupied watching the Sea Sprite dizzy his opponent to meet his face. "Too busy watching the Agility Challenge?"

"Watching?" smirked the man.

"Pay a little respect, Darren," said Steven, "you are speaking to a twice Agility Challenge champion before his retirement."

Darren nudged the man playfully. "Would you believe this nonsense? Not a drop of blood spilled. Give me a club and I'll give the kiddies a good show."

The men rolled their eyes. Upon rendezvousing with the rest of them, they made their next move east from town square, away from the noise, passing many a row of ivy-infested home.

"I'm surprised the chief administrator hasn't condemned this one yet," remarked the tinkerer of an eerie brick manor, with a lot four times the size of its neighbors.

Steven peered through a worn-out fence out front, cut through an old oak tree and some untamed shrubs. "Doesn't look like there's anyone home to evict."

"That's the old administrator's estate. Back before they decided to build a castle on Vina," said Barron, "it's pre-meteor."

"Back when they were still running for the Raknias," added Remus under his breath.

"It smells like dead rabbits here," grimaced Myleyn. Followed by Myleyn, the friends descended into the Quincunx's mist, carried by the spellbinding sounds of a fine-tuned harp.

On the stone platform surrounded by water, a single tear slithered through the freckles on Savannah's face, taking in the delicate strokes of an expansive painting, etched across the surface of one spectacular canopy. "It's incredible."

"It is incredible. I mean they even figured out how to filter all this running water into storage using those sluices there," the architect remarked, his attention clearly elsewhere. "Quite the operation if you think about it."

She flashed a befuddled smile.

"Come," Steven grabbed her hand, refocusing her gaze on the tableau. "This tells the story of the Quincunx's origin. This flaming rock over my head is the Great Meteor of 515 F.Y."

"It's why the lilies float here, right?"

"No one knows why the lilies float here," he said, "nor why the fish live tremendously long lives. Though they did not do that before that flaming rock came along."

"Let's get a pint somewhere before they run out!" interrupted Darren, drawing stares from the Floating Lily's patrons.

Barron walked behind Steven and Remus, giving their ears a good reaming before Darren caught on. "...He's your responsibility."

"Let's go, Darren," Steven said, passing the floating lilies for the same steps from whence they came.

Save for himself, Myleyn, and Remus, his lowborn acquaintances couldn't even get into the upmarket establishment if they tried (or at least according to Barron, who was in no mood to burn any bridges with the owners of his favorite establishment today). Sadly, judging by the rundown exterior of their alternatives, which leaned over the riverbank above, the slumber wasn't very kind to these cedar, nautical-themed taverns.

"Flying Fish Tavern! Ha. Remember we used to come here during preparation, Barron?" said Remus.

"Unfortunately," sighed the man.

"It's not ideal," whispered Steven, "but I say we make the best of it. Who knows, maybe Murr will even give us a discount for stopping by."

An unforgettable odor of exhuming rats and soiled ale filled their nostril passages as the friends entered to an unpleasant creak. "A discount?" Barron looked about, catching stares from a few unsavory patrons. "For what? Falling through the floor?"

Out back a half-rotted picnic bench awaited them at the precipice of the fall. The tables were mostly occupied by commoners who, unlike Barron, whose cloak was folded in layers between his rear and the splintered bench, didn't seem to mind the location, nor the warm ales, one bit.

"Is Murr working today?" Steven asked the tavern wench.

She pretended not to hear him, before whispering something in his ear.

"What did she say?" they all asked, almost synchronously.

"Murr's gone. Slumber got him."

"He's gone? I don't believe it. She didn't mention anything about a discount, did she?"

"Quiet, Remus," interrupted Barron, switching the table's focus off the tavern wench to the balcony propped up by soggy beams of wood. "Don't look now, but a few characters are staring at us from up there."

The rest of them, unfazed, leaped their eyes above to the balcony, where mangy men, wrapped loosely in disparate pieces of cloth and leather, stared back.

"How do you know they're staring at us?!" casually replied Savannah aloud.

Barron closed his eyes and shook his head. "They are now..."

"Now their hoods are up."

"Aren't they dying from all this heat?" questioned Myleyn.

"I can't tell," squinted Steven, "I am starting to think your optae is making my vision worse, Remus."

"Then stop wearing that darn thing," whispered Savannah.

Troubled by their lasting glares, Myleyn scooched closer toward her date. "Perhaps we can get going soon?"

"What's wrong? Aren't you having fun?" he said, rolling his eyes.

"Please," whispered the girl, her eyes staid.

"Yes, we can go. Remember, it's *Camille*. Don't forget it."

Remus folded his arms obstinately as the rest of them finished the last of their skunky ales and rose. "We just got here," he groaned. Upon his next sip, Darren tilted the butt end of his mug over the peak of his eyebrows, sending ale shooting from both his nostrils. "Let's go, Remus."

"One of them looked me dead in my soul," said Savannah, "I could have sworn he was possessed or something. His eyes were rolled up in the back of his head and pale like snake eggs."

"Elixir fiends," said Barron, in the face of an unforgiving sun.

"Do you think we should tell this patrol?" asked Myleyn.

"And say *what*?" chuckled the nobleman, "that there are creeps inside the famous Flying Fish Tavern? They'd be out of business yesterday."

The girl delivered one ruffled glare.

Only several hours out from sundown, and not a minute sooner, their prayers for shade were staring back at them, as they exited the east gate of Maldinax to a familiar sight. There it was, nuzzled between two plum trees, on the opposing end of a sunny brick road; his carriage, driver, and his mother's old mares.

His guests entered first. Barron remained outside, inspecting his father's old carriage tediously for nicks and dents.

"Anything?" knelt Prescott beside him, causing him to jump.

"Nothing." He swept his getup of nonexistent dirt and stood. "Just how I like it."

"Onwards to the sacrifice, my lord?"

He felt a burn coming on, so he tightened the knot on his tunic and, reaching for his forehead, started nodding.

"Barron, come quick, it's your favorite!" shouted Myleyn from the cabin, where a very much welcomed but by no means unexpected bottle of Frostberry wine bobbed its head in a bin of chilled river water.

"Splendid."

Eastward from Maldinax, into the heart of wine country, the carriage returned to a full gallop, permitting a nice tangy breeze through the cabin.

To those whose eyes had not yet seen its true worth, wine country might've seemed remote.

Yet this was not at all like the xeric dominion of Varakai, nor the diseased grasslands of Taranchia: more of a lost kind, the sort in which commoners may only dream of residing. They were the estates of the old families, whose lines were as embedded in the rocks as the minerals that got them there; commanding the highest hilltops and vineyards on this side of the river, from valley to sea.

Myleyn, upon noticing a look of hopeless envy in Steven's eyes, inched closer to her date, grabbing his frigid hand. A few chalices later pebbles crunched in the spokes as they dipped downward into the golden bowl of the Northeast Canyon, where a draught of dusty wind trailed not too far behind.

Foot and carriage, they were just in time for more provisions.

From the windows and Prescott's dusty roost, the high plains stretched well into the bloody horizon like islands on land. The fog excluded most of Market's beauty from one's imagination, but not its lower half of grass and side-winding trees, the skirt.

They veered westward against the mouth of the canyon, away from the tactless funnel of the Merchant Guild's makeshift bazaar, towards the infant foothills in Residential's shadow.

Amongst an already crowded line of eager faces, Steven, Darren, Remus, Savannah, and Myleyn wasted no time in plopping down at the first open spot they could find along the ledge, in sight of a lifeless crater on the tail of a ravine.

Barron remained on his feet, scoping out the other viewing options dispersed about the capacious basin; aiming first for the skies athwart, to the alcoves of the Great Bulwark. Within Market's skirt, a rare window into the Tumsibs' elaborate inner network of tunnels lay bare. They were the fortunate few born low, but most certainly not lowborn. Their great galleries were held by tortuously sculpted rods, with unsurpassed views of Gromula's Cave, loaned exclusively to the highest bidders on this special day.

Barron eventually settled on the ridge; though his facial expression described someone who had just swallowed a lemon whole.

Three hundred feet below their legs, they watched torches being planted on the upslope to Gromula's Cave. From their great vantage point, the shoeless hunters—this year's volunteers—looked like mere children, swathed to their necks in fur, their faces concealed behind replica hunting masks.

Upon overhearing Darren's fictitious rendition of the Gromula Day origin tale, Barron couldn't help but sneer.

"There were nine!" shouted Darren.

"Yes," said Barron, "there *were* nine. The original tale, however, tells of a group of eleven hunters from one of the last remaining tribes in the canyon; or what was then still known to the fading few as 'Pyrithia.'"

"Go on," said Darren, half-listening with his arms folded.

He cleared his throat. "The hunters set off one late afternoon to gather rations for their kith and kin. They waited until sundown, that's when the animals came out of their dens. Anticipating rainfall, the hunters sharpened their stone-tipped spears, garnered their bone-wrought masks, and in a hurry set off for that same watering hole you see below—or what's left of it. At the time, Pyrithia's Sol River was still thriving, albeit losing traction. Attracting Tethia's many creatures around the last greater pools to hydrate and wash.

"They became lost in their sun-touched surroundings, singling out a herd of long-horned sheep from the congregation, but they refrained from striking just yet—the animals were far too clumped together. Striking would only cause confusion for themselves and their unsuspecting prey. But time was of the essence. The animals likely felt it, the disturbance in the air, the pressure dropping. They had begun to break off from the watering hole, back to their caves and their holes in the ground. But some sheep lingered, letting the rain seep deep into their fur as they grazed upon the clover.

"The lead hunters reached their bony arms out from underneath their furry cloaks, sending them in a thrusting motion. The other hunters were edging closer towards the grazing mammals. Meanwhile, the rainfall started picking up and so the hunters stepped carefully as to avoid joining the runoff, now chasing into the crater below. The new-found slipperiness caused one of them to lose their step, sending him sliding into a brittle lip. The impact alone triggered a chunk to release and with it a nasty echo. Before the hunters could even move, the stragglers stiffened their horns and retreated inside Endurian. Rather than tucking tail without their harvest, the Pyrithians regrouped. In a last-ditch effort, they proceeded inward through the cavity to pursue their favorite prey. Their element of surprise was now thrown away, however, and a few of the hunters protested. Of course, ultimately obeyed.

"Beyond a small translucent stream cut through stalagmites, the hunters extended out their feelers—"

"What do you mean by *feelers*?" interrupted Darren. "Hands, don't you mean?"

"You never wondered what that extra hole was for in their mask? You know, the little one right above their nostrils?" scoffed Remus.

"All right, all right, proceed," sighed Darren, eyeballing Remus bitterly.

"Right, well, outside the entrance from whence they came, their next choice was simple: turn right or left. But only one passage possessed the scent of wet fur. So off they went, left, into an even dimmer passage. So very dim in fact that the lead hunters were forced to sap much of their stamina to find a way forward with their feelers. Thankfully for them, they were picking up on a large convergence of odors at the end of the left passage, where the duo linked arms with their blind cohort and advanced. Sooner or later the cave became so stifled of noise, save for the occasional rumble of thunder, that nearly every one of their missteps could be heard bouncing on throughout the cavern.

"A baa came from ahead, and again—its echo. As if the hunters weren't already uneasy about their own steps, they began projecting muffled sounds and even started tugging on the line. This, however concerning, would have little impact on the first and second hunters, who pressed on with a new concerted conviction. They were closing in on a distinctive meaty trail.

"But the arm tugging became so very forceful, and more of them were losing their step. Before the hunter in the fifth position could determine what was to cause, he was jerked, this time the opposite way, causing the release of one feral grunt. The second hunter finally turned around to confirm what the fuss was all about. As he locked his gaze onto the hunter behind him, a sudden and inexplicable fear washed over him: the hunter' mask was being removed (which, as we all know, was considered a great taboo in their culture). Taboo enough to capture the second hunter's attention. As he squinted his tiny little eye sockets to reduce a nearsighted glare, he found the trembling hunter's ears erect and his feeler retracted.

"'*ENSIDA*!' shouted the hunter, before vanishing in the blink of an eye. And run they did, as fast as their little legs could move. Foolishly, however, the first hunter stopped, in an attempt to demystify his second's sudden reservations, I guess. A grave mistake, and a fatal blow to his psyche, revealed within but the faintest strand of light: a funeral of blood. And not just blood, but innards, and hide, too; and spears. They fled through a narrow end on the far wall, left with but the faintest of cries from their own.

"There was usable light in the next cavity, coming from a standing slit, obstructed courtesy of eons of calcium buildup on the floors and ceiling. It was their exit out of the carapace-tingling burial ground. Yet despite safety being so close in their grasp, it didn't take much long before the first hunter's guilt had set in, causing him to rush the other way. The fool. He was met with a guttural sound, liken to the burst of a ripened grape. Upon realizing the other's absence, the second hunter turned frantically in search of him. Meanwhile, with his spear at the ready, the first hunter disappeared into the noise. Right before he could advance any further, however, he was yanked back into the light by his companion. Good timing. That was when they got their first glimpse of the nightmare-inducing arthropod. Its antenna first, followed by its thick-plated skull. Beneath a pair of eyes that could not be reasoned with was its gaping mouth, oozing undigested sheep's fur and well…" he smirked, seemingly losing his thought.

"*Gromula,*" whispered Savannah.

"Monster he was indeed."

"What happened to them?" she pried naively.

"Well, Gromula had himself a far thicker exoskeleton than their spears could handle. They yielded, not surprisingly, leaving a somber *paas*—goodbye—to their fallen brethren as they fled from the monster's lair." He wet his lips, grimacing at another regrettable glimpse of the queen's rented alcove. "Years later and here we are, still dropping an offering to Gromula like they did in the years that followed."

"So that the beast would never think twice about leaving its lair," whispered Steven to Savannah.

Following a healthy sip of wine, and another glimpse at the queen's ostentatious entourage, he shrugged.

CHAPTER 9

A CALCULATED ENDEAVOR

Weary from the sun's influence, the six thought it wise to join Lord Duncan's camp further south down Endurian's ridge. His seating accommodations were far too inviting to pass up on.

From where the friends were now perched, it was as if the mountaintop had extended out from the dehydrated mountain for their selfish convenience. And with an even greater view of Gromula's Lair for the coming run. Huddled like kings upon a stilted cot in the shade of Duncan's awning, the friends made quick work of his sundry assortment of meal spacers, wines, and elixirs.

Thus far from what Barron's observed of their host, the chief administrator's son was more sensible than he had envisaged. A bit self-absorbed, yes, but who was he to judge? Product of a family as old as his. Just one look at his crimped blond hair, tights, and plum-sewn cape, almost anyone would think him a twit. And yet judging by her nervous hair twirling, and the obvious glow upon her dolled-up face, Andrea seemed chipper than the rest. From her powdered forehead down, she and her sister both looked primed as ever for the ball in their floral pattern corsets, with naked laces running up their unblemished white shoulders to ensure their fledgling breasts were perched in place. It was a typical getup of a maiden of noble stock, albeit some minor sometimes major variations, depending upon the occasion and weather.

Eventually, the pre-celebratory drums and hums and horns had seized, sending the party-goers refocusing their gazes upward, onto the great open alcove front and center, where the queen's closest, her council members, and their lucky family members arose.

At the edge of the open balcony, between two limestone columns a portly man garbed in an unflattering silk robe and a bright gold toupee, emerged in front of a cowel with his chalice held high. "Maldinians," he shouted unimpressively, seemingly testing the reach of his voice, "I bid thee welcome to the one hundred and fourteenth Gromula Day sacrifice!" Cheers followed—particularly from below, where thousands of peasants tussled for their slice of the Great Bulwark's shade. "Technically the one hundred and sixty-fourth celebration, however let's not confuse our descendants with that noise."

Barron averted his eyes from the grand emissary, searching for Myleyn's, now far too preoccupied with making a fix to Andrea's crown-styled braid, which humidity has since relaxed into a blind bee's nest. Elsewhere, he had found a far more amusing scene. Remus and Steven were mid-attempt at weaseling their way into another of Duncan's elixirs. And yet the more the two tried softening him up with their perceived knowledge of alchemy concoctions, the more he distanced himself from them.

He came upon Barron with a vexed expression and a half-empty pema elixir in hand. (It was likely not his first elixir, there were dark clumps of sweat on his cape, which stuck to his back like sap. His pupils, on the other hand, were engorged.) "You know it was Lord Geldrin's father who initiated peace talks with Starik long ago? The old man stopped a bloody war," he blurted as if he had just spoken a single word fast.

"Ah yes," he turned, meeting two bulgy green eyes with a half-cocked grin, "for the same desert gems he had convinced the old king to wage war for in the first place."

Duncan let out a laugh. "You know, you are welcome to try any of my elixirs, Barron. I am told that you are something of an elixir connoisseur yourself."

Barron feigned a smile, returning his focus to an unreserved alcove up high, where Tumsib drummers began to set a new scene with the hilts of their palms.

Thunder.

Joining them were their human counterparts, lined about the washbowl, where they pattered the rims of their Neuvian drums, liken to the same mounting rain of legend.

Below the torch-lit path of the monster's lair, the volunteers were forming up. They held their spears up high, some with sharpened rocks corded upon their ends, and torches, and there were two tussling with an unruly horned sack.

Amidst a storm of cheer, the eleven volunteers charged headfirst into the inner cavity with their offering. "Give it up for our brave hunters!" echoed from the queen's alcove.

It only took a few minutes before the antics had come. "Do you feel that underneath us?" said Remus, in a deprived attempt to scare Esca.

Myleyn scooched underneath Barron's arm, while the second builder investigated the grainy surface beneath the cot.

"No wait, I think he's right," said Darren, "I do hear something down there," his ears now pressed firmly against Endurian's surface with a dubious smirk. Duncan grabbed his date close (the poor girl was on the verge of tears).

Then came a sound resembling that of a disturbed bullfrog, out from beneath the balding builder. Even those sitting feet off the ground could feel its wake. Duncan laughed first, followed by the rest of them, but not of course poor Remus who, at this juncture, was quite through with his friend's antics.

Another twenty minutes had gone before the ceremony gong afar was smashed. "A resounding feat for our brave hunters!" shouted Queen Satina Rook, her voice muddled within clapping hands and cheers. Steven went rushing his way over to the far ledge, dodging flying suds and drunken advances on his way.

"I count eleven," he said, fumbling his chalice to his lips for a sip.

Catching Barron's attention, the man leaped off the cot to have a look at the result himself, finding little outside the hunters' departure passage of legend but a now motionless instrument and a few jumbled-up figures. But based on his colleague's pupils, at the present three sizes too large for his head, not to mention his now miraculously cured eyesight, it was clear as day that he had consumed a potent far-sight elixir.

"That's odd," murmured Steven under his breath.

The humidity rose like waves off the walls as he squinted once more, to no avail, at Endurian's exit cavity. "What do you see?"

"I can't say for certain, but the hunters look different. Shorter, leaner."

"Shorter? Perhaps our canyon-dwelling friends have returned from the dead."

"I'm serious." Barron was already back at his date by the time these words left his mouth. He like the rest of them drank away the hour, until darkness had swept across the crevice land, leaving but a few stragglers along the dusty ledge.

Gromula Day's end was near and the air was cooling, leaving but a single activity left in the evening—Of course, after a sizeable consumption of a Stainberry wine there were two; three if you count sleep, but that was out of the question—it was time for the Gromula Ball. Down the spine of Endurian, the friends marched beneath a blood orange vista where, within, a violet dust glimmered lucid as the stars. A mystical sight to behold, causing the party-goers to stop, speechless, in wonder.

"Follow the music!" interrupted Andrea, soaring slovenly down the hill upon Duncan's back.

"Nice cheeks, sis!" jeered Esca.

His mood sobered as they chased up the bowl in a newfound dust storm.

There it was, painted repulsively on both sides of an adjoined marquee tent, at the end of a torch-lit path, the nation's newfangled flag. He found the regrettable sight halfway up the bowl, where the presence of peacekeepers was as ubiquitous as horseless cabins—indeed, horseless, requiring the use of a cranker. A bugger it was they truly were, but it could be done with a man of stamina, and a pump, a great pneumatic billowing pump.

He could do little but chuckle, as for all that armor and weaponry at the lawmen's disposal, they could do very little to scrape the egregious image from his head, nor, in their power, stifle the feigned adulations of glass-clinking ass-kissing taking place within. Thankfully at the meeting place of the canyon and valley, discretion wasn't all that necessary. Not amongst the social elite, the "Maldinites" that is. And with lords of the old families in front, Duncan and Barron's acquaintances, titled and untitled alike, had no issue entering. In the company of old capes and collars, their poor friends even blended in somewhat (notwithstanding the occasional brow furrow and glare).

Darren and Steven were not one to let this rare opportunity pass. The two darted right past the dance-floor, for a banquet table captivated by bees. There were pies, wines and savory treats present, arranged neatly as the line, like a cheap promotion.

All Stainberry, all sneaky as the clever bees.

Amongst the various pockets of conversations, the insufferable open-mouth laughter of Lady Stainberry herself pierced through. And as too did the hoarse sound of his name.

It resonated uncomfortably within him when Marrin said it—like it was no longer a name, but a patronizing sound. Either way, it was the moment he had been waiting for. There he was, the overseer, a drunken glow upon his chubby face, alongside his wife. After acquainting them-selves with his date, another man approached: Nero's long lost man, the lead engineer, Lord Devyn DuSprite. It marked the first time he had seen him since the Awakening. Shorn of his typical work getup, with an uneven tan behind his bulbous head of sappy hair, he looked as bored and underfed as the last known images of him in his head.

It didn't take much long before his feign politeness had waned. "…it was a pleasure meeting you, Myleyn. I hope to be acquainted again soon," the overseer said to Myleyn, causing him to grin.

It was on the crowded dance-floor where he and his date had found an open spot to spread their wings. He couldn't prevent it even if he tried. As for all the spellbinding sounds wrought by the Tree Sprites' careful hands, the *cyldrical* was by far his favorite, the spherical log with clever holes. To the girl's surprise, the man's legs had become possessed by a force the likes of which she had never seen. Herself, dreadfully off-beat with the rhythm of the deaf, failed to keep pace. Despite this, she couldn't seem to shake her giddiness; and nor could he, smitten to the bone by his classmate of old.

Barron and Remus later observed a queer scene on their way back to the tent from a quiet toke, drawn by the monumental glare of a faultless white cabin. It was the queen's entourage, which arrived with a laugh-ably needless force of arms. First ahead of the rest was a squat-looking man in a slick black suit of armor, roosted upon the saddle of a flightless blue bird with legs as thick as a human's. He had a bored spell cast on his stubbly face, commanding the many soldiers to create a perimeter around the lively tent.

"Aren't you glad our tax crowns are being put to such great use?" smirked Barron.

"The elusive apex screecher. Aha. Guess the warden found his old friend," commented Remus, whose tunic thanks to a little fizz was now entirely rid of its red stain.

"How do you figure it's the same one?"

"One does not simply come upon an apex screecher, much less tame one in the matter of a few months."

They observed the more eager of the bunch poking their powdered faces out from the flaps, like milkmaids upon a teeming cow pen. "I reckon this might be the most unmemorable Gromula year yet."

"Maybe if you asked Esca to…"—Barron said before dropping his thought. For good reason. One brash yellow light lit up the sky, like a beautiful firework gone rogue. From a curious silence came a troubling boom, which stirred the canyon's declivity into a full tempest of tumbleweeds, gravel, and dust, powerful enough to blow out their torches and send their loose articles flying. Unlike the big bird, with its ears erect at alert, the Maldinites began one fatal screech, sending the lot of them plugging their ears. A whole mess of them rushed out of the tent flaps for their getaways.

Beyond the bowl, the two watched the tail end of the yellow light, crashing down somewhere on the northwest horizon. They then watched Duncan rush through the heap, drawn determinedly on an expressionless man with a mushroom-shaped hairdo and the same plum sewn on his cape. "Father!"

"That's Lord Plumscint," whispered Remus, "that ought to have been Maldinax's emergency flare."

"Better yet, what was that noise?"

The chief administrator said nothing as he turned, scanning his son's face with a regrettable frown, before proceeding towards the warden. Duncan threw his arms in the air, approaching Barron and Remus for a synopsis of what they just witnessed.

"Back inside you moths!" they heard the warden shouting, balking at the crowd upon his beaked pedestal.

"They saw it, Father!" exclaimed Duncan, "the emergency signal. Shall we take our leave?"

The chief administrator's face scrunched upon meeting his son's dilated green eyes, a second time. Over their heads advanced a winged messenger.

"I ride for Maldinax," said Lenox to his son. "Return to your date. Make sure she gets home safe."

"Lord Frostberry," averted the chief administrator, singling out an absconding nobleman in an unflatteringly tight robe and a white ruff, followed by a tetchy young woman and two of his grown offspring.

Lord Frostberry gave him a contrite look, before continuing into a giant blueberry on wheels.

"I'm coming with you, father."

"...Fine, then make yourself useful. Gather our men."

The blockade on the upslope made a valiant attempt at preventing the carriages from dispersing. But not all of them were so easily subdued. More and more were leaving. "Your funeral!" the warden through his fist up, after watching Lord Frostberry almost barrel through his blockade.

While Remus filled the group in on his favorite theories, a now hysterical Andrea Vement set her sights on Barron, who, with little success, provided little for affirmations. *Clearly she wasn't in the right state of mind*, he thought, as she continued to spew her deepest darkest fears of losing a man she had only ever known for a month, maybe two, now presently in route to Maldinax with his father and some seventeen of their right-hand men.

"What's going on up there!?" yelled Lady Stainberry, stomping towards the warden while sloppily spilling her sixth chalice of wine.

The warden shoved her away, sobering the scrupulously dressed collection of celebrators silent. "Fools, all of you. Maldinax is under attack."

"I called it," chimed Remus proudly amid balled-fists and casually tossed obscenities.

There was powder running down Myleyn's face. "Why are *you* so upset?" quizzically Barron approached her.

"Because I'm scared, Barron. How are you so calm?"

Despite unrivaled safety, several of the more outspoken party-goers fled up the bowl, unwilling to wait for the queen's call.

More and more were getting that same itch, and, as time (and conversation) plateaued, so too did the ball.

"Please!" shouted the queen from the stairs of her white cabin, an unrolled piece of parchment held in her veiny hand. "I ask that you all remain calm. We don't have a *who*, a *what*, or a *why* just yet, but we shall. Our finest soldiers have been dispatched to Maldinax. For now, I advise you all caravan south with me, back to the city." She held her breath and stared long towards the warden.

"Yes, she did say south…South as in *through* the canyon," he joined. "This exception is for your own safety, though, I do warn you, the canyon is much darker and far more rugged than you can ever imagine without the light of the sun. Remain in your vehicles and keep up."

With that the queen lifted her favorite dress and entered her cabin, her driver giving way for a macro wagon to join the growing caravan. "The canyon? What about Gromula?" panned Andrea anxiously, "oh I wish Father were here."

"Do you think we'll run into him?" turned Steven's date, half-hoping.

"My father? No dear, he's sick."

"*Oh*, well do send my condolences," said Savannah, turning into Steven's ear, "I did mean Gromula, though."

Myleyn looked to him for a decision.

"I'm leaning towards the alternative," he said, longing up the slope. "I just know my poor old carriage is going to need a new set of wheels after trekking through the old city," he sighed. "This is a family heirloom. A fine wine, I might add." At that Myleyn pulled the man aside.

"You heard the noises up there," she snapped, "we can't possibly go that way."

"The further you are from harm, the closer you are to harm," he overheard either Steven or Remus slurring words, triggering a grin.

A warm sweat formed on his neck as she pushed on him some more. The rest joined, turning at him in almost perfect cadence, causing him to close his eyes and sigh. "Fine. Canyon it is," he said, halting his nervous chin-stroking to elaborate. "But let me be clear, if anything at all happens to my carriage, make no mistake I will take meticulous time expensing whatever it is, however big or small, to each and every one of you. Do I make myself clear?"

Filed in with the rest of the convoy, the queen exited her cabin, gripping the banister of her primly white perch.

As for Prescott, even half asleep the old man wasn't foolish enough to relinquish an already swelling tip for a bumpy carriage ride through the capital's underbelly. After all, who would willingly pass on such a rare event?

"*Ahem*. Horns, if you will, please," said the woman, turning her attention onto the macro-wagon beneath her—the same one filled to the brim with dancers, musicians, and idling musical instruments. Following her advice, she threw her hands by her side and cleared her throat. "I will reiterate, keep up and stay in your carriages!" She sent a smile to the horns before descending back into her horse-drawn cabin, and off the fifteen overworked landaus went into the mouth of the Northeast Canyon.

"Are you sure you want to sit there?" Esca said to the girls resting upon Barron and Steven's laps. "I really don't mind."

"It's no problem," said Myleyn of her bony seat. "Right, Barron?"

"Hm?" To the tavern that reeked of exhumed rats, his mind was, wondering long and hard who it was that had occupied that balcony, and, if they had acted upon Myleyn's hunch, where the Plumscints and his two extra guests would currently be. *She would never live it down*, he thought to himself, burying the intrusive thought deep down where it belonged.

"We can always switch off halfway," chimed Remus, his feet faced towards Esca, "if you need a break, that is." Barron and Steven popped their heads out in almost perfect unison, with the same silly grimace spelled upon their plastered faces.

"I'm sure you'd like that," said Darren, stealing the very thought from the tips of their tongues.

Slow was their pace upon the uneven terrain, where no such comfort as roads had ever existed. Yet save for the creaking, the clumping, and the rocking, their overworked trundles were managing thus far. It was almost peaceful, if not for the unspoken air of fear that dimmed their pathway across the monster's lair, where a few ascendants nervously pointed their lanterns.

By the time the glinting fleet had reached the void between Market District Plateau and Loarea District Plateau, most of the convoy was still awake, especially the performers, whose rears most certainly felt every last bump into the later night. Obscured invariably by the unscalable faces, helped not by the encircled glare of lanterns on their unmarked path beside the ravine, Barron too remained awake, for he knew well that not another chance would ever come to gaze at these parts again. The Sol River wasn't much for looks, but there were a few weeds in there, maybe a few puddles where the sun occasionally shines. Otherwise, he had longed to witness it in its heyday.

"Here already?" asked Myleyn, blearily awakened to a jolt.

"Stay in your vehicles!" they heard guardsmen shouting down the line.

"Prescott," whispered Barron into the interior panel, "why have we stopped?"

"Something's caught the warden's attention," the driver said into the vent. That's when the friends started taking turns sticking their heads out of the cabin, doing their best to interpret any semblance of news from the passing guardsmen.

Soon enough news came of an attempted breach into the old entryway into the Loarean mine. Together Barron and Steven spewed a handful of follow-up inquiries—follow-up inquiries neither the guardsman nor Prescott had answers for. Of course, when that didn't work, the two excused themselves outside for a call to nature.

Not surprisingly, a peacekeeper approached the men rather quickly, and questioned their inability to follow simple instructions.

Luckily for them, Prescott was listening, and, following a helpful reminder as to which family the old man drove for, they were set free. (In Barron's defense, he did have to go.) They crossed beyond the ravine, away from the immediate light of the convoy, to the cold hard touch of Loarea Plateau. While the architect situated his pants, the other crept on through rock, moss, and web, using his hands as a guide. Even with his far-sight elixir, the old city was far too dim for any one man to handle.

Luckily there was light enough ahead outside the old mine, where the warden and the few soldiers in his midst scanned about the ground.

He watched his friend creep closer until he could no longer; there were newfound lights, so he yanked him to his knees. Unlike the Northeast Canyon, the Northwest's security detail was much too daunting to be caught snooping around. And no, not just for today's occasion, but every day of the year. In addition to a roadblock perched upon the upslope mouth, there were leviathan moths, unseen, wisping their dirty wings in the dark places high and low.

"What is it, Lord Fortier?" approached the queen, her crown crooked and her bun half undone. "The convoy grows impatient."

"Show her," said the warden. The ranking soldier, an arbalist with three stripes on his left shoulder, pulled a mask off a body they had lain atop a lopsided stack.

"Are those bodies?" turned the cartographer, his tongue clicking, and sticking to the roof of his mouth.

"Your breath reeks," whispered Barron.

The warden shined his lantern on a dead man's face, one with furrowed tan skin and a clean-shaven head. Dry sweat still clung heavily to his skin, and so too did a crossbow bolt, hanging off the side of his neck, one which the warden unshyly extracted with his bare hands.

The queen shrieked, gripping her throat, "Who are these men? These aren't our volunteers..."

"I knew it," turned Steven to Barron.

"Shh."

"We got 'em just in time," spoke the ranking arbalist, before being interrupted by another gasp. The queen had just then noticed a hole in one of their chests. "And how did *this* happen?"

"Not sure, my queen," he said, "some kind of sorcery, I gather. Almost blew out our eardrums, though."

"An Imian plunger," knelt the warden.

The queen tilted her head. "A *what?*"

"An Imian plunger. A creative little mixture of flammable ores and under-island gases. Yet another demented invention of Imia's finest. Stare miners pay a pretty price for these concoctions: save them weeks of digging. The best part is they don't even need a flame to activate. Just water," he said, pushing another over for a closer glimpse at the gap in his diaphragm.

The sobering process had begun to hasten, inviting paranoia as he listened in from the shadow of the big rock.

She placed her hand on the soldier's shoulder. "From the beginning, but make it quick, it's been a long night."

"Of course, my queen," obliged the crossbowmen, "there were about a dozen of them. Imians, by the looks of it. They were trying to get into the old mine—"

"If I may," interrupted the queen unassertively, reprimanding the man about the dangers of spreading unsubstantiated theories.

"...as you can see, they were able to get one of their concoctions off. Luckily our blockade held."

The warden waved a sticky chunk of rubble in the air. "Karnip sap. You can thank your grandfather for this idea," he said to his queen, "in normal circumstances, just one of these could have easily imploded that seal out like hay."

Riled by the warden's aimless distractions, the queen turned her attention to the ranking soldier for a body count. "...Ten, my lady. They probably would've gotten more of them off too," he continued, "thankfully, even with their borrowed garments, one of our moths picked up their salty trail."

Barron switched his gaze to the barred mine, where the warden shined his lantern. The entranceway was plugged to the brim with boulders and chunks of rock of varying shapes and sizes, with a few smaller gaps now missing.

"And when did this incursion happen?" she pressed him.

"No more than an hour or so ago, my lady. I take it our message wasn't received?"

"Carrier must have just missed us."

"It did seem to us like a coordinated effort." Overhearing this, the warden returned to the bloodied mound of carcasses. "What do you mean by that? Speak quickly."

"They came not long after the garrison was called up to Maldinax. It seems they had assumed it'd be smooth sailing from there," he chaffed with an air of smugness.

"Dandy craftsmanship, striper," praised the warden, "only, there's just one problem, one of them got away."

The soldier scratched his chin.

"*No*? *Really*? Do you forget what day it is?" With that, the queen pulled the man aside, a quiet desperation in her eyes.

CHAPTER 10

LOREA

Maldinians,
I want to extend my gratitude for yet another memorable Gromula
Day holiday. As for our many loved ones whom we have tragically lost to the
Deep Slumber, and, sadly, could not be there with us in person to celebrate
this vital tradition, make no mistake, they were present in spirit. As your
queen and rightful ruler, I wish to inform you also of an act of malice. One
that has struck the very heart of our nation in the late hour of our celebration. While our great vassal of Maldinax valiantly thwarted an attack by
a force of unknown invaders, the foundation of our sacred capital, which
many of this fertile nation call home, was tried by a band of rapacious
assailants.

The queen took a sip from an unlabeled vial beside her, then, letting
out an uncomfortable cough, she resumed, elaborating on the effects
of such a brazen attack. As she wrote, a lean shadow, lost in the sun of

her desk-side window pane, watched her closely as she reached again for her quill.

As we work to unwind this heinous act, I ask you all to report any pertinent leads to your nearest authorities. It is our chief imperative to find our missing volunteers, so they may return to their families and loved ones; and so too this outstanding assailant, so that we may bring them to heel.

A cloud passed over her window, allowing her desk-side candle a turn. Over her shoulder, a revealed Lord Vanic yet loomed, leaving a terse grunt, before folding his trench coat beside him and parting a farewell.

Queen Satina Rook, signed the woman, easing her rear slowly into the back of her chair.

She tossed the last of her vial into the back of her throat and slouched.

At some point in an impromptu trance, her bleak expression became slightly more animated—alive, almost, like a slice of cake on an empty stomach. She climbed to her feet and wandered into her throne room, where a stark consecration of reds bled hot as her hearths in winter. Her steps were answered with echoes. Especially profound as she approached a massive stained glass window on the east wall of her keep.

These same echoes continued throughout the marble hall of her forefathers even after she stopped moving, grazing the disjointed rows of chiseled white columns, before finishing with a light snare upon a chandelier up high.

Her face was pressed close to the window when Lady Knish approached her from behind, studying the wet letter in her hand. "Is everything set, my queen?"

"Yes." Sweat was leaking through her milled façade, revealing a glow of youth, unfounded for a woman in her later middle years, as she pressed her face longingly against the glass and watched young ascendants swing their training swords outside the Ascendency's barracks.

A colossal statue of the Great Founder met her gaze.

"Did you need anything else, my lady?"

"My lady?" she asked again in silence.

No matter how hard she tried she couldn't shake his stare—that warm broody sureness plucked suddenly by a transient cloud. "…The Great Founder sees all." She turned, returning toward her bedchamber.

Later that same morning, the warden came upon the throne room with an update on his investigation. Not alone either, but with a group of solemn-looking soldiers in dark leather coifs in tow. Investigators of the Special Investigation Probing Bureau, or "probers," as they are more often called. Their armbands and vests were marked with a strenuous black eye.

Against the west wall, she quietly panned from one expressionless face to another, firstly to her regent, and the usual humorless trout, High Treasurer Ogden Vodgar. There were guests present too, frequent visitors from the major guilds: Guild Master Degas of the Merchant Guild, Guild Master Encore of the Art & Historian's Guild, Guild Master Aeseres of the Mining Guild, and Master Alchemist Vanic Dacmaster of the Alchemy Guild.

The queen seemed to be the only one to have welcomed the warden's sudden intrusion. "Come, Warden. Let's hear your report," she said to him, receiving impatient looks from a few more faces than one.

He started with an update on the investigation underway in Maldinax. Some headway, in the form of an admission by one of the heathens who had thought it wise to torch a vassal yet overcome by the costly effects of the Long Years. They were Taranchians. Avarices. Hired by forces unknown. And a bit of bad news too: his failure thus far in sniffing out the fugitive.

"Continue," she said, causing the others to dance impatiently in their seats.

He lowered his head, causing her to tense. "What? What did you find?" Her tenseness was more like fret now. "Xander?"

"It was an ambush. Those men never left that cave. Heathens… though I might have something, a lead. We found a pit in Gromula's Cave, below a hardened stack of clay, only it was made to look like a rock."

"Warden," smiled Lord Encore, "if I may. I believe you may have just uncovered a Pyrithian burial pit. A great find. I know a few students in mind who would jump at the prospect of such an enticing excavation."

"Was there a struggle?" she perseverated, her eyes wet with tears.

He shook his head. "We found Lumina mushrooms too, not far from the corpses. Our 'sacrifice' was munching on them," he remarked to mixed gasps. "…The mushrooms that is."

"Warden, you're aware that there are hundreds, mayhap thousands of fungi species that call these temperate caves home?" redacted the master alchemist.

"I don't need a vial stitched on my jacket to tell me what a glowing mushroom looks like. But perhaps you would like to take a look for yourself on your way out to seize another home?" As the table broke into debate, the queen inched herself into the red light. She listened helplessly for some time, like a timid child during a family conflict.

"Please," she said, revealing a lithe frame as she stood.

She placed her hands on her lustrous karnip table and exhaled. "I think we could all use a break."

Lord Fortier pursed his lips and watched smugly as the guilds' profit ambassadors packed up and left. Once gone, Lady Knish anxiously organized an unruly mess of papers into a stack.

"With your permission, my lady, I would like to take my men back to that pit for a more extensive look around," urged the warden. "Once I have concluded my investigation, Lord Encore and his students can have at it. Forgive me, but I'm still a bit skeptical that eleven foreigners could have snuck past our defenses unnoticed."

She stared at the light in her window and, sipping from her wine, turned with a quiet eye. "No-no. You've done enough. Who am I, Xander, if I can't keep my people safe?"

With a slow, reluctant nod, he folded his arms.

"Focus your efforts on securing our border. Those were Taranchians who attacked Maldinax, as you said. The last thing I need is a revolt. Lady Knish," she turned away, "what do you think if we assigned our new intelligencer this investigation?"

"I think it's a grand idea, my lady," she said, causing the warden to scoff.

"Draft a bounty. These heathens could have crumbled that entire rock, and for what? Residue?"

That same day citizens from all across the capital flocked to their nearest news boards to gaze at the latest. More specifically, an update on what manner of sorcery occurred in the late hours of yesterday.

While patiently waiting for Barron to finish reading the queen's attempt at damage control, she skimmed through the rest of the crop on Residential's news board. There were rumors of giant roving mushrooms in the north, a profile on the realm's newly appointed intelligencer, and a bounty post, though none such trifles tickled her interest. The reactions on the other hand—"Imians," she heard people whispering—she was fully in tune with.

"Whoever they are, I'm willing to bet they were out here looking for bloodstones," said one voice. "Seems they know something we don't about that rock."

"Wouldn't be the first time the Imians have tried it," chimed another. "Did you ever wonder where Leo's armor went?"

"It doesn't matter what they were looking for. Murdering innocents doesn't justify an end."

"Bloodstones," repeated the man aloud, rather drearily. *Let it not be my treasure.* He shuffled his way from the noise with a feverish look on his face. *That can't be. Everyone knows the bloodstone veins are long gone.* His ears were ringing. While nowhere near in dire state of crowns, a few leftover veins were hardly worth the effort. Despite this, he was not unequivocally sold on these bystanders' theory. He even went as far as questioning the rumors; though this simple fact did dawn on him: his knowledge of local history was only passable at best.

He had a queer glint in his eyes as he reapproached her. "What do you say we take a little visit to the library? Just like the day we re-met."

"For what?" She looked him over suspiciously, received only by silence. "A compromise, then?"

He left her face. "So long as it doesn't involve trying on my mother's jewelry..."

She veiled her disappointment well behind a snooty pout. "My family would like to meet you, Barron. Oh, and speaking of my family, how is your mother faring?"

"What do you mean?"

"Are we going to pretend that the realm didn't get attacked yesterday?"

"Right, but she's miles from Maldinax. Plus, we have a full-time guard outfit," he reassured her. "Though I suppose we could pay her a little visit. She doesn't get a whole lot of company these days." Before making their way out to the valley, she as promised made a stop with him at the Viamar Library, where Barron dispatched *The Complete History of Maldinia*, volumes six and seven. What he needed above all else was precedence—anything and everything Loarea in the Age of Prosperity. The real truths behind the fireside tales.

As they departed from the library, the two bumped into his subordinate, First Architect Garvey, back from the daunting renovation initiative he had been assigned, for the short holiday. Their timing proved impeccable. His subordinate informed the two of a travel restriction, enacted while he was perusing the hour away in the library. While this may have sobered Lady Thornrose's rudimentary plans, Lord Alarie was internally gleaming.

"How's your assignment in the harbor going?"

"A lot of work still needs doing in the shipyard. Homes, ships, the whole port really. Even the stop gate was destroyed."

He looked at him with uncharacteristic eye contact. Garvey spoke again to him unto deaf ears: "Congratulations on the dam, by the way."

"Hm?"

"I was just congratulating you. A single trip too, I hear. Great Founder, Selvin must've gotten quite the sketch off you."

"Let's just say I wear more patches than one."

"Well, I'm off. I have a date with Malyptah," he said, thumping the cover of a familiar-looking book.

Myleyn sighed as she joined him on a quiet bench on the Outer Circle.

"It's too bad about the travel restriction. I'll tell you what, once this travel restriction is lifted, we shall pay our families a visit. You can try on as many of my mother's jewels as you like. Even my great-grandmother's brooch, that is if you are into that sort of thing."

She smiled, exposing the outline of her bones beyond her slender pink cheeks. "I do love a good brooch."

By supper time he had tackled several chapters from Volume 6. He topped off his chalice to the brim and sipped into the back of his sofa, transporting himself to the year 697 F.Y.

Into dusk they dredged, up and down the conjunction, digging, piling, and smelting limestone and twin dolomite alike, until by chance uncovering the most beguiling mineral of them all, the bloodstone. A suitable gift and sign of good fortune, King Pontis believed, with an even greater use case for the prospective palace being built in his son's name.

But why such a grim name for a valuable specimen? the king's constituents speculated. *Was it due to its crimson exterior, or by the omen spawned by its cursed chance discovery? As for the case of the young Prince Loarea, the firstborn son of King Utazeb Pontis and heir to the throne, witnesses claimed to have seen the boy cast into the abyss by the Great Founder himself. Other witnesses recall a similar story, yet it was not an eternalized entity that had any part in the terrible act, but a lone penal drudge, dreadfully weary and rightfully resentful of the king's decision to claim the sanguine minerals for himself. Following his son's untimely death, the still grieving King Utazeb decided it best to end the development of the cursed "Loarea Palace" altogether.*

Interestingly enough as he read on, despite the king's initial reluctance, mining of the native minerals did not just end there. This was only a precursor to an eventful twenty-year-long hemorrhage of the then-unnamed plateau under Market's right wing.

Following this initial discovery, and of a new smelting method to shape the priceless ambiguity, the following pages exploded with one architectural feat after another.

Yet of all the various morsels of events from this time, Barron perseverated on one, from within the same sequence of oddities that had effectively overshadowed the nigh entirety of the early 8th century F.Y. *In the year 701, King Utazeb's nephew, Lord Leo Pontis, was given a chest of the fresh-cut gems as a reward for his completion of the Market District-Loarea District Connector, successfully bridging the gap between the king's ruling place and his newest treasure trove, the newfangled "Loarea Plateau."*

The famous engineer, and later Nero overseer of legend, decided it best to take his humble two hundred pound share of the red gems and melt them down into a blazing suit of armor, unknowingly creating the greatest marvel in all of Maldinia's history and, naturally, conversation piece, for as little time as it lasted in his possession.

Further into the second volume, stories like Leo's were all too familiar. And not just stories about theft, but of squabbling, scheming, conniving sons, nephews, daughters, wives: plotting, even murdering over their shares of their inheritance.

Catching wind of this toxic trend, the old families with enough sense began offloading their gems as quickly as possible, meanwhile praying to the God King Xardrescu for a delayed expiry.

Later, he scooped up a mystery stew from the first line-less food stall he could find in Market District and continued reading.

On week three of the fourth month of the year 709 F.Y., a mining shaft collapsed, burying seven miners alive.

Piquing the man's interest, he absorbed the next paragraph and the next; in the process, further enriching his knowledge of Loarea's present erosion. Several non-mining-related events were glossed over as well. Most notably, a section highlighting the completion of Beau Nero's workshop, in 711 F.Y., to which was built in the same section of rock once reserved for the young prince's castle.

As he read on, he discovered a disastrous shaft collapse in the year 717 F.Y. This would be the last of the self-inflicted mining calamities, as directly following the incident, King Pontis enacted a ban on plateau mining altogether. Unfortunately, the damage was already done—all in all, in the bloating nation's chase for their savory sanguine talisman, a total of forty-eight miners were buried alive.

As tragic as these easily preventable deaths were, the overall growth Maldinia saw in these years was enough to thrust the nation onto the grand stage. A long shot from the once scoffed-at Neuvian holdout. "Maldinia" was now a kingdom worthy of conversation.

By the end of volume 7, he had discovered several more enlightening nuggets of history from the 8th century. One in which would include an image of the original letter of intent for the *Voyage to Maldinax*— Overseer Pontis' overzealous vision to repurpose a portion of the now exhausted, and idling, mine shafts to build Loarea Tunnel.

However, none hit him so profoundly as King Pontis' obituary, buried amidst the skunky contents of two pages.

Of his dying words, *"A shade has come, and to me it has spoken: 'Fret not, for it was an anchor for this vessel, so thou shall grow.'"* Tipping back the last drop in his cup, he released a sigh, one of both disappointment and relief. *Bloodstones.* He suppressed the word like an embarrassing folly, unrooted from a distant past, but he would not despair. For even if it is just a sparse residue left of it in that rock, then at least he may close this chapter forevermore, beyond a shadow of a doubt.

CHAPTER 11

TO THE RIVER

The cloud-dwellers suffered so dearly into the next day that Marrin was forced to send the men home early. He had little choice. On days like today, the Sibs shimmered like the sun on glass: pinks, reds, golds, and blues. An amusing sight; though the *glow* was anything but funny for any one man to withstand. The oxygen levels were already so low that the city dwellers would often, and at random too, drop dead, visitors especially, who had not yet properly adjusted to the altitude. Luckily for him, he would not need to worry about such trifles in the cool comfort of his tower, where already he had whittled away at several of his more pressing obligations—a letter first, sent to his mother of his desire to wed the young Thornrose girl.

By the time the workweek came to an end, the remain-in-place order was lifted: a most welcomed announcement, if not perplexing, for the Gromula Day perpetrator was still yet to be found—and a soon-to-be afterthought, for a separate, even more unexpected announcement had been shared by the queen. The Lumina Cleansings were now officially over. The many roads of the alchemists' analyses have led to the same harmless destination: the Lumina mushrooms were benign. Of course, further tests were to begin in hopes of determining any medicinal properties, if any.

Not surprisingly, emotions were running high from the same citizens evicted from their homes. They have not so easily forgotten the furnishments gifted to strangers, financed by their hard-earned tax crowns. At least for now, most were just content with returning to their old lodgings and storefronts. Barron himself for the first time since showcasing his pulley system was eager to return to his workplace, the real workplace, where he had a door that locked. But not quite yet, for he had a promise to keep.

Beyond a gritty iron fence tended by armored guards, lay a brick road through a meadow.

"Edwin," Prescott greeted one such guard.

"Welcome back, Master Alarie!" replied the man, returning quickly to a humdrum spell.

The sun was a welcome shy, but the crows were most definitely not, stalking the few hilltop canopies scattered about the Alarie's riverside estate for a long glimpse at the inbound carriage, and the unwavering competition staring back at them from his roof.

Myleyn stood to her feet for a long look over the river. "You never told me you lived on the border."

"The Pebblewood River *is* the border."

"Oh. Right…"

"Friends and I used to race down it on makeshift rafts. The Taranchian children always found it funny. One time Remus and I came pretty close to falling off Sprite's Drop too, had it not been for some Trawl fisherman and his well-timed net." On the river's edge, a great walled enclosure loomed beyond a man-made fall. The gate was ajar. There a slender woman with long dark hair waved them in.

"…The Thornrose Estate was a sight to behold, mother. Roses for miles. Get this: they even utilize their unused acres to grow crops. Isn't that something? Speaking of which, our property could use a little love, don't you think?" he admonished, within a tight squeeze.

"We could always use another farmhand," she winked.

"Your home is lovely, Lady Alarie." Myleyn took her time studying the various structures scattered about the courtyard. There was a barn and a stable, just like any other farm, and good strong soil amid the decares of swaths. But this was no farm. Real farms reeked of dung. This was merely an idyllic image of a country getaway.

She took Myleyn's hand. "Let me take you inside, dear, we can freshen up before dinner. I hope the two of are hungry."

Barron dawdled behind at the carriage. "What do you make of all this lunacy, Prescott? Do you think the Alchemy Guild knows something about these mushrooms that we don't? Seems odd, setting this whole witch-hunt aside so suddenly like."

Prescott shrugged. "The girls go crazy over them."

Barron scoffed. "What do you mean? You've been feeding them to our horses?"

"Them two right there," he pointed to Quinn and Raine (the only two horses present at the stables), "they buck like ponies when we happen upon them. Puts a little pep in their step."

Fascinated, Barron turned to the horses, examining their long faces with a thoughtful expression. "*Is that so?* Well then, ladies, would you like me to see if I can root out a few more for you? Xardrescu only knows I could use a break from these courting frivolities."

They stared back at him curiously. "Knowing my poor mother, she probably has plenty of them floating around."

"Barron!" shouted Myleyn from the castle up the hill. "We'll meet you inside!"

"May not have much time, sir," said Prescott, pointing out a dark patch of clouds up high.

Determined, he fetched a spade and waltzed rearward across the river crossing. He hung a left, following a faint path up the nearest hill, into a patch of willow trees, where the crows cawed at the vaguely reminiscent face.

"Hullo to you too," he said to them, slightly frazzled.

A leak sprung through the canopy as he putzed about the hilltop in search of the glowing ones. Then came a grumble. "Good timing," he exhaled, catching a glimpse of a pale glowing object on the exposed root of a collapsed willow tree.

As he approached it, he noticed not one, but three stump-huggers on its hollowing trunk.

Unlike the little one found in his yard, the stems on these were a few feet tall with a head meatier than that of a cabbage. He stuck the edge of his spade into the biggest one's stem, causing not a blip in its conviction. Hearing Myleyn calling out his name, he gave it one last shove, severing its head.

On his way off the hill, he took heed of a few more, glowing cold through the patch like the winter sun. "Stay there," he said to them.

Back at the stable, the horses were growing uneasy. "Easy now!" intercepted Prescott, failing to soothe the frightened creatures with his usual tricks.

As Barron approached, he attempted to halve that which was in his hand. Yet it wouldn't budge. No matter how hard he yanked, bent, and pulled on it. He shook his head, observing the storm nigh upon the acres, then tossed it whole in their trough.

"Come now, girls," said Prescott, "what do we say?"

He observed them inquisitively as they sniffed their meal, finding it hard to believe any living creature's eyes could twinkle so brightly for an unwashed mushroom. "Pep in their step," Barron repeated aloud. *What's the Guild hiding?*

His normally snug-fitting pants were about to burst at the seams following a filling spacer meal of duck pate, crackers, and wine. Not eased one bit by the main course either—rather, a full banquet.

"I see potential in many of the girls, my lady, though I find that class is something that cannot be taught," remarked Myleyn snidely. "Well, at least not overnight. Speaking of which I am supposed to be at an appointment in Maldinax, come Firstday. Now I am not so sure."

"It's a shame what happened there," remarked Irina. "The Quincunx has been left in a blight of balky soot and oil."

"Not just the Quincunx, I'm afraid," added Myleyn.

"So, you've read the news boards too?" Barron chirped under his breath.

"Andrea's there as we speak, helping Duncan and his family salvage what's left of it. Now that the travel ban's been lifted, progress has only slowed. People are leaving for the desert in droves."

"Do you blame them? If the queen can't protect her borders, then who can?"

"What's this I'm hearing about Xardinia now too?" asked Irina.

He stretched out of his father's head chair, brushing the brace upon the canary-gold ceiling with his fingertips and making subtle eye contact with his mother.

"Myleyn, why don't you join me upstairs," suggested Irina.

Finally, he exhaled.

As Myleyn satisfied her wish of trying on his mother's old jewelry, he went outside, listening to the thunder and watching the rain funnel out from the gutters. He noticed two of his guards holed up beneath the stables; and another, visible in the turret that eyed the bridge. As for the rest of them, he wondered if they also had found a roof over their conductive shells.

When the rain had finally stopped, the crows and the critters raced like mad to the muddied fields before the few farmhands could scare them off.

"Thank you kindly for allowing me to try on your jewelry, my lady."

"Any time, my dear. I am just hopeful my grandmother's old brooch turns up before your next visit," regretfully Irina said, as she caressed her brown-haired mares with the tips of her fingers. "I assure you, it's beyond."

As the wheels began churning, he prodded the girl about their visit; more specifically as to whether she had taken a liking to any of his mother's jewels. To his dismay, it seemed she did not, at least based on her pursed body language. Part of him wasn't entirely surprised, as he knew her to be a bit particular. Still, she spoke very little of it.

Finding it difficult to contain his unrest, he cleared his throat. "Those were relics of my grandmother, and her mother before her."

"I'm sorry, Barron. But if I am going to wear something for the rest of my life, then it better be something I am content with." She shied her gaze to the wet streaks upon the windows.

He kept to himself for a long stretch of road; eventually breaking his silence with an exacerbated sigh. Upon hearing this, she relocated her golden head of hair to his shoulder. "What troubles you, Barron?"

At that moment, betwixt dueling acres of wet flowers and poppies, it had occurred to him.

He couldn't stay mad at the girl. The fact that his mother had, at will, allowed her to try on her heirlooms was a blessing enough. "Nothing," he smirked, "you're just picky."

CHAPTER 12

A SNEAKING SUSPICION

He paused before entering.

A normally unsentimental man, he couldn't help but feel an inexplicable wave of emotion crash over him, as he gazed upon the oblong brick factory swallowed whole in ivy. He was nervous, evidenced by an irregular heartbeat and a sudden urge to urinate. Some discomfort and nostalgia, too—like returning to your childhood home for the first time in a long while. But there was also another emotion: eagerness. Eagerness, of course, to see the place he had only merely existed in for so very long.

A dusty, distorted N was cast upon the marble floor of a reminiscent lobby. He couldn't see it just yet from behind the enormous, eternalized statue of Beau Nero. But he could surely envisage the woody smell of his desk, his firm leather chair endowed by his father, and his evocative window view of the clouds out yonder the outer wall.

Save for the dirty footprints left behind by the alchemists', and the stacks of discarded wood leaning against the brick walls, his old stomping ground appeared mostly the same as he remembered it pre-Slumber. It was a stark contrast from the befuddled state it had been left just four and a half months ago to the day. Then again, he had only yet seen the lobby.

He heard men whispering his name as he waltzed through a small crowd towards a stairwell, cleft around both sides of Beau's image like a scarf.

"There's Barron," he heard Marrin whisper to Selvin. "Barron, have you seen Devyn anywhere?"

"Can't say I have."

"There he is," pointed Selvin, "about time." The lead engineer approached indifferently with his head down and hair messy, triggering the company leaders over the railing.

"Men," began Marrin, quieting the lobby in an instant. "Before you run off to re-acclimate, I just want to say a few words. These past few months have been a real test and a true testament to our resolve as a company. I know it hasn't been easy. I for one vow to never set foot in a tent ever again," he said to unremarkable laughter. "We lost some good men to the Slumber, hard-working men, brothers." He exhaled hard and tapped his knuckles on the railing, before whittling off the names of the deceased like a true bureaucrat-in-training. "...Now that we are back, I ask that we all respect the Alchemy Guild's wishes and steer clear of the roped-off sections. This is only temporary, I assure you, just until the Guild finishes patching up our floors. And yes, I am afraid that means you cartographers, the basement is OFF-LIMITS. In the interim, I have set aside a table in the warehouse. The rest of you, mind your noise, would you?"

The man had only just acclimated to his office when a fat knock had been delivered to his door. He knew who it was. Marrin was the only one brave enough to bother him with his curtains shut. "What can I do for you, Marrin?"

"There's a problem at the Mining Guild."

It took every ounce of him not to lecture him.

It was the guild master's fault for his failing infrastructure. A short walk through his warehouse was evidence enough: The walls and floors were sopping wet and heavy with a layer of coal, and now beyond warped. As for the roof, Lord Garrick Aeseres had a makeshift skylight in his warehouse—not at all like the iconic N cast upon his lobby. This was a result of years of neglect. Much worse than Marrin led him to believe.

"We'll see what we can do for you," said Marrin, grabbing the Mining Guild leader's hand.

He couldn't wait for the old goat to retire. He was already nearing the realm of unsolicited stories. As he waltzed beside him down the miners' rotten stairs, Marrin looked at him with a sad smile, as if waiting for him to volunteer for the repair so he would not have to do so himself. A good part of him wished he would fall through the floor. *Perhaps an early retirement was exactly what the old goat needed to stamp his prosaic footnote in the annals of Nero's history,* he mused.

The following day he and his subordinates, First Architect Garvey and Third Architect Robert, whipped through the repair mock-ups, all the while, making sure not to leave any rotted brace, sunken floorboard, or jutting nail unturned in the miners' battered warehouse. Thoroughness would be the only way to keep Marrin and Selvin off his back.

He killed every sconce in his office, and shut his curtains, leaving only a small sliver of light as he leaned his back into his chair. Somehow someone didn't get the memo. "...Come in Marrin."

"I just wanted to drop by and thank you. I am sure you hate it, but the miners should consider themselves lucky to have you overseeing their renovations. Those mushrooms were the least of their worries—"

"Marrin," he spoke impatiently, "now that you are here, do you have a moment?"

"Of course," Marrin grunted into the chair opposite him. "What's on your mind?"

He had an itch just then and there to get up and shut his door. And yet seeing that sloppy, unfazed grin on his face, he would allow the full transparency. Better yet, wear it like a badge. "I don't think we should be doing the realm's grunt work any longer, Marrin, much less for the guilds." His mouth was so dry that his lips were sticking to his gums.

"I hear you, son. It's funny, I often ask myself what your father would do in certain situations; however, it seems there's plenty of him in you." He grinned fondly before getting up unexpectedly. Even more unexpectedly, he shut his door.

"The unfortunate reality is we're hardly breaking even as is. Sure, Devyn's sold more crankers this month than any other, but, and this is between you and me, but I don't think this trend will last much longer: horses are cheaper, and they don't require a whole Sib to operate. The treasurer mentioned to me just yesterday the defense work would be slowing down too. He claims because of the headway that's been made, 'All thanks to our help,' though I am beginning to think we've out-priced them."

"Forget the drudge work for just a minute, we need to create real demand," he spoke with a spark of tenacity. "Just recently I was brushing up on a little local history. I couldn't help but notice all of the archi-tectural feats made by our company in the Age of Prosperity. Did you know that the Grand Palace of Imia City was a Nero creation? Fascinat-ing, right?"

He folded his arms and chuckled. "What are you suggesting?"

That you quit. "Right now? Hard to say," he stuttered, "however, I've been hearing more and more rumors about this Xardinia lately. They're calling it the 'City of Wonder.' Might be worth exploring, get a little inspiration for some builds while we're at it."

Marrin flashed a smile.

"We need something big—something historic to put us back on the map."

Nodding, Marrin scooched upright in his seat. "How about this… with Selvin and his team now off fixing that mess at the Mining Guild, I need someone I can trust to supervise the renovations downstairs. Selvin's found several defects already in the basement, so I am not taking any more chances. Once the Alchemy Guild fixes all of the blemishes they've left, as they promised they would, I'll lend you a few men. Just need to figure out where on Tethia this place is."

He bit his tongue, reasoning. "Fair enough."

"Good," said Marrin, "now until then, let's keep this conversation between us. The last thing we need is our men worrying about their jobs."

"Understood."

He winked and climbed to his feet, grunting the whole way up.

Come first sign of dark, he locked his office, and off he went out the double doors with a hopeful pep. Tonight, he had a supper arrangement with Myleyn's family. Fitting his hopeful mood, he swapped his work jacket for a fine woolen overcoat. (He would most certainly need it where they were headed.)

Five of them congregated inside a dim-lit alleyway in the South Market, where an off-duty peacekeeper halted arriving pockets of noble families. Present from her immediate family were her parents, Landon and Marie, and her younger brother Naxwell.

"Names!" warbled the Tumsib peacekeeper, a gargoyle of a specimen with colossal limbs and head. Directly behind the guard, a bookish man sat with a tomb spread upon his lap.

As Landon stepped forth to speak their names, the bookish man started whisking through his tomb to verify their nobility, naturally enough too, as if the pages were intertwined with his memory. He then pivoted to a hole in the wall beside him, where he stuck his head and shouted unshyly, "Alarie and Thornrose!"

"You may enter," he said. And with that, the Sib yanked free the cellar door, and down they went. Inside—in a sense. But this was not a room of humankind, but an opening into the vast network of tunnels within Market's mantle.

"Welcome to The Cove," a pearly Tumsib female with a shrill voice greeted them. She tossed a bell back and forth over her exposed shoulder, unbeknownst to them alerting the rest of their staff of the inbound, upper-stratum guests. "This way, please."

They descended through a series of flowstones and columns, on an incongruent path into a great open room.

She extended her pearly arm into a colorful nook lit intricately by hidden lanterns, where Landon hmphed. "This'll do," he said to her (as best one could over the steady hums and drums emanating from the ascended pillars unseen up high).

While they indulged in their favorite Neuvian comforts, Myleyn's mother delved into just about every faux paw under the sun.

Barron didn't mind, for there's little to nothing to learn from someone through filler talk.

"What do you make of this mess in Imia?" out came her next question, returning to her Stainberry wine and huffing it like a fresh flower.

Neither Myleyn nor Barron spoke up immediately. Instead, they gave one another a look as if the woman had two heads. (In Barron's defense, he was still a bit flabbergasted at how similar her and her daughter's faces looked next to one another—he was now quite certain that her pink hue and dimples had come from her mother's side.)

"In what regard, Mother?" replied Naxwell.

"Am I the only one who's been following this whole ordeal? According to our new intelligencer, the island's populace has seemingly gotten up and vanished."

"Rubbish," said Landon, "their population has been on a steady decline since the Great Earthquake of 515 F.Y. And now this Slumber…"

Barron set down his chalice and wiped his lips clean. "And how did Maldinia's latest nepotism hire stumble upon such knowledge?"

Landon twiddled his mustache in quiet agreement.

"Everyone knows they had a part in the Gromula Day infiltration, the queen's just too meek to speak it aloud," she whispered, "it's not the first time they've tried something so brazen."

"I for one admire the Imians' resolve," said Barron, "managed to outlive the fate of their fatherland by a couple hundred years. I wouldn't count them out just yet."

On the second to last day of the work week (Fifthday, as the lost descendants of Neuvia call it), he bumped into Remus on the connector to work. Even odder than his punctuality today, his hair was combed wet, and his undershirt was tucked in. It was the first time since Gromula Day that he looked his age. "Meeting Esca for a date after work?" he teased him.

Remus scoffed. "No—*did she say she wanted to*? I am sort of low on crowns right now."

"Aha. After a promotion then, are we?"

"I suppose. My father promised me not a single crown more until he croaks…"

"Still wasting all your money at the taverns, I see."

He shrugged but didn't dispense any energy in denying it. "I'm not sure if it's even worth the effort. I've only spoken to Lord DuSprite once, maybe twice. I'd be willing to wager he doesn't know my name."

Barron pursed his lips and made his best effort at an empathetic nod. Else, nothing. He had little words of encouragement for the waste-of-talent slacker, nor desire to vouch for a waste-of-talent slacker. "Well, get out there and invent your next optae," he rolled his eyes.

The air was ripe with sawdust and chatter when he said his farewell to the warehouse, then vanished through an unmarked door.

Fifty steps later he had found his footing within the murky shadow of a cobweb-infested sconce, where he stooped low and studied the floorboards beneath him for defects. He had a funny feeling, a slanted pit in his lower stomach, recalling what Marren had said about Selvin's initial findings, about his concerns with the floor-work. Warranted. For the floor here in the basement was hollow, built crudely over the remnants of a forgotten mine, which wobbled from side to side as he walked upon it as if an idled vessel not far out at sea. A cause for wonder, for most wise men with a brain, especially now after the Alchemy Guild's botched extraction.

Only, for their part, the Alchemy Guild wasn't entirely to blame for this mess—the little holes in the platform were left by the Glowers. Like a hungry worm's tunnels in an unclaimed apple, they attuned.

He braced himself as he continued past many a dusty shelf, arranged like a blind man's maze, with some mounted on the walls, others broken out into piles on the floor. "What a mess," he coughed.

This was the archive, after all, where engineers' gizmos, builders' manuals, and last year's schematics went to die. It was also possessed, some have claimed. For generations, the occasional lackey, sorting, storing, or sifting through the archives, has claimed to have heard voices coming from Loarea's innards; whether from the trapped souls of the lost miners or the voices in their heads, none could say for certain.

He made sure not to linger on any particular piece for long. But mostly just the planks lost to the shadows. That of course was quickly becoming a commonplace, as he made his way through a maze of holes, to the far corner, where the alchemists' work-hands were hard at work patching one such hole. This one was rotted before the Slumber, and now it was gaping. But if the Guild didn't know that, they should have known that. Today it spewed a look of hungering darkness, leaking bitter air onto his ankles as he slid over a chair to oversee the first replacement planks being fastened. And oversee he did—just not the renovations. For as much as he tried to forget about the shrinking prospect of his treasure, he couldn't. And why should he? Better yet, how could he? So far beneath the surface, he could almost taste his treasure. He would need a distraction, and fast, like drawing castles and daydreaming of Xardinia.

It was a start.

It was a place he could now visualize, high up in the mountains, though not dizzying high like the plateaus, just nicely perched where the air was rich with hope and promise, where innovation was an old buddy of yours you shook hands with before outmaneuvering them in a battle of wits.

Come first sign of dark, there were two of them left: himself, and an underpaid guildie with an overworked tool-belt.

"Should be all done by tomorrow, sir," the workman said on his way to the stairs.

He panned about, unconvinced. The gaping hole was now considerably less gaping. But that was still gaping, wide enough at least to slot a Darren or a Steven through after a good Gromula Day feasting. "*Right.*"

En route back to the basement, heavier a hand lantern and an awful excuse of a dinner, he found the cartographers hard at work at their temporary workstation, amid the builders and their innocuously loud chatter.

"Do my eyes deceive me or is that our savior of the Eastern Dam?" inquired one of the cartographers, a man with two green stripes on his ill-fitting company jacket. They called the man "colorless," of course if ever there was a contest for the palest Neuvian on the whole of Tethia, Second Builder Daemon would surely take the prize.

"Steven finally decided to let you out of your cage, Daemon?"

The second cartographer chuckled.

"Sure, that is if we had one," remarked Steven bitterly, over the sound of sawing. "What's it like to have your own office again?" It seemed obvious that his old friend was not himself today: his eyelids shined a dark purple, as though he had himself a late-night argument with the missus.

He took a bite out of his dinner (i.e. the dried buzzard wing no longer crammed in the back of his desk) and shrugged. "Ask me again later. I have to oversee that mess downstairs—I'm sorry, I did mean your 'office.'"

"Hilarious." Steven joined him back at the unmarked door. "Don't look now," he whispered, noticing Remus and Darren inbound.

"Do you think I could go down? Most of our stuff is still down there."

"No. That's your fault for not taking them with you after the Awakening. Just tell me which ones you need and I can get them for you later."

"It's not just maps," he continued.

"Fine, fine," he said, pretending not to see the two coming their way. "You can come downstairs. Just grab it quickly and leave...I swear if Marrin finds you in here." He closed the door but not before delivering an "absolutely not" to the tinkerer and builder.

Steven started his search within the immediate shelves, dodging a sloppy mess of discarded floorboards, petrified rats, and nails.

With his lantern out, Barron poked his boot into a location where a shallow hole sat only hours prior. Although the replacement piece didn't budge, he didn't want to test it with his full weight. So off he went to the next spot, "great," and the next, "fine," until he had finally reached the chasm.

"Yikes, I don't remember *that* being here."

Startled, Barron sent the back of his hand into the soft portion of the man's gut. "Looks like you found your journal. That's good. Now you can leave."

"What about our books? Our maps?"

"The sooner you leave, the sooner you and Daemon can return to this cesspool. Now would you let me finish my work here in peace?" he said, resigning to his seat. Despite his objection, his old friend had no plan to turn back, not before a wee look inside of the chasm.

"Ruh!" charged the man angrily, "ruh!"

"No? Aren't you just a little curious? Did you bring that map of yours by any chance?"

He shoved him away from the hole, causing him to fall.

Sweeping dust off of his hands, Steven returned to his knees. "Well?" he replied, receiving a death glare. "Right," he sighed, "I have a few other things that need doing before calling it a night anyways."

"Sure, you do." The room fell into its first silence, allowing him to return his face to his notepad in peace. He lifted his head to confirm his solitude, only to find a vulgar act of stupidity. Steve's chest was lain half-way inside the chasm. "You don't listen, do you!" he shouted, grabbing him by the crease of his jacket (in doing so, causing the man's journal to slip from his front pocket). It teetered over the edge.

"My journal!" he returned to his feet, making one valiant attempt at catching the illusive journal. A great success too, if not short-lived.

Crack!

The replacement plank beneath the man's upper torso had severed. He watched Steven's body flop like a fish out of water, off the edge, belly up, shrieking the whole way down.

Then came another crack. Desperately he tried pulling himself up, though the floorboard supporting his left elbow was caving in. His left arm joined the right. A victory. No. A rouse. The one rotted plank of wood preventing him from falling in gave in too.

He fell six long seconds through a windless hollow before the lower half of his body was inflicted by a mess of bee stings. "Where am I?" he muttered meekly, scanning a rangy mess of hardened clay and debris that had swallowed his legs whole.

The cartographer had no words. He lay slumped like a flattened doe in the same pile of rejected residuals. An unconscious jerk from him caused his borrowed lantern to roll off the unstable mound. It illuminated two great walls of tenderized rock, and a few more towers of stacked debris, before shattering.

"I think I'm paralyzed," said Steven, finding the strength to reach his hand underneath his ribcage. "My ribs, I think they're broken."

"Good, you just ruined any shot I had at overseer."

He attempted to free himself, only to find the pain too unbearable. Every tug and wiggle sent his pain receptors into a tizzy.

"Remus!" shouted Steven, whose futile cry was stifled in the blanket of shrapnel. "Darren! Anyone!"

"Would you stop that?" Barron scanned the excavation pile with their only remaining light. "These mines haven't seen light in well over two centuries, you're going to cause a cave-in."

"We need help," wiggled Steven.

"No one's coming, Steven. And no, we're not waiting for the Guild to save us tomorrow. You're going to find us a way out of here, so you can fix this mess, and then I want you to rethink your life." Evaluating the distance, Barron yanked his body free and began descending the teetering tower of Tethia. Following a missed step, he met a firm surface with a painful reminder of his braised and bloodied legs.

Steven cried out in torment the whole way down, triggering one disturbing echo after another. But he powered through.

Huddled beside their only lantern, the bludgeoned men gawked at the hole up high. Without a ladder or rope anywhere, Steven floated the idea of adding to the pile—of course, any energy expended would undoubtedly be their undoing: poor airflow aside, they had not a single drop of water on either of them. Moreover, their only light source, outside of the weak glow emanating from the few basement candles, was as good as borrowed time.

As Steven scanned the capacious shaft, the man simmered on the repercussions of such a foolish act. *Even if the imbecile takes the fall for the incident, it will still surely tarnish my image*, he thought. "You've done it now, Steven."

"Why do you want overseer so badly, anyway? Seems like an awful job with more responsibilities than I can count."

"Why? Because in a realm starving for hope, the Marrin Vander's of this world have found a seat at the table. Do you really think Marrin's old brother-in-arms will bring this middling company back to the promised land? Pfft, Selvin has the imagination of a rock. How about Devyn? A step up, but Marrin would never allow it."

"So then, a champion of the people, are we?"

"Oh, shut it. So, which way, *cartographer*?"

"West. Nothing except for a wall that way."

"Lead on." Broken pales, sifters, and picks were among the little that remained in the narrow confines of the excavated path, where time moved eerily sideways. The pillars of throwaway nuggets were not gone, just morphed into whichever construct or fantasies were present in one's mind. Further west, he couldn't help but perseverate on his recent readings. More specifically, the cave-ins. "Forty-eight," he mumbled the death count to himself aloud.

"Hm? They had to get in and out somehow, right?"

His words fell on deaf ears.

Forty-eight. "Now which way?" he asked, at a fork in the shaft.

Steven paused before blurting out the first thing that came to his head. "West should take us down the whole of Loarea Road," he said, "to Loarea Tunnel and the outer wall. North...I suppose that would take us underneath the guild compounds."

He pondered his choice silently to avoid wasting any precious saliva.

"West seems the obvious choice," Steven continued, "but if we can't find an exit, a costly one."

He groaned. "I'm going to die in here, aren't I? Don't answer that. Northwards it is then." The two went right, into yet another abandoned shaft. The shaft was noticeably narrower and the walls were far more abused.

"Bloodstones," said the two synchronously, noticing red flecks on the opposing walls.

"This must be it!" said Steven, rushing eagerly ahead.

"Only one way to find out," Barron said, hesitating afar with his map.

"I knew you had it!"

There was evidence all around them, but the longer they took in their sanguine surroundings, the sooner the image faded from their heads. Their eyes were playing tricks on them.

"Maybe we're getting closer." Steven's eyes were steadily fixed upon the treasure map's coordinates, distracted enough to absorb the butt end of a pickaxe.

Hearing a grunt, Barron turned. "What was that?"

He wheezed in pain.

"You poor thing," he said sarcastically. "Wait, did you hear that?" He rushed his ears against the west wall, followed begrudgingly by the other, where they slowed their breathing and listened.

"What is it?"

"Sounded like voices," whispered Barron.

Steven scratched his head, getting another look at Barron's map. "We must be underneath the Alchemy Guild."

He tapped his fingers on the red wall, which was received by an echo. "We shouldn't even be able to hear that," he said, "the wall must be thinner than we thought."

"That could be our exit," eagerly remarked Steven. Northbound they set forth, until, in the limit of their shying lantern, a massive pile of debris shone, extended twice their height, to the roof of the red shaft.

"A roadblock," spit the man sulkily, "great, just our luck."

Steven watched him slump to his rear, a sad look in his eyes. "I'm going to get us out of here."

He said nothing, tossing a rock at the newfound wall.

"Let me have a turn with your lantern."

"Not a chance." Despite ill lighting, the mapmaker was hard at it, clearing a crevice round enough to poke his head through. And before long his torso too, and even his legs.

As they entered the next atrium, fine streams of light glimmered like stars through many a puncture hole. It was the outside looking in. Despite this, the chill, that inescapable bitter chill, remained.

"What's wrong?" asked the mapmaker, finding the other stooped ahead.

He beckoned his colleague to the ground beside him. "Look." Within the center of the left wall were rows of slits carved crudely out of the rock itself, and one enormous open aisle. Beneath them, more levels of traversed dig sites than either could count.

"It's incredible," whispered Steven.

"Let's go." The two came upon a stairwell, wrought, just like the makeshift windows now guiding their path, from the bulwark itself.

"Barron, this is it. This is our chance. There are hundreds, maybe thousands of levels beneath us. One of them must have something."

He looked now to the weakened wick of his lantern, then to Steven, then back to his lantern. "…Fine, but we don't have long," he said, catching the other off-guard. "Let's see if we can find this treasure once and for all."

With Steven leading the way, the two found another tunnel just like it below them. Again, red walls of dust—mind tricks. Eventually, mind-numbingly deep they descended, losing track somewhere in the triple digits. Some of the lower levels had small carts chasing along rails for miles, guided by a healthy number of Luminas, but no treasure. Some walls were mined so very intensely that there wasn't even any red dust left on them.

Sadly, it was time for them to cut their losses, for the light outside had grown murky, along with their only wick.

The stairs had come to an end in an ample open cavity, with a floor of solid rock and an upstretched ceiling filled with fledgling straws. Away from the stairs, they slumped their backs on an enormous crystalline column where they reasoned.

"What a waste of time," lamented Barron. "How could I be so naive?"

"What do you think *that* is?" asked Steven, chasing a strange coil to the ceiling, like a bug to a light. Barron joined him, advancing beyond the column, only to find their jaws dropped. In the very back of the cavity stood a massive vat, filled with pale green glowing liquid, suspended by shipyard chains.

As they stared in awe at the mesmeric vat of liquid, their eyes began to buckle. It was far too much to bear.

"Do you...do you think this is—"

"Yes," interrupted the architect, nodding with a grim, sobering stare. "But why?" Hearing voices coming from the stairs, they quickly concealed themselves behind the vat. He had no choice but to snuff out his flame. Though it was not like they needed it anyway: Up close and personal, the vat's liquid was like milk siphoned from the udders of an ethereal star. Closer as the footsteps approached, they could make out the strangers' voices.

"I reckon," said one of them, "it's only a matter of time before they're all gone." A pair of frighteningly pale men in bulky leather jumpsuits appeared briefly before disappearing past them. *Alchemists.* They carried with them wooden crates, heavy enough to require both hands. "How many did you get today?" they heard one of them say.

"Fourteen," replied the other.

Once the voices had silenced, he wiped a cold stream of mucus running down his nose and readied. This was it, their best and quite possibly only chance at an impromptu escape. They followed the duo closely but not too close to where their footsteps could be heard, onto a man-made platform filled with curiously glowing coils, beakers, and other alchemic apparatuses.

While awaiting the guild members to proceed further through the mysterious lab, the man scanned an enormous, compartmentalized bookshelf wrapped around the mouth of the laboratory, shaped like a great horseshoe.

Out of the blue, a ladder came nimbly around the bend, right beside them. "How did we get stuck gathering like a couple of penal drudges?"

The guild member navigated up a level where he placed his crate, marked it with a pen, and descended.

Pausing for the other to offload his crate, Steven snuck a closer look—one of the lids was not tightly fastened, allowing him a look inside. To both their sneaking suspicions, inside was a heap of tightly packed Luminas, fledglings, their hyphae tangled like yarn.

"Psst." The architect pointed forward, for one of the alchemists was removing a panel from the wall—a passageway.

They scanned behind them from the revealed doorway. "I don't think they should be that far behind, right?" asked one of the alchemists.

"Explain that to Wendell…" An arm extended back into the cavity, startling the two behind their cover.

The passageway had suddenly gone, so the men rushed over, familiarizing themselves with the strange panel.

They heard a reverberating slam on the other end of the panel, turning speechless to one another, before lurching their sweaty palms onto the wooden panel. As with only a trickle of help from the puncture slits, and a now obstructed vat of Lumina nectar, it was but a race against time to find something to grip.

To make matters worse, more voices were nearing from the stairwell. Finally, the two moved the panel out of the way.

On the other end, the two scrambled to slide the door back in place (revealed to be a bookshelf, filled with half-empty vials and dusty tombs). "Just leave it, let's go," remarked Barron.

Joining the other, the two snuck blindly around a dank cellar for an exit. A trial and error process that saw them bumping into one another through aisles of empty vials, before finding a trickle of hope; Barron bumped his head on something hollow. "Up here. I think I found the door. Follow the sound of my voice."

Somewhere below the long flight of steps, the other bumped into another noisy shelf.

"Who's that in there?!" they heard a voice shout from the laboratory.

"We have to hurry," spewed Steven. "They're coming, Barron. *They're coming.*"

A lantern, followed by another, came upon the cellar. "Did one of you open this?"

"*Barron.*"

The hollow door shook as the clasp released in his hand. "Got it!" Barron shoved one side, followed by the other, sending a rush of humid air inside, and Steven running.

Unable to ignore the emergence of outside light, the alchemists began shouting indiscriminately, "Wait up!"

Their eyelids tremored as they slammed the cellar doors shut on them, retreating in pain towards Loarea Road, leaving the upside thumb of the Alchemy Guild's headquarters in their rear view.

CHAPTER 13

PLANTING THE SEED

Swept in the wind on the northern border, a leviathan moth's sensors were met with an anomaly: a natural aroma—like dirt, masked by elixir stains and sweat. Up and down the river, its faint cry alerted several of its friends, along with the half-snoozing guardsmen in the roosts of the watchtowers beneath them.

And like the effortless spread of a late-summer wildfire, the watchtowers of the Pebblewood River came alive with some unnerving bells that early morning; disorienting fish, bees, and birds from their homes, out into the open; the warden among them, dashing northeastward from Vina Mountain upon his flightless bird.

"Taranchian thieves, sir. Should we bring them in?" inquired a watchtower steward, his men clenching a collection of pasty northerners.

Lord Fortier scanned the cravens up and down.

There were some children but mostly meek-looking men, with filthy rags covering their extremities.

He singled out one such craven in particular, a gangly, middle-aged man whom the younger ones regarded as "Skalk." His eyes were nigh colorless, with the slightest hint of yellow—the only exposed part of his face he could see, save for his feet, which were plagued by blisters.

"What was stolen?" he inquired.

A soldier handed him a glowing bag, causing him to scoff. "Afraid of the dark now, are we?"

"The little one over there stole a few plums too."

The warden, fighting back the urge to laugh, looked to the guardsmen like they had three heads. "If you'd like to walk them to jail, be my guest. Otherwise, you know where they live."

"On second thought," he balked, stopping one of the guardsmen in place. "Not him." The thief with the authority of a leader received the man's gaze. He said nothing, he simply stared at the cold reflection of his sickly yellow eyes in the man's tight-fitting breastplate as the warden dismounted from his great bird.

"Leave us," commanded the warden, causing the guardsmen to scatter.

The warden shooed his screecher away from the wet blades of the river bank, pulling the scavenger close into the heat of his lantern. He then snatched the scrawny man by his arms and rolled up his sleeves to ensure his stringy restraints were still in place. In doing so, the prisoner recoiled in visible agony as the rope came in contact with one of his many warts.

He kicked his bag over, sending several Luminas rolling into the water. A stubborn one teetered over the edge, one roughly seven inches long, cap to stem. That's not even counting its stringy hyphae, which stretched almost twice the mushroom's size in length.

"Perhaps you can tell me what's so special about these mushrooms, in particular? Besides the fact that they glow?"

Unfazed, the scavenger sniffled.

"Not much of a talker, are we? Do you understand Neuvian Proper? You know, the same language our kinfolk spoke of old? The same language I speak to you now in..." The northerner remained silent.

"…The way I see it, you and your men trespass our land. You set fire to Maldinax; now you skulk and steal our crops while our children sleep. Now I could have you arrested for trespassing, not to mention for thievery—oh yes, it was indeed the chief administrator's land you and your friends have stolen plums from—or you can spill. The choice is yours, however, I must say a man of your stature won't make it much long in a Maldinian prison. A Tum could chew you up and spit you out like a pema root."

The scavenger averted his gaze onto the gills of the mushroom just out of his reach.

"Okay then, patchwork spearhead, how's about we find you a nice crowded cell?" At once, the warden yanked the man closer to his bird.

"We aren't burglars," spoke the man, causing the warden to stop. "We're just hungry is all."

"Oh, so you do speak? Do you prefer crop-snatchers?" he replied, hoisting up his meager loot. "Personally, I prefer a bit more variety in my diet. More protein." He dragged the bony man through the grass by his bindings, causing him to wince in agony, and his bird to buck in excitement.

"Most of our land is still tainted," he said, causing the warden to pause. "We do what we can to get by…If not for the Guardians, we'd likely starve." Judging by his pulse, which thumped irregularly through the palm of his hand, he was confident he was withholding information.

"And whose fault is that? Your families went mad. The Great Founder's rule was no longer yours to lambaste, so, naturally, you turned against one another. A devolution is what it is." He narrowed his eyes. "What do you mean by 'Guardians'?"

He shrugged. "They waltz about at night, their spores feed on the blight left behind from the war. When the few lucky among us on the river awoke, their spores were everywhere, busy at work; and as were yours."

"Well then, since you have humored me, I can have you on your way back to your merry little mushroom gang in no time. I just need to know what's so special about the glowing mushrooms. It seems you know something I do not."

"From what I hear? They make your pecker grow."

Grabbing the scavenger by his neck, he held it just below the bird's gravelly beak. Saliva dripped through the hairs around its mouth in anticipation of his master's gracious offering. "Is that why you're raiding our land for them? Huh? Choose your words carefully."

"I don't know. I didn't ask questions. Some old man in a boat shows up on our shore, and promised us a share of your land if we helped them out."

"A share of *our* land?" he scoffed. "One of yours?"

"A foreigner. Offered us gold for the glowing ones. 'Heavier they are,' he says, 'larger the prize.'"

A look of reluctance shrouded the warden's face, sending him to free his clammy grip. At once, the patchwork spearhead crawled safely away from the beast's reach. The warden threw the man his emptied bag and spit. "The next time I see you, you best be thinking back to this day and how lucky you were to have been given a second chance. I'm not as forgiving as the queen nor naive enough to allow a perversion like this to happen again."

The man nodded then plopped with a splash into the moon-light's gaze.

Once rid of him, he collected the few mushrooms left in the grass, only to be startled back to reality by an unsettling rumble, from across the river.

It was some time after noon when he arrived back in the city with the latest.

"Hello, Warden," greeted Lady Knish from behind a busy pile of documents. "Pardon, but I didn't realize we were expecting you today."

"You weren't. Where is she?"

The queen popped her head out of her bedchamber with a sedated look, before beckoning him inside. Save for a weak glare, leaking through her dusky stained glass window, only a single candle flickered in her room.

She had been sitting in her rocking chair, he knew: a shadow of its hind legs rocked back and forth from the corner of her dreary space.

He took a step closer in her direction, causing her to shudder. "What is it that I can do for you today, Xander?"

"Apologies for the disturbance. As I am sure you might've heard, we've had a string of incidents earlier this morning," he said. "It would seem that our benign, glowing mushrooms have captured the attention of our dear neighbors."

Sending the displeasure in his undertone, she rolled her eyes.

The clouds soon passed beyond the butte, causing Xander's eyeballs to bulge. "My Lady, you look *different*," he commented.

She chuckled, exposing a healthy glow within the creases of her powdered face. "I do hope that is a good thing. I've been trying some new remedies."

"Remedies," he nodded with a feigned smile (though the thought did cross his mind whether he had been talking to the queen or some double of hers from decades past).

"I was informed of these incidents as well," she began pacing around, "though it wasn't *just* the Luminas that were stolen. Did I hear that right? It certainly wouldn't be the first time we've caught crop-snatchers on the river."

"Not just the river, I am afraid. The Sprites apprehended a few of them in the forest too. I was told they had several glowing ones in their possession, alongside a few empty night-sight elixirs." He took another half step closer to her, causing her to slink meekly into her rocking chair. "Why the glowing ones?" he continued. "The Pebblewood River is home to a platitude of palatable fungi. Not just on our side of the river either."

She rocked in her chair, revealing an old toy chest beneath her seat. "What are you suggesting?"

Suggestively he raised an eyebrow, causing her to sigh. "The grudge you have for the Alchemy Guild is well known. However, I remind you this: The Alchemy Guild has been nothing short of a divine intervention these last few troubling months..." He had a look of disgust when he finally bowed out of the door. Before he could exit, she stood and extended her chilly hand. "*Wait.*" Finding a vulnerable glimmer in her eyes, he paused to listen.

"I apologize, Xander, I-uh I don't sleep very much these days. How about this, you focus your efforts on keeping our borders safe from scavengers, and I will keep a closer eye on the Alchemy Guild's doings." She fixed a subtle yet perturbed stare onto his shadow. In his absence came another guest, visibly as perturbed as she.

"Our worst fear has come alive," was the first thing out of her mouth as she closed her bedchamber door behind the master alchemist, "it won't be long until all of Tethia knows about this; if they don't already. The Imians, the Stares, they'll all want a piece."

"King Carliga is dead," he said, "his children are now grown children. As for Imia, you saw the intelligencer's report, not a single fishing ship could be found in their waters. It'd be a miracle if King Marinus is still alive."

"All the more reason for them to want to get their hands on the Luminas."

The master alchemist repositioned himself in the window's glare, stroking his chin.

"Now is the time, Vanic. I have to let my people know of their true potential. We must begin redistributing to the lot of them. And before you say it, I know, I am privy to the Guild's secrecy policies. But no more of this, keeping my people in the dark will only stir resentment."

He bit the inside of his cheek.

"Until then, look at me! I can't go out in public looking this spry. They'll string me up for sorcery."

"And in due time to supply, my lady."

Frustrated, the queen moved to her credenza where she furiously downed a lazabloom elixir. "No more delays. It's quite time for our people to become acquainted with the Lumina's true potential."

He fixed a patronizing smile. "Of course, my queen. However, we must be choosy in whom we distribute to. If we open the floodgates completely, we shall unknowingly place the world's biggest target on our backs. Just look at Loarea, centuries later and the Imians are still skulking around that hollow rock. And for *what*? A few crumbs left of a pie?"

"In your own words Vanic, the Lumina's spores safeguarded us from the effects of the Lull. They're likely the only reason you and I are still drawing breath. Our people deserve this gift for all the sacrifices they have made."

His face uncannily tensed. He exhaled and smiled. "Well, and what better gift than a nice big fat tariff? I assure you, my lady, in time you will see this once flagship nation returned to the glory of your forefathers."

She tapped her heel in swift succession. "The general and our emissary should be returning from their Starik visit before month-end. How do you think applying tariffs on our enemies would bode with an already fickle armistice?"

While he absorbed her words, he subtly transferred the mud from his boots onto her rug.

―――――――

Behind his locked door, Barron and his friend gazed out his back window towards the alchemists' tower afar. "This is corruption at the highest level, Steven. Not only are they breaking the law by trespassing inside of Loarea, but they're stockpiling those things!"

Steven's eyes wandered about his friend's tastefully bland walls, where not a single piece of art was hung. "I am just as angry as you are about this whole thing, but let's not forget, they're technically legal now to harbor. You might be reaching a bit."

"Polemist. It's been what a couple of days since they've stopped calling it an outbreak? I find it hard to believe that facility was erected in just the few days following. Those shelves were filled to the brim with Glowers; oh, and not to mention that vat. Please tell me you saw that coil being fed from it into the ceiling?"

Steven chuckled. "I figured you would be more rattled about your foiled treasure. You're *sure* there wasn't enough sediment to make some money with?"

Barron jerked his mouth to the side. "That wasn't sediment, that was sediment's sediment. Buyers want something substantial: a fat gem, or better yet, a suit of armor. Those tracks we found were new. Newish. The Mining Guild got there first, who else?"

"What if that vat *is* our treasure?"

"I did consider this. However, the timing doesn't match up. Those seamen must've been led astray."

Steven shook his head, relocating to a seat at his desk.

"What we need is a do-gooder, Steven. Someone to expose their little operation. The best-case scenario: word gets out, and the queen, Dacmaster, and the rest of the Alchemy Guild get Loarea'd off this rock. Worst case scenario, whomever we send to do our dirty work comes up missing."

Steven shook his head concerningly.

"I know…then we would need to find another sap."

"You never know, the Alchemy Guild may have gotten permission to run their tests in there. Maybe the Luminas have to be kept at a certain temperature."

"Regardless of the location, the alchemists are still actively foraging for them," he said, "why allocate all that time and effort on a so-called 'benign' mushroom?"

"The queen did say the Alchemy Guild would be running further tests to determine any medicinal properties. Perhaps they're on to a breakthrough?"

"Yes, but what I'm saying is, what if they are already three steps past a breakthrough? You saw it yourself…they had enough Lumina nectar squeezed to perform hundreds, maybe thousands of tests. The alchemists are selling them, I'd be willing to bet on it."

"So who would willingly do our dirty work for us?"

Barron looked at him, his eyebrow raised musingly.

The morning after he awoke in a puddle of sweat of his own making; the sort in which one might only conjure after an elixir bender. As he leaned down and twiddled with his homemade leg dressing, he heard his voice being called out from the hallway.

Myleyn poked her head into her bedroom. "About time," she said. "Your breakfast is going to get cold."

"Splendid," he smiled, "I like my milk how I like my Frost-berry: cold."

"Very well," she smirked, "but on one condition, you must tell me again about your 'fall.' I woke up with your blood on me."

"I shall tell you in detail, but you must promise me not to speak of it to anyone; not to your mother, father, nobody. But first, my milk."

They relocated to the dining room where Myleyn's once reluctant expression turned into one of bewilderment. He started with their initial discovery at the Eastern Dam, ending eventually with his impromptu venture inside of Loarea. "I'm rarely speechless," she said, embracing him. "I am so sorry this happened to you."

He thought he could hear her chuckling as she held him taut, and so he loosened his hold on her. "What? Are you laughing?"

"Nothing," she said, "you're just far weirder than I thought."

"I'm full of surprises."

"We have to report this. The Guild is breaking the law."

"I put my trust in no one, Myleyn," he said, "if this somehow comes back to me, I'll lose my job and promotion."

"Surely we have to do something."

"Yes. I have thought about it, and I have a solution. It's quite simple, I write an anonymous confession from a 'concerned alchemist'; one with a conscience, one who could no longer bear the guilt of lying to his family about his Guild's doings. I'll make enough copies to fill the Sol twice over."

She nodded dubiously.

"Then I'll have Steven disperse them. The man owes me a life's debt for the stress he's caused me. The Alchemy Guild knows something that we do not about those things. It's red as the rocks in the day. There's a reason they're still scraping those tunnels for Glowers. They're hiding something, and if the queen doesn't act, the people will."

Onto the surface of her dining room table came a stack of paper. "Well?" She met his gaze. "Where do we start?

CHAPTER 14

WATCH THEM GROW

As the early morning sun rose, so too did Lord Alarie's master plan. Yesterevening as he slept, copies of their scathing confession were posted on two separate news boards in Market and Residential. (And, for the high likelihood that their confessions are taken down, slid discretely beneath the doorways of homes and storefronts across the Inner City.) As per Barron's wishes, the bulk of the stack was reserved for neighborhoods with a high population of residents and formerly displaced. This of course being commoners. A demographic not nearly as helpless as peasants nor, on the whole, half as detached as the nobles; one composed primarily of humans, who outnumbered the titled fifteen to one.

As for any extras Steven managed to retain, he wedged enough of them between the cracks in the cobbles in the West Market to be dangerous.

It was the top of the fourth week of summer, and the anonymous exposers went about their day like any other. The heat, on the other hand, was not like any other. By mid-morning the sun was nearing full force, sending a hail of unfettered rays down upon the mountaintop, mesa, and plateaus. Close to the sun, even a leisurely barefoot stroll through the unshaded sections of the rocks shall send the soft layer of someone's soles burning bright red; any longer, the skin may very well blacken.

Despite the oppressive heat, the always neatly dressed and jovial etiquette teacher's face radiated all the same as her first lesson, as she and Barron said their farewells and parted ways. A lesson on the Crown Butte for a client of great importance, she was off to. A lesson she did not intend to be tardy for. Unfortunately for her, and her unscathed punctuality record, an angry mob of citizens severely threatened her chances at a repeat customer.

A similar story further west around the bend of the Outer Circle, where swarms of citizens charged their way down the Market District-Loarea District Connector, only to be halted on the downslope by a wall of peacekeepers.

His plan was working much fairer than he had thought. The only thing preventing the realm now from falling into complete chaos was just a couple of choke points. And although no public sentence or usurping had come to pass, a second wind was stirring from within.

"The men grow restless," relayed Selvin, his hands heavy upon the guardrail.

"Regardless of what may occur out there," replied the overseer, "we will remain focused on our work *in here*."

"There won't be any work left if the crown falls," said the lead engineer.

"I can't prevent any of them from leaving. However, if we lead by example, then perhaps we can persuade a few of them from leaving."

No soon later did they catch stares from stripes in the lobby, and so the four of them moved their impromptu huddle inside of the overseer's office, where a warm pitcher of water and an all too familiar sight of unfiled letters and invoices awaited them at the overseer's war table. "Barron, unfortunately, your venture to Xardinia will have to wait. I'm going to need you and your teams at the ready if any destruction comes to pass."

The man clenched his teeth, averting his gaze from the huddle. He was frustrated, but less so regarding Xardinia—a mere distraction from his real goal of wearing the coveted silver jacket—more so, because he still wore it.

Devyn slid Barron the absentee list as Marrin mowed through yet another maintenance proposal from the treasurer. Excluding the lucky ones away on assignment, today's absentees were two three-stripe builders and a tinkerer-engineer. He knew who it was before even seeking out the latter's name. It wasn't the first time Remus Gezdin went missing on account of a self-inflicted liver injury. And yet now, with upheaval in the air, this oversight of his may very well be his last. For now, ignoring the clamor in the lobby was no longer possible.

The company leaders exited back over the railing, where they surveyed powerlessly.

The overseer's eyes were about to bulge out of his head when he finally saw how many of them were in the lobby, chattering like bored housewives, most without their jackets on. "What's the meaning of this?!" he exclaimed. A few of them received the overseer's glare, peering upwards through the gaps in old Nero's arms. And yet not a single one of them spoke up. This was quickly becoming the happiest day of his life.

Noticing some red within the blend, the lead architect casually waltzed down the stairs where he halted a young architect before his apparent escape. "What's going on, Robert?" inquired the man, almost too obliviously of his constituent.

"Demonstration is fixing to take place at the alchemists' tower. Don't know what else it'll take to get the queen's attention."

"I see. And you were planning on tagging along with your friends here?"

The third architect's face went red as his stripes, and yet little did he know beyond his cold façade Barron was internally gleaming.

Flummoxed by the blatant dissent, the overseer intercepted the lead architect for clarification. He of course pleaded ignorance, lest he disturb the swelling tide. There was little he could say at this juncture anyway. The warehouse was clearing out by the minute—those poor hook racks had never felt such a weight.

Outside, a similar tale was unfolding; smelters, butchers, stone-masons, weavers and spice men were wandering from their workshops and mills by the hundreds and growing. This was no demonstration, he soon realized, watching the distant demonstration from his second-floor window, but a siege of attrition. Working men, previously displaced and the like, in union as one; their sights squared upon those responsible for their evictions, starting with their flimsy tower of warped wood. Fortunately for the men of Loarea, the lawmen were all too preoccupied plugging the same holes these hard-working men were permitted freely to enter only hours prior.

In the throne room, the queen and her council were hard at work trying to cull the immediate threat. "We have a mob at our doorsteps," said the queen, her eyes wandering to and fro the anonymous guild member's confession, and her council members' trepid faces.

"Where's the warden?" asked the treasurer.

"I've sent word," she replied flimsily. "For now..." The way her advisors stared at her (more like gawping, actually), it was obvious there was something off about her today. Within the crimson pools of the west window, her powdered face glowed more than a rock plopped into a boiling pot of water.

"Might I remind you that the general is back," started the recently returned grand emissary, Aloc Geldrin, "we should inform him at once. We have three thousand foot soldiers at the ready, only a few bridges away. Once the mobs are dealt with, and tempers have simmered down, we shall allow the Guild to prove their innocence in front of an audience."

Lady Knish's focus swayed from the emissary, back to the frazzled queen. "If I may, my lady. Mobilizing might be our only option to prevent the realm from falling into disarray."

"The last time this happened we spilled blood, the blood of our people, and for that, my late husband and I are marred. My daughter would never forgive me, not any of us if this were to happen again." A brief silence washed over her table as she fumbled about for her chalice. "I apologize, I just know how easily these affairs can get out of hand. Where does our intelligencer stand?" She searched the quiet corner of the assembly table, where an expressionless, silver-haired man sat with his arms folded.

He received the woman's desperate gaze and inhaled, resigning his arms to his side. "I think we should do nothing." Their eyes fell upon him; this elder son of Claudius "Blind Eye" Flumen. Only a junior pupil at the time of his father's passing, Oleander came garbed in a pewter trench coat with a black F sewn on his left breast. "I could be wrong, but last I checked, it's hotter than the sun out there," he continued, "and yes, those *are* humans out there, mostly. And humans, as we know, need water to live." He cleared his throat and sat up. "I guess I just don't see the harm in investigating the matter ourselves. From what I recall you saying, my lady, the Alchemy Guild was to run further analyses on these Lumina mushrooms for 'medicinal purposes'; however, no exception, nor amendment—at least any that I'm aware of—would permit the alchemists to operate inside Loarea. My home was safe from the toadstools, though I can empathize with their plight."

"Well, we're not getting anywhere with that mob down there," redacted Lord Vodgar. "My lady, I must reiterate, we have crop snatchers in the North Valley, murdering infiltrators; and now miscreants within our walls."

She sank into her chair, murmuring under her breath, "Yes," she turned hollowly, "yes, I have to do something."

In the Nero Company's headquarters, a low rumble was causing sediment to rain down from the ceiling. *Was it thunder?* he wondered. The sky was indeed graying and there was even a little rain, but this noise was not from the sky. It was lower than that, deeper. (Quite like Selvin's gravelly voice was now, bouncing about through the warehouse.)

"What's that noise, Selvin?" asked Barron from the rail.

"They're mobilizing."

Marrin followed behind the lead builder. "We're getting the men out of there, Barron," he said, eyeing the lead architect and engineer. "If either of you would like to help, come along. We must be quick."

Not good, he thought. Too late, however, to sway him otherwise. With Devyn now joining, he had little choice but to tag along, lest he appear a coward.

All was quiet in the alchemists' tower.

Outside, the men of Loarea were hollering, banging on its soot-swept siding for Lord Vanic's head. Marrin feared little of blank threats. He marched straight through the mob with Selvin at his heels, fanning out in search of familiar faces. Even without their jackets on, Marrin not only was able to pinpoint several faces but also convinced several of them to turn back. Barron thought it impressive if not a moot point.

As he refrained cautiously from a safe distance, he noticed a glare: a reflection on their cellar doors. They were wide open and bent wildly out of shape. It was only a matter of time before the overseer would notice. Men were rushing inside in droves.

On the surface, the quakes plateaued.

A curly, blond man, clad in stiff gilded armor and an ostentatious purple cape, came forward in a seeping ray, sliding a karnip fiber whip from his pocket, before unraveling it with a quick flick of his wrist. Soldiers filed in after him, creating one great ring around the lab. He then cast out his whip, piercing the chatter. "Round them up. The prison's filling up fast."

"General Jarcentinia?" spoke Marrin, turning to Selvin with an eyebrow raised. "He hasn't aged a single day…"

"So, the rumors *are* true," the warden entered, filing past the general with a unit of probers in tow.

Angered by a lack of cooperation, the general broke through their shoulders, followed by his stripers. He grabbed a jeweler by the seam of his tunic and tossed him out of his way as he forcibly entered the lab. "Vander?" greeted the general, scoffing. "O, how the mighty have fallen."

"Before you drag us away, you ought to take a look at this. It's a log," pointed Marrin. "The Alchemy Guild has been doing test trials on two of our own."

"And?" he chuckled, "I see no alchemists here. Nor a 'glowing' vat either"

"They emptied it!" someone shouted.

"Damage control," chimed Steven.

Barron looked to his old friend with several shades of malice as Marrin moved unshyly towards the general, shadowing him like a cloud. "According to these test logs, the Lumina mushrooms possess age-traversing effects. 'Unripening,' as Test Subject One calls it. The Alchemy Guild has known of this for over a month now; look here, they're all dated."

"Clever," said the general, subtly signaling over his guardsmen, "just wait until the queen finds out that her favorite bridge repairman was behind this break-in. Forging phony documents," he frowned, "all in some elaborate ruse to frame the Alchemy Guild. I've heard quite enough of this nonsense. Arrest these men!"

"*Us?!*" shouted the gray jackets.

"What about the Guild?" added Second Builder Darren, joined by jeers.

"Tell me, Dandikauf, how much are they paying you?" scolded the overseer.

On their way out of the cove, the general glared over his shoulder at the warden.

"Reginald, Rowan, Xardwin collect any evidence you can find in here; anything to incriminate this sham. Victor and Anvel let's find out where that coil leads."

Amid a heavy downpour, a swift-moving prober with thick curls leaking from his coif darted inside the cellar where the others awaited his report. "General left behind a few of 'em—just cadets, I think. Shouldn't give us much trouble, Warden."

"Catch your breath, Lamb."

They sent a few knocks on the front door and waited. But nothing, nothing but the faint tremor of fleeting footsteps.

A man with a plateau-shaped eye-patch covering his right eye sighed, his only serviceable eye studying the few leftover infantrymen on watch. "What's our next move?" Victor was this one's name, the Special Investigation Probing Bureau's lead investigator—a position the warden himself too once proudly held.

The warden paused over a rumble of thunder. "My orders were simple. To bring order to Loarea. However," he continued, with a funny expression, "who's to say the poor alchemists aren't under duress?"

Around back the probers found success picking a door lock. Unfortunately, a padlock was preventing them from entering the building just yet. As luck would have it, Victor was quite knowledgeable in the art of infiltration, a reformed burglar himself. Despite the absence of his thieving tools, there was an ample supply of mud brought forth by the amassing rain. He reached his now muddied blade through the crack in the doorway and pressed it firmly onto the metal chain. And with a little patience, and some luck, his blade stuck, allowing him to slide the locking mechanism out of place.

They tasted a foul stench within the fibers of a long drab rug, following every one of their steps, as the three of them split up for the coil's source; jiggling door knobs, poking their heads in and out of the many rooms flanked about the ground floor. For now, the rain would mask their presence. As for the smell, the suffocating mixture of ammonia and decomposing plant matter was here to stay. As if it couldn't get any worse, inside a room labeled "Supplies" the warden was welcomed by a swampy stench.

As he waltzed forward with his nostrils plugged a great glob of a creature came lurching eagerly into the bars of its cage. He smacked its holding cell, and turned to the cage beside it where a pair of curious yellow eyes emerged from the tiny pool of water, just briefly, before disappearing.

"*Psst*," he heard Anvel signaling from the hallway.

Footsteps were heard and a voice was calling out, "Anyone else need anything from the kitchen?"

"An ale will do!" someone replied from the floor above.

"An ale," repeated the alchemist aloud, chuckling to himself as he fished for his keys. "Good one!"

The warden poked his wet head out. Followed by his men, the three scanned a now quiet stretch of hallway, its walls filled with portraits of guild masters of old. "I suppose we'll have to do this the Imian way," whispered the warden.

Fortunately for them, the distracted alchemist had forgotten to lock the door of the "Kitchen" behind him; and one after the other, the three tip-toed their way inside. Only this was no kitchen, but a storehouse, filled with alchemic contraptions and alphabetized storage shelves, containing thousands upon thousands of bottled elixirs.

There were two voices, they discerned, as they crept closer, somewhere in the distorted light of the center aisle, beyond a profuse collection of lazabloom elixirs. While their steps were yet concealed over the sound of raindrops, their shadows were not. They held, peering through the gaps in the shelves, observing a guild member as he cranked an awkward lever. He rushed over, helping another guide a flow of pale glowing liquid into a bushel of empty vials.

This was it, the mother-lode, a thunderous symphony of incriminating evidence, topped with a percussion of rain.

It took every ounce of the warden's compendious frame to restrain himself from punching the lackeys' teeth in.

Instead, they watched and listened for some time longer, before slipping out the back door. "Warden," they heard a voice say to him, "come with us."

CHAPTER 15

LIMBO

The blustering winds leaped and crashed like waves upon the table-top peaks, frightening the last of the brave little Tumsib children back into their cozy rock dens. Assailed too was the mesa, where underneath the canopy of the prison courtyard, a heap of detained agitators watched the rain collect amidst the colorful flashes of lightning.

For their part, Steven, Darren, Xarlen, and Krieg were hailed as heroes for uncovering the Guild's illegal operation. Barron shared little in their excitement, for there was not a single alchemist in attendance, not one, despite his plot allowing first-hand knowledge of the Guild's clandestine dealings to spread.

It most definitely was not the result he was hoping for. Rather, an enlightening confirmation of the crooked system in which they all inhabited.

"You know, I do seem to recall you telling me about what you would do if you were ever thrown in prison," Steven said.

A flash of lightning illuminated a conical expression on Barron's face. "Oh, shut it."

"It's not all bad. Just listen to them, there's hope in the air. We did a good thing today."

Barron shushed him with loose eye contact, pulling him away from the crowded awning into an empty cell. "What we needed was Change, Steven." His eyes drifted to the overseer, much too quiet since their recent detention. "Sadly, a virus cannot be thwarted until its source is rooted out."

The cartographer scratched his head.

"Will the following inmates step forward!" interrupted a guardsman's voice, "Marrin Vander, Barron Alarie, and Devyn DuSprite!"

"What's this about?" he heard Marrin pressing the guardsmen as he approached.

"You're being transferred to the jailhouse. General Jarcentinia's orders."

Marrin continued prodding them, to no avail. A breath of fresh air: The guards didn't recognize his authority. He spun to Devyn and Barron for a semblance of clarification, which they too shrugged off. Unlike his counterpart, however, Barron did not intend on living Marrin's historic blunder down—he would archive it like a good quote from a treasured novel.

Needless to say, their tenure in their newest cell was initially quite awkward. There was still no word on a verdict. Nor a sentence. What they did have, at the minimum, were three blocks of wood and a pillow of hay to rest their heads on this evening.

"Vander." A figure approached. "I do hope your sleeping arrangements are more suitable to your liking." The overseer spun guardedly to the bars of their cell, where the general stuck his head through. "Not even a 'thank you'?"

"What's your angle, Dandikauf? And why us three? Last I checked we had four company leaders and over a hundred men in custody."

The man smiled, exposing a pearly mouth of teeth. "Selvin will manage, as have I," he alluded to a faint scar on his shapely chin. "I've brought the three of you a little gift." He sent a whistle down the hallway, rousing several guardsmen.

"I'm sure you are tired of sitting in those wet clothes." A guard fumbled open their cell door, while another one snuck by and started lining up some crates. The first contained a bowl of fat-heavy slop, a handful of bread, and some overripened citric slices forgotten in the sun. The second crate had some fresh clothes, and another blanket for them each.

They peered off the edge of their beds, for the last one appeared empty. Upon closer inspection, however, a single piece of parchment appeared at the bottom of its dusty web—a note, or maybe a letter, Barron thought it.

"What's the meaning of this?"

"I am glad you asked," said the man, turning towards the guardsmen, and flicking them away.

"What are you even doing here? The prison, the jailhouse, these are the warden's jurisdiction."

"Vander! Where have you been, my old compatriot? The Armory District is under my domain, it has been since before the Slumber. The warden's duties have been, shall I say, consolidated." The man squeezed his face closer into the bars. "Now, I have strict orders to detain the lot of you agitators indefinitely, but you and I, Vander, go way back. We served in the Desert War together."

"So, you're letting me go then?" replied Marrin. "And how about my men?"

"Not so fast. I have brought you a deal. A bargain, let's say, in exchange for your freedom."

"And what about the rest of my men? Are you going to let them go too?"

The general sighed. "Just read it."

The overseer scooped up the note and plopped his rear onto his slab, causing it to rattle under his weight. The general waltzed to his left, observing Devyn's unamused expression, then to his right, to Barron's. The lead architect was paler than usual. He had a cold sweat running down his forehead where most of his bangs hung.

"So, your Overseer Alaire's son, are we? The savior of our wells I hear."

The architect opened his mouth, but nothing came out. Utterly dry was it, as if he had swallowed a glob of fresh paint. His head was spinning too.

"Is he all right?" he turned to Devyn, answered by an uncooperative shrug.

"*Well?* Do we have a deal, Vander?"

The overseer arose, waltzing to the caped man, causing him to flinch. "What is this?"

"I urge you to consider—"

"A gift?" he interrupted, "you want me to convince my men to play nice? Or else you'll what? Tell the queen I am your mastermind behind this break-in? How much is the Alchemy Guild paying you to look the other way?"

The man turned to the opposing wall, and back to the iron rods that separated them, gripping them with a fierce scowl. "I don't think General Konnix would stand to hear his star pupil slander a fellow commander. Oh, and if you must know, you are absolutely correct about one thing: the law was broken." He shook his golden head. "Only the Alchemy Guild is not culpable in any, at least, for their part, for trespassing, nor their perfectly legal crown-sanctioned test laboratory. I'll urge you this once, Vander, think it through."

He whistled to a guardsman, stealing a pitcher of water from his roving meal cart, which he tauntingly drank.

As Barron watched his throat move, he felt his tongue go numb, then his vision. The lights were all but gone, and so were the walls. And from this darkness came a voice.

"…Father?"

His sun-cooked eyes were shuttered by a glare when a pale figure with a wiry mustache, with shoulders as wide as a Sib's, marched forward across a now empty mesa. The glare obstructed its face. "I am not your father."

He searched for features within the outline of the stranger's face, only to find its floating body slipped from his grasp. "Who are you?" he panned the red surface, only to find a few tumbleweeds.

"I have been called the Great Founder by some," reappeared the figure, "others, the God King Xardrescu Morthanix."

"God King? HA. You are no deity of mine, but a figment of my present dream."

"You're certain of this?" replied the man.

"That's right. Though I'll give it to you, in life, you were a man of extraordinary conviction, who conquered the greatest master stroke our people have ever known," he said, alluding to the plateaus up high. "You are our Neuvian savior; a symbol of our people's resilience,and our insatiable appetite for innovation. For a time or two, I suppose."

"You are correct," he said, "but if I may ask, what is a deity, after all? In your own words…"

"I don't know, something greater than man?"

"Well," he started proudly, "that, I can say."

"Something supernatural—immortal, I guess."

"Hundreds of years it's been since I instituted this great nation, and here I am still relevant in your mind, am I not?"

Tongue-tied, the man folded his arms.

"A deity, yes. Though so are you"—he darted at him, his wispy finger out—"it's there, in the pit of your human soul, guarded by your deepest darkest fears."

He found himself alone again. "Where has the rest of the dream-scape gone?"

"Look around you," returned the figure, "what do you see?"

He set his eyes first for the barren caprock of the unconquered mesa; then a sluggish cloud. "I see a blank slate. A canvas for my designs."

"*Yes*! What else do you see? *What do you hear*?"

He inhaled, catching a morsel of a voice, followed by another, corned on the edge of the northwest shadow. The voices resonated in his ears like whispers in a forest.

"You hear what you hear, Barron," said the figure, "remember that."

"You're an invaluable asset to this company, son. You have more potential than any of them, I know. But it's not your time yet."

The hairs on his neck stood up straight in secondhand anger.

"And why is that?" countered the other voice—one vaguely remi-niscent, like a fragment of an old dream. "I've proven myself time and again. You know what I think? I think my father should never have given you the company reins."

"I am sorry, Barron, but Nero needs someone with a bit more expe-rience. Someone with the assertiveness necessary to run a company of this size."

The figure approached as he stood there seething. "Do you want to know why I left Neuvia all those years ago?"

Allowing a moment to shrug off his anger, he opened his mouth and exhaled. "Yes, yes, we all know the story. You came upon the oneirocritic with some 'great dream.' A 'prophecy,'" he scoffed. "How about what the story fails to imply? Like growing fear of a Stare invasion. How about your telleum veins drying up?"

"You aren't entirely wrong, though our telleum reserves are just fine. Were, at least. My father, the king, spread all sorts of lies to lessen the target on our back. Do you want to know the real reason why me and some fifty sturdy men, your original ascendants, trudged through the desert all those years ago? I'll give you a hint, it had nothing to do with our telleum reserves."

"Go on."

"I was a young prince once. But not one to sit idle. I fought tooth and nail, for seven long years, staving off the Imiandrian threat. And if the stories you heard are true, we were successful in thwarting their plans for a foothold here on Pelegra. But war heroes die war heroes, Barron. And stale are war heroes, brave or not. But don't ask me, ask my fallen brothers whose dusty bones and ashes may still yet grace the sands of Old Neuvia." The landscape turned quiet once again, allowing the man to dwell on his prolonged vision—only briefly, however, until a great blinding light tore through the sky.

Awakened with a mug of tepid water by his chin, he was back in his muggy cell amid a familiar sound of rain.

"Drink this," said Marrin, "you fainted."

"You all right, Barron? You managed to scare the general away for a good while," chimed the lead engineer.

Barron lurched his mouth around the mug, gasping the water down like a broken dam. The pain was already diminishing. "This tastes like metal," he said, "is the best a fellow 'brother-in-arms' has to offer?"

"We used to call his sort tenters; dispensing their orders from afar," he scoffed. "You know the type, the Lord Geldrins and Vodgars of the world…In turn, their soldiers hardly knew 'em. Don't get me wrong, I was a bit thick in my early days, I said my fair share of unwise words. Ancient history now. Though I don't suppose he's forgotten any less. Why else do you think Selvin's not here—"

"Good! Alarie's awake," interrupted the general, peaking his face around the corner pryingly. "Now, where were we? Oh, that's right— your decision. What shall it be, Vander?"

The overseer huffed and shook his head. Otherwise, nothing. *Perhaps he finally caught on to the lingering aura of distaste*, Barron thought. Either way, it was his turn. "You're bluffing," Barron joined in clear, unfettered speech.

"Excuse me?"

"You're bluffing."

"Tell me, in what way am I bluffing?" redacted the general.

"You've inferred that the alchemists' secret hideout was sanctioned by the council. However, I don't seem to ever recall any special amendment to *Fin De Mine* in well over a century. If I remember correctly, *Voyage to Maldinax* was the last—our Loarea Tunnel."

His compatriots looked at him, positively and pleasantly struck. They relished as the general's smug self-satisfied mug warped into a crooked frown. "...Who said anything about an amendment?"

"Careful, general. Don't want to implicate yourself," added Marrin.

The general pulled his cape close and scoffed. "Fine, then. It matters not. Enjoy your bed bugs."

"*Fin De Mine?*" turned Marrin, gazing as the general stomped away, "where did you learn all this?"

"I read a book," he said, piquing both his and Devyn's curiosity.

"...Well?" pried Devyn, "which book was it?"

He scanned the now hushed silo, inhaling. "Bluffing a Bluffer."

The men burst, unable to contain their laughter; howling even louder after hearing the echo of a slammed door. Marrin had never looked so proud.

In the throne room, council members, guild representatives, and the warden had returned to the assembly table after a long break. "I'll be making a speech tomorrow," were the first words out of her mouth.

They looked at one another, particularly perplexed. Lord Vodgar was the first to respond. "My queen, forgive my bluntness here, but I think that would be a grave mistake," he said, puffing out his tiny frame. "Hundreds of disruptors are in custody as we speak. Maybe thousands; many of whom I will add are pertinent funders to our drying coffers."

"All will be present," interrupted Lord Vanic, "even the miscreants." His eyes fell upon the warden.

"Hm," replied the warden, "and what about the Alchemy Guild, my lady? Do blatant infractions to *Fin De Mine* not exempt them? How about that mysterious vat they've decided to empty just in time—"

"The Alchemy Guild is to pay handsomely a fine for their infringement," replied the queen, "this has been decided."

"And what of looters?" jumped in Lord Degas. "Whilst the rioters were out there being wrangled up today, the markets were ransacked by thieves. Now a speech? If I can't ensure the protection of my merchants' assets, then what good am I for?"

"While I can't ensure there won't be any looters, Lord Degas, I can assure you of this: security measures will be augmented tenfold."

The intelligencer appeared disturbed in thought, but his lips were open. "And what will be the topic of said speech?"

"I will be unveiling a gift. A second beginning. For all of us," she eyed the master alchemist. Before her advisors could gather their thoughts, she switched her attention to the warden who sat with his arms folded. "Friend and foe will be among us, make no mistake about it. For this, I will need your help. We must find the ones responsible for orchestrating this rabble, and this hoax," she alluded to the anonymous confession.

Out from a lull, he coughed. "*Me?* I thought I was your prisoner."

The woman forced a chuckle, causing the others to follow suit. "You are not my prisoner, Xander. You have been escorted here for a briefing."

"And still I haven't been told why."

"*Why?*" she quipped, her voice audibly strained. "If you must know at this very moment, I provided you specific instructions to remove trespassers from the alchemists' compound. Not to skulk and loiter around past due."

He unfolded his arms and tilted his breastplate onto the table. "And what else did the general tell you?" Her ascendants inched closer, anticipating a call for the man's removal.

For his sake, the queen was spent. She fiddled with her dress and resumed, "I sincerely apologize if I have broken your trust; however, if you avert our council meeting again, I will be forced to remove you from this table."

He eased back unhurriedly in his chair with a charmed grin.

At around midnight, following an eleventh-hour briefing session at the Probing Bureau, the man returned home to the Outer Circle, to a brick manor with a fence as tall as his front door. A homely manor for an unhomely man. Despite a late return home, his wife was more than happy to keep him company around a warm fire, as he spilled, in ambiguous detail, a timeline of his eventful day.

"You should have seen the look on her face, dear. It was worth all the trouble. Now she seems convinced that there's some grand conspiracy afoot to topple her regime. How rich is that? Coming from the woman whose crown should have never even touched her head. If only she stepped outside once in a while and saw what we all saw." He disappeared into his kitchen, returning with a stiff drink and a plate of cold sausages. "Loarea was something out of this world," he said, propping his rear closer to where the wood crackled with his drink pressed close to his lips. "I would have liked to see more of it before the erosion."

After downing his drink, he grew quiet as he stared at the flames. "I fear for our children," he slurred, "and their children too. The rocks, dear, they're beginning to crack." Following a full-body hiccup he grunted his way up to the mantel, where a dizzying swirl of bloodless air met him at a family portrait.

Staring back at him from within the confines of a fine-looking silver frame, was a less cynical version of himself, with a full head of hair; his dear Octavia, and his then two young girls, Anya and Fiona.

He sipped from his drink and, stretching his hand out onto the portrait, set it gingerly onto his wife's face. He let it linger for a brief, fading moment, before surrendering up to bed.

CHAPTER 16

WATERING THE GARDEN

With the storm clouds gone, the *glow* was finally right back to where it belonged atop the rocks.

Two hours out till noon and foot traffic was showing no signs of slowing atop Step Mountain, Loarea Tunnel, and even more astonishingly, the Lift. While mention of the Alchemy Guild's deceit in the now infamous "anonymous letter," and the ensuing riots, had drummed up all sorts of speculation, it was this surprise "gift" of the queen's mention that had brought Maldinians hither to her courtyard on this smiling day.

"Single file!" echoed a guardsman's voice from beyond the Nero leaders' cell.

Marrin was standing by their cell door, visibly ruffled by the influx of footsteps inside and out. "What's the meaning of this?" he asked a passing guard.

"It's your lucky day. Queen decided it best to give you non-violent offenders a second chance. You are to report to the courtyard for a declaration, however," he said, slipping a metal key into their door.

Barron could hear detainees chattering in the holding cells adjacent. Perhaps today was their day... "Not you lot!" clarified the guard, escorting Marrin, Devyn, and Barron into the sun where a few familiar faces were being lined up.

Nero men and the like, most were still garbed in their muddy work uniforms, extended from the prison yard to the Hub. Darren and Steven among them, who hadn't even gotten a chance to throw on their shoes yet (their poor feet singed).

There was a heavy presence felt beneath the railings of her rose garden, where her council members nervously loomed. She could feel it in the ground, all the way up the pathway of her throne room, despite very little sound seeping through the walls of her fort.

She stood alone by the vibrant glass pane of the east wall, where a nasty red glare obscured her face.

"Don't look so excited," she heard Lord Vanic say to her. He reached out his arm, almost invitingly.

Outside, the cathedral bells were ringing noon. The faintest glimpse of the crowds beneath her sent her recoiling back into the shadows of her garden. The courtyard was almost full. Too full for her liking. She watched the master alchemist step forward to the podium, drawing a smile as he pulled his ensigned trench coat close by his side. "Maldinians!" His voice bellowed out the bowl of the Nero instrument, bouncing off the shield wall below him like a snare.

"My thanks for your cooperation with the Lumina cleanup. I know these last few months haven't been easy, however, as a result of your patience, we have been able to rule out the mushroom from our list of Slumber culprits. This is good news." With his chin faced up, he continued, "For those of you who have lost your homes due to disrepair, or perhaps temporarily as a result of the outbreak, know this: salvation is upon us." As her queue neared, she started dancing in place, tucking her long legs between her favorite elaborately sewn purple and gold dress, which today had fit her like a glove.

"Now in order to cull your suspicions, my father has asked me to clarify. Yes, the Alchemy Guild has been utilizing the cool inner chasm of Loarea to conduct our latest tests on the Luminas. We broke the law, and we hear you loud and clear," he paused over a shrill gasp. "Due to the Guild's secrecy policy, I nor my guildmates have been able to share what I am about to show you. That is until now."

He reached his hand toward his front pocket, at which point she had come to realize the full weight of her advisors' scowls—much worse than the thorns pressed upon her back.

They watched him as he pulled a three-sided vial up over his head. "If someone could just block out this horrid glare for me, that would be helpful." He forced a laugh. Upon removing his trench coat, he placed it over the vial like a makeshift awning. "Behold!" he shouted. "The Lumina Elixir!"

"Crook!" they jeered, followed by a wave of unsavory words.

"Extracted from the same fungus which we once foolishly wrote off as dangerous!" he continued even louder. "The Lumina Elixir will not only preserve its consumers' natural aging process, but in higher doses, and with help from several other ingredients that I am not at liberty to disclose." He smirked. "Decelerate it!"

The crowd, now fully up in arms, shouted down his claim as blasphemy. He appeared flustered, but still pressed on. "We have tested this product in small doses on two brave citizens, whom I can't thank enough for their help. Without their bravery, it's possible we wouldn't have this delightful fruit to bear."

"Liar!"

"I understand your reservations, and as a student of science myself, I applaud your skepticism. However, I bring you *PROOF!*"

Out from the garden's shadow, she emerged.

"Now, it is my utmost privilege to introduce our very own Queen Satina Rook!" Her regent's mouth had nearly dropped to her breasts. For the first time in a long time, there was not a single drop of oily silt or root powder upon her face. A natural glow, burning of youth, had torn through its veil. "And long may she reign," he concluded snidely.

"Thank you for your introduction, Lord Vanic," she approached timidly. "I am sure many of you still have many questions for myself and the Guild—questions that I do intend to address in the days to come. But first, I would like to start by saying it has been my honor to serve you all as your queen. Truly, an honor. Even now, in the overgrown wake of the Deep Slumber, I act in your best interest. This decision was made not only for the prospect of a better Maldinia but for all my peoples, so that we may flourish as one." She began tearing up, almost tickled by her noble deed. "I hear your frustration! I do. But this is our great guardian angel, whose spores have safeguarded our nation from the effects of the Slumber." She bowed her head, tuning out the noise with a low hum.

The peacekeepers rerouted their resources toward the rowdier clusters, making their presence well known to any who dared.

"The Alchemy Guild has worked tirelessly to prepare samples of their newest product for the lot of you. And so, at this time, I ask any of you interested in a taste of immortality to politely file into your nearest line!"

Not surprisingly, the once relatively non-violent courtyard assembly had escalated into a stampede of shoving and shouting in a race to secure a spot in one of said four lines. But not all. A herd of disruptors came crashing into the shield wall, screaming for the queen and Lord Vanic's head. Rightfully distraught they were, providing the two with an alternative set of instructions. One which involves inserting their samples where the sun does not shine. They of course were only moments away from breaking down like the rest of them.

Her words pierced him like a blade. He extracted the mortal instrument from his mind, but the hurt lingered. All the lies, a mere afterthought in the presence of a brighter bauble.

"Going to lock up the factory, at least until tensions simmer down," turned Marrin to anyone listening.

With such a small chance of finding Myleyn in the frenzy, it seemed a better time than any to get a head start on his newfound break. He did not intend on spending the rare opportunity baking underneath the hot sun. His first venture as a free man saw him sauntering far from the depravity. But not alone. His path was being followed by a pair of men in dark leather coifs. He spotted them in an alleyway on his walk home, around the northeast bend of the Outer Circle.

A fast walker, he forced the two to pick up their pace at the mercy of their discretion.

He was now very much aware of the only footsteps outside his own on the quiet road. He would have to run. *But where?* Within the inner barricade, the Market District-Residential District Connector was in view. There an armed and ready unit of peacekeepers stood guard.

Rather than drive through the checkpoint, he continued around the bend, southward past Myleyn's house, erratically consoling himself. *They must know of my involvement—but how?* He started fidgeting with the skin beneath his nails until he couldn't take it any longer and turned. "Who are you? What do you want?"

They said nothing as they approached him, studying his behavior. *Probers.* "Where were you headed off to in such a hurry?" one of them inquired.

"What is the problem, investigators?"

"A *red* emblem, huh?" inspected one of the probers. "I never seen one like this before. You were with the other inmates, weren't you? Why didn't you get in line with the rest of them?"

Am I required to drink that carbonated con water? I have a date

"Am I required to drink that carbonated con water? I have a date with a book and one frothy glass of wine."

"Very well." And with that they let him go.

He patrolled about his yard that afternoon, pondering the probers' true intentions, his father's old crossbow looped around his neck. That was until he heard voices on the other end of his gate, at which point he had dropped to his stomach and prepared his aim. "Who goes there?!"

"There he is!" answered a voice.

"So much for an hour in peace," he sighed, shouldering his crossbow. "What do you want, Remus?"

"Hello to you too!" shouted a female from behind the shrub wall (more than likely Esca's, her voice soft like honey).

"We have a gift for you, grumpy!" chimed Myleyn, "now that you are a free man after all."

"Please tell me it isn't one of those elixirs," he replied, freeing the latch. "It's poison. It's what you people deserve." Remus, Steven, Savannah, Darren, Esca, Andrea, and Myleyn entered unshyly. "Even better," approached Myleyn, planting a wet kiss on his cheek.

In the far reaches of his backyard, the eight of them continued conversing in his summerhouse. "…I'm curious, how many of you caved?"

"What, you mean you didn't get one too?" teased Steven.

"I feel ten years younger," chimed Esca.

"You look great. I mean, well, for a twelve-year-old—where did Duncan go, anyway?" Remus deterred, "he disappeared on us earlier."

"He and his family had to go, I guess. I never even got to say hi to them," frowned Andrea.

"Odd. I didn't see them either," commented her sister.

Visibly tried, the man wandered off toward his front gate, checking every nook and cranny on his way.

"What are you still doing looking for Luminas?" trailed Myleyn with a laugh. "They're legal to harbor now, you know that."

"Legal," he said dismissively, "just wait until the Guild runs out of them. What then?" He poked his head out his front gate, where he scanned about the ridge for probers. "If you must know, I was questioned by the Probing Bureau on my way home from the assembly today. I think they know somehow of my involvement in the anonymous letter. Why else would they stop me at random?"

"How could they know?"

"I don't know, I just know Steven has a big mouth." He heaved a sigh. "I am overdue for a victory."

"A victory? Don't be so hard on yourself, Barron. We did the right thing by exposing the alchemists' illegal operation. That assembly likely would never have happened because of you. I'd call that a victory."

"And what do we have to show for it? The Guild got off scot-free. Still have a dolt for a queen, and oaf for an overseer; crippling taxes, mounting emigration. Nothing will come of this. The people have their bribe, they can go on about their day like any other. Maybe even get a good night's rest."

In Loarea District, the warden and his trusty band of probers were hot on the trail of an individual who, according to their latest intel, "left casually the assembly with a few 'suspicious-looking bags.'"

"*This* is the highlight of my career," facetiously the warden said aloud to his men, returning to the window of their borrowed cabin.

They made their descent into Loarea Tunnel with some safe space between them and the suspects' vehicle; a lordly piece of craftsmanship with two embossed plums stamped upon each door. Bad timing it proved. A horseless carriage whirled right past, bringing tears to the warden's eyes.

"Nimble things these crankers are downhill," whispered their designated driver, Reginald, from the roost. (They did however eventually pass the carriage once the slope lightened and the sun disappeared.)

On Layer 11, they found their mark, parked in the shadow of the downward slope.

"Looks like an exchange," whispered Anvel. "One of them just offloaded a chest into the other's cabin."

"…They're leaving."

The warden perked up in his seat. "Go back up a level, Reginald."

Anvel gave the warden a look as if he had two heads. "They'll get away, Warden."

"No, they won't," reassured Victor ominously.

"*Plopper*," whispered the other probers.

The warden nodded. "We were never going to catch him with these old mares."

Upon the pedestrian path of Layer 10, in the light's forgotten shadow, the men approached a narrow crevice marked with an illustrious Nero *N*. Wrought as unsubtly as Malyptah's famous watermark, the nook was home to a whirlpool-shaped fixture with a hole at its base the size of a grown man's head.

"Start brainstorming a cover story," said the warden as the rest of them watched the greenhorns, Lamb and Rowan, instinctually approach the long-dormant emergency communication device.

Through guano and web, the young probers pushed their arms inside a slot, where together they began to dislodge a heavy rounded stone into the light of their torches. Once the object reached the top of the bowl, the warden gave them the signal. That's when the two of them gave the stone a good shove.

A pounding *knock* answered, followed by a grinding swirl, as the object began one wide swim around the bowl.

Eventually, a hollow thump and a whistling echo were all that was left of the poor rock when it finally stopped circling the bowl; plummeting the lonely road toward a gong, two hundred levels beneath their feet.

"Not as loud as I remember it," sniffled Lamb, leaning his back casually against the Nero invention of old.

As the men made for their ride, a piercingly loud pang came rushing up the bitter shaft, causing the young man a good jump.

Once they arrived at the surface, the warden wasted no time filling the bewildered tunnel guards in on the situation. "A jewel thief was on the run," was the explanation he gave them.

The gate was down, and a fair number of other carriages were halted in the darkness. He was no fool, he knew the Plumskit family's carriage by memory. He had them right where he wanted them: distracted. The real search had just begun.

"For those of you just arriving, I'm looking for a jewel thief who slipped into the tunnel. A young blond-haired rascal, about yay big." The man gestured. "I am hoping one of you can help me find him."

A whinny interrupted the man mid-thought, sending Victor and Anvel to join the guardsmen to investigate.

"This particular thief took it upon himself to rob a jeweler whilst the owner and everyone else in the city for that matter were conveniently preoccupied in the courtyard." The warden paused, allowing citizens to lend their insights. "No?" he continued, received by a resounding shrug. "Pity. Search their cabins!"

"I've had enough of this, I am leaving," stirred a portly nobleman in an unflatteringly tight yellow ruff. "Do we look like thieves to you?"

The guardsmen rerouted the man back in line, causing the warden a good laugh. "You're not going anywhere," he said. "Lord Frostberry, is it? You almost ran over my soldiers' feet. Search his cabin first."

The nobleman scowled. Just then Anvel escorted an arriving vehicle's stowaway into the mix. The skittish young man with curly, blond hair shuttered as he joined the irritable line of noblemen. (He, of course, was Lamb, disarmed, in his everyday clothing).

"Are you hard of hearing or what?" barked the warden.

The laggard opened the side of his mouth, shrugging.

After emptying the man's pockets and shoes, they discovered a convenient pouch tucked away in his pants pocket. "Well, what have we here? Here be our elusive jewel thief!" announced the man, clasping the overstuffed pouch of pebbles firmly between his fingers. All eyes looked upon him as another carriage came galloping down the dim bend.

"Very good. Raise the gate!" At once, an explosion of light came bursting through the repurposed mineshaft. The warden watched the crowd of antsy noblemen leave, then, returning to his carriage, his men filled him in on their findings. Quite astoundingly, Lamb's act of theater had worked, allowing the others ample time to confirm which cabin it was that ended up with the chest.

Reginald slid open the front panel, capturing Xander's attention. "Where to next, Warden?"

The warden paused, taking in a strong whiff of something pungent in the air. "You smell that, Reginald?"

The man flared his nares. "Smells a bit like berries."

He relaxed into his seat. "Follow that smell."

CHAPTER 17

TROUBLE ON THE RIVER

Nearly three hours had passed since the last Lumina Elixir sample had been dispensed, and the fresh-faced queen was still on edge. Her paranoia only seemed to worsen after receiving word of trouble on the river.

"I bring word from the Tree Sprites," she overheard a young courier say to her guards at the door of her keep.

Spotting the familiar face, Lady Knish signaled him over.

The errand boy's eyes widened as he familiarized himself up close and personal with the youthful face of a woman he once comfortably recognized. But no longer. "Speak freely, Sid," Lady Knish smiled at the young man.

He adjusted his bonnet and swallowed. "Sapson of the forest vanguard sends word. The northerners are raiding the North Valley," he said, received by mixed gasps. "Imian ships have been spotted off the coast of Taranchia too."

"I should think this timing a bit peculiar, wouldn't you think?" remarked Lord Flumen.

The queen sank into her red chair with a barren frown. She then tilted her neck onto the messenger with her eyes crossed. "What do you think we should do about it?"

The boy started groveling, triggering Lady Knish to spare him from the senseless torture. "It would be wise if we sent reinforcements, my queen."

Lord Vodgar groaned, releasing a winded tangent on his distaste in expending yet another resource they did not have on the realm's defenses—a reluctant vote of favor nevertheless for Lady Knish's cause.

"The Taranchians are becoming more brazen by the day," added the emissary. "We should wipe them out once and for all."

"They don't act alone," chimed Lord Flumen.

Lord Vanic looked at her, nodding.

Unwilling to empty her canyon garrisons with the Gromula Day heist still fresh on her mind, the master alchemist proposed an alternative approach: simultaneously distracting her from the manic stupor that she had found herself in with yet another reminder of the Imian embargo still active, whilst presenting an alternative solution to cull the present intrusion.

"Lobbers!" screamed a lookout from the roost of a watchtower on the northern river, as if a great tidal wave was nearing. "Flee!" he added, climbing like mad out of his shoulder-high roost, and again, over a guardrail, leaping crudely into a clump of horse feed.

For a moment, an object came blocking out the sun.

This, however, was no eclipse. It was a war barrel, infused by gifted deviants, hurled like a feathery horseshoe out from an old hand-cranked Taranchian barrel lobber.

The scout rolled beyond the pile of hay and watched vulnerably as a barrel came crashing into his stilted outpost. The impact was as loud as one might dread for an otherwise quiet afternoon, startling the panting scout speechless; but not nearly the worst of it. He watched the brave ones struggle their way from a now evaporating structure, a sad purple sopping banner going down with it. And quite like the little metal rings now bursting off his compatriots' hauberks, their flesh gave in a bedlam of curdling screams.

Many an acre west of his fallen outpost, between dueling corn farms, the scout emerged to share this gruesome tale, pinpointing the warden's inimitable black armor, and a band of probers, cross-examining a great blue carriage's sole passenger. As the probers pried him ignorantly of the situation at the river—to whose tale had been relayed to the ranking prober, and so on, to the warden—Xander nonetheless resumed his cornstalk interrogation of the suspect vintner, for his failure in the tunnel to comply with his authority.

"…I am late as it is for a meeting," sighed Lord Frostberry.

"Fair enough, you're a busy man, I get it." The warden nodded, wandering off to the frightened scout for a chat. "Do you know whose carriage that belongs to?"

The young striper shook his head.

He caressed the few hairs on his head in a disarming manner. "A forgivable offense, I suppose, when factoring in the haste in which you fled from your post. Yes, I guess that would be enough to make any man lose his wits." The soldier gave him a regretful look as he came upon his ear. "Tell anyone about this stop and I will have you tried as a deserter."

Once gone, he and his party joined Lord Frostberry in his glitzy cabin, where the warden poked around nonchalantly through the many fragile contents in his interior cabinets. "So, what sort of fool would sell wine during a raid?" he dangled a gold chalice upside down, "better yet, what sort of fool would sell wine to these same raiders during a raid?

That's where you were going weren't you, to Taranchia? Of course you were, why else would anyone drive so far north."

"I am not going to entertain this. Shouldn't you be more worried about chasing the crop-snatchers away?"

"Oh, no—you didn't hear? The queen's got a special job for me today," he said, drawing pleased grins from his crew. "Fergus, why do you sweat so profusely?"

Victor eyed an ornate chest across the aisle, which their host nervously guarded beneath his slippers. It was the same bulky chest from the tunnel: clinking around like ceramics whenever one of his subordinates moved around in their seat in the slightest.

"Seeing as you haven't answered a single question truthfully, I believe you owe us a ride-along."

The nobleman averted his attention to the window, then, following a genuine laugh, returned his attention to the warden. "Indulge me, Warden. In what way am I not being truthful?"

"A chest full of wine sings not like this," he said, forcefully rocking the cabin. "Not so clever, are we?"

"Warden, you must understand the clientele I am dealing with here. They are not ones to be left waiting."

He nodded, throwing a hand onto the bloated seam of his leg. "Then how about you help us understand."

"I go to my grave, then."

"Don't be so dramatic, Fergus. Besides, none *such* grave exists."

Unwelcome to his sarcasm, the vintner scowled.

"Well, what are we waiting for?"

"This isn't a macro wagon. My driver will be showing you gentlemen out now. *Felix!*"

Amused, the warden shut his door and scooched his rear right next to him. "He can't hear you. Now the way I see it, you have two options.

You either take us with you on your little exchange to Taranchia, and I will try to overlook your insolence back in the tunnel, *or* we can return this nice little carriage of yours to the capital where you will be acquainted with a cell. Oh yes, I'm quite certain the queen will be tickled to hear all about the samples you and your friendly helper, Duncan, have amassed during the assembly today."

"Is that what this is about?" he chaffed. "Unless I missed something, it's not illegal to buy up others' free samples."

"No, it's not. But conspiring to cross the border during a battle most certainly would."

It seemed to the warden just then, as the other prepared a redaction, he had also swallowed a bug whole. "Fine, you win," the nobleman said tetchily, "you can come along; however, you must all promise me to be invisible once we cross."

"Not a word from me," he said, raising a finger to his lips.

"Felix!" shouted the nobleman, "double up!"

Living up to the warden's presumption, his authority was anything but necessary when Lord Frostberry and his unwelcome guests had reached the only conduit between Maldinia and Taranchia; the Pebblewood River Crossing (an otherwise last-ditch effort at a courtesy between King Pontis of Maldinia and the last vestiges of the Trawl family during the final days of the Taranchian Civil War). It was all too clear to him that this was not Lord Frostberry's first time across. He certainly underestimated the breadth of the man's influence, but not so much his reach of pocket.

Despite troubling circumstances downriver, there seemed very little worry about on the opposing end of the Pebblewood River. There were locals in the river, unencumbered by the burden of their rags, casting their nets into the current, filling their clay pots, and checking their traps. Just beyond—of course, not nearly as far as the footsteps of

Raknia Hill on the cliffs afar, but amidst the lifeless craters of the Central Plain—a thin haze of caustic residue endured. A self-inflicted plight upon the puddle-shaped kingdom of Taranchia, which several generations later would avoid.

As ruined as it was, the civil war-scorched nation came slowly alive with noises at night, the locals rising from their slapdash river huts and dens to savor the last few hours of daylight. There were bugs too, lots and lots of bugs. Enough to rouse Lord Frostberry's steeds to the startling speeds of an angry apex screecher.

Further east the sounds of battle were especially apparent as they encroached upon the realm of the river's end. Profound, to say the least, outside Bastion, the once prosperous cliff-side harbor of the Trawl family, now a shanty town swallowed in the tall grass. Although their family's presence was all but lost, some of their stalwart creations remained. Most notably the great stone fortress of Trawl Tower, with a view unrivaled on the edge of the world.

Its war-torn inhabitants appeared to have made several iterations of repairs to its battered integrity, as best as they could with whatever they could.

Lord Frostberry fiddled nervously with his ruff as they exited onto a hill on the outskirts of town. He cast his eyes over the western gate, finding top-heavy huts of recycled blocks of rubble and wood, thatched with many a hole, complete with window panes of crudely fastened shards of shattered glass.

He began pacing as Felix set the chest down beside his slippers, calming his breath some as he set his sights out yonder, to the East Sea, where the sun dipped below a veneer of red flecked clouds, layered in slits like rings on a volatile planet.

"Not a word of our presence," whispered the warden from the downslope of that same hill, where he and his men were concealed in the tall grass. Not thirty yards south of them, the crickets hushed as a wheeled wagon brought forth another round of war barrels to the river dike.

Meanwhile, in town, whispers spread as a muscular individual, veiled save for his eyes in sand-colored cloth, emerged from the cliff. A few more locals appeared, sliding down rusty rods protruding from their rooftop perches, walking ahead of the veiled figure beyond the limits of the last flimsy wooden gate in town.

"Should have stayed home," scolded a fair-skinned Taranchian man aloud, with a face as wart-ridden as his brothers to his side.

"Yeah, well, what's with this mischief on the Pebblewood?" redacted the man.

The Taranchians began meandering around his carriage suspiciously.

"Hours late!" shouted the voice of the veiled figure approaching, a male, a devious accent superseding the contents of his inhospitable tone. "I hope you have a good reason for this, Maldinian."

The nobleman forced himself still, dabbing his forehead with a sweat rag. They began to form a half-circle around himself and his driver.

"Let's just hope you have brought more mushrooms than your last visit."

"I brought you something even better today."

Athwart the river Pebblewood the probers gazed as a barrel came crashing down upon a friendly watchtower, followed swiftly by a few blood-curdling screams as its foundation began disintegrating. They repressed their anger; biding; eventually relishing as the deadly arbalists answered with a volley of bolts upon the Taranchians' ill-fortified dyke.

"What are you waiting for?" pressed the veiled man, watching Lord Frostberry nervously fumble a key into his chest.

The veiled man shielded his mud-colored eyes as the nobleman squeaked open the chest. For a great beacon of neon light came shining out. (Never before did the locals' teeth look so white.)

The veiled man leaned in. "What do we have here?"

Lord Frostberry busied his trembling hands with an unplanned demo. "I have brought forth your favorite stalk. Not only in solid form but in liquid form too," he began shaking an elixir enticingly. "This, my friend, is the Alchemy Guild's newest product, the Lumina Elixir."

"Why have I not been informed of this?" He advanced threateningly.

Lord Frostberry jerked his lips into a smile. "That is why I have come."

"No, it isn't," he pressed upon him, stirring his gloved fingers through a grimy gold sack. "This is why you have come. Tell us, wine man, how was it you were able to cross the river with a raid afoot?"

Lord Frostberry opened his mouth to answer, though in remembering his unintended tagalongs in the tall grass, he would refrain. "...Felix here told the guards that we were on a peace mission."

"*Peace*?" cackled the man. "The same courtesy your people offered to the Pyrithians after sucking up their precious Sol...*Peace*!" He cackled again. "Spoken like a true Maldinian!" He composed himself, staring suspiciously at one of the samples. "How do I know we aren't getting cheated? Can probably piss more on an empty stomach."

"These are concentrated," said Lord Frostberry, "this will save you the trouble of extracting the nectar for yourself. So," he continued, eyeing his prize.

He lowered his mask some, revealing the face of a sun-kissed man in his middle years. "You were late." He shoved his fist into his pouch, offering the nobleman the residuals—a life-changing sum of gold by most accounts. "There won't be a next time if you are late..." Fissures interrupted the man mid-threat, shaking birds and insects from the brush. The warden and his men most certainly felt it; of course, were far too distracted by the grunting struggle of yet another war barrel being loaded to give it much thought.

Finding their way back to the crossing proved far more difficult than he imagined. There was a strange pollen obscuring their path, causing Felix to miss the bridge by a good two miles. A good opportunity if any to pry. "So, who was he? I know he wasn't Taranchian."

"I don't know his name," he said to the warden, "he's kept his identity secret."

"That man was Imian."

Victor chuckled. "All Imians sound the same."

Lord Frostberry attempted to scooch his rear to the corner of his bench. He was blocked unsuccessfully by Reginald.

"Your product is in every wine cellar in Maldinia. Including my own, admittedly. If you're so strapped for money your obtuseness knows no bounds." A lull washed over the cabin. "Felix!" shouted the warden, "drop us off at our carriage, we have work to do on the river. As for these fine gentlemen—Reginald, do please take our hosts on a stroll to the Armory District. I am sure we can find you two a nice pile of hay to lay your head upon tonight."

Lord Frostberry's face went pale, the bridge hovering in view. "Prison? We had a deal!"

"Just wait until the Alchemy Guild hears about this," scoffed the warden. "Losing the Guild money will most certainly not sit well with them."

Lord Frostberry took his handkerchief and scooped the skin beyond his neck curtain.

"It's getting cold in here," arose the warden, reaching over to shut the man's window.

"...Fine...what do you want to know?"

The man stared out his window. "Oh look, the bridge is nearing," he inhaled, "would you look at that."

"Okay, fine, *look*, I made a deal with someone in Varakai," spoke the man, reluctantly pocketing his rag. "The wine business is rather lucrative—it wasn't always this way. Alas with all these travel bans and embargos, my profits aren't model. And in the company of whose taste for the good life knows no bounds, I might add."

"Go on."

"Right, well, in exchange for an absurd amount of gold, these men wanted to know the whereabouts of our bloodstone veins. I'm well-read enough to know there isn't anything left in that rock; of course, they don't know that. At least, nothing that they accept as factual—'Maldinian lies,' I quote them. All the same, I gave them the coordinates of the last (rumored) unmined avenues left in that rock. Fifty years and some later, the same old foolish policies are still in place. So, what do I do? I go to the neutral zone to resume trade. Sure enough, Slumber hit that place harder than anywhere—it's a ghost town now—"

"Let's back up a little, shall we?" intruded the warden, "so you just provide foreigners classified information on a whim? That's an odd habit. Where did you even obtain such obscure knowledge of our mines? Did you call in a favor to Lord Aeseres? Or was it your father-in-law you coerced this information out of? Oh yes, I am well aware of your newest little wife, Mitzy, of formerly Encore."

"Don't talk about my wife," snapped the man.

"That would explain the Gromula Day escapade...Fergus, you've been selling information to foreigners; Imians. The writing is on the wall. Unless you are prepared to spend the rest of eternity behind a cell, I suggest you start spilling everything and anything you have, and fast. I have a border to secure after all."

"It was a long time ago, I don't know," he continued, "I guess I remember hearing one of them mentioning something about bartering Stare women for breeding? Not enough Imian women to go around on the island, I guess. Mind you this was before the Slumber, before Starik's populace withered. Unlucky fools. As for the Gromula Day business, that was not my doing. You said it yourself in the tunnel, I was at the Gromula Ball that night."

"Continue."

"Back to my most recent visit, these old men scooped me up, and in broad daylight too. They blindfolded me, and accused me of murdering their 'treasure hunters.' I hadn't a clue what they were on about, but I pleaded for my life all the same. They were willing to overlook their foiled treasure hunt, contingent on a steady supply of the glowing mushrooms. And before you say it, no, I did not disclose the existence of the Luminas. Not that it matters now, everyone knows about the famous 'glowing mushrooms of Maldinia' now. Anyway, I knew what the alternative would entail, so I complied. I have a family after all."

"And let me guess, that's when you approached the alchemists, right? Of course…who else would have such a bountiful supply of those things."

The man heaved a sigh.

As a single tear fell from his eyes, it was almost hard for him not to pity the man. An imperfect opportunist, he was indeed, but so also Human. Flawed in the worst kind of way, but not irredeemable.

With still many a question outstanding, he and his driver were soundly escorted back to his North Valley chateau where, from this day until the very last, his every move shall be monitored by the Bureau. (An information spring, the warden believed, would prove far more useful a role than an enemy.)

"Warden, you might want to see this!" shouted Reginald later from the reins.

Not five miles out from the river, over the fence of a daunting stainberry vineyard, the warden jumped to his window, gazing at an anomaly within the last few muddy specks in the red-blotched sky.

"Those are Sprites up there," remarked Lamb.

"That's old man Stainberry's estate," joined Victor. "What are they doing down here?"

"Making me look bad," quipped the warden, "hurry now, Reginald! We'll cut off the heathens before they reach the Pebblewoods."

Following an unheeded warning shot, they watched the vanguard spearhead, Sapson, toss his karnip spear with tact through a raider's shoulder, rousing the rest of the locusts into the fold.

Spears no sooner fell from the sky, with the Sea Sprites joining, and their sea glass bombs: foxing the heathens like mad from old man Stainberry's finest product-to-be.

By the time the warden and his men swooped in, the latter half of the vintner's estate had been left in a gruesome aftermath of bitter juices.

CHAPTER 18

A TENACIOUS SPROUT

"Three fallen watch towers and thirteen good soldiers dead. We're at the precipice of war, Xander," vented the queen, milking her chalice of wine with several shades of worry. "We need proof, not some vague conspiracies."

The warden bit his tongue, pacing about the throne room floor. All the while, inviting unwelcome stares from her throne room guards. "The Sprites have twenty cold bodies as proof. Would you like me to bring you chunks of the avarices' flesh? Or would you prefer to wait for an endorsement from King Marinus himself?"

An uncharacteristic anger rolled over her eyes, causing a vein to emerge beneath the peak of her crown. "Bite your tongue," she said.

A heavy set of footsteps came upon the warden's blind side, ones he didn't so much as blink in the presence of.

"It's nothing," diffused the woman, returning her chalice to her lips. "Look, I am aware of the Taranchians' debauchery. Lady Stainberry made extra sure to send me a detailed list of all their damaged goods. And that's just one of them." She sighed. "I am also aware of the Imian sails," she continued, averting her gaze to her chandelier. "It's obvious the Taranchians didn't act alone; however, before we go and invade Imia, we have better find ourselves a refutable catalyst. Better yet, a purpose."

"And ships," chimed the warden under his breath.

"Imia is an old wart that must be dealt with, though if it isn't clear, we aren't exactly popular on the grand stage. War invites attention, and never the good kind either—"

"Who said anything about war?"

"What then? Peace?" She sank her head between her legs, before curtailing her feet to the unmarked room beside her throne.

"Shall we?" she said, opening her hand.

Inside he searched about her comely abode, gravitating with the woman to her credenza where she helped herself to a healthy mouthful of lazabloom.

"What were we talking about again?" She yawned, removing her shoes.

"The Imians," he said.

She stumbled her way off her carpet, one shoe off, the other still on, revealing her shapely form just beyond her purple-hemmed dress. "Right." She settled on the edge of her bed where she collapsed in a slow, dramatic fashion. As the blood rushed to her head, she gave her shoe one last tug, and turned, as if invitingly. (Whether or not his original intention, he took the hint.)

With improper airflow behind a closed window and door, the two lay in each other's sweat, unembellished, contemplative for some time. "As much as it pains me to say this, I think we ought to consider lifting the embargo on Imia. The Imians want what we have, and they will do anything to get it. It is for this same reason I don't put a chain on my bird. He may appear to tolerate it, temporarily, but he doesn't forget."

Particle-actuating shapes of refracted light entered through her desk-side window, her head now drifting to the far corner, where light seldom traveled, to her daughter's old doll, resting atop the chest beneath her chair. "Not you too," she resigned.

"Let's say we do lift the embargo on Imia. Then what? We allow the same aggressors who orchestrated this raid to buy up as many wines, pies, horses, and elixirs as they like?"

He bit his tongue, sifting through his words carefully. "They can buy anything. But not before a little shakeup." She perked her back off her headrest and turned at attention. "The guilds have benefited from tax reprieve for far, far too long. And yet unlike the monks of our cathedral, for example, the guilds are a business, operating as a business would. I mean this with no offense but why else would they maintain operations here in today's economic climate? They are as good as a weed in an empty garden."

She clenched her jaw, jerking it from side to side. "Let's say I do comply with your terms, how are you so sure that the guilds won't just get up and leave once the dust settles?"

"I can't say for the whole lot of them, though based on Bryce's behavior during our last gathering, I'd say his mind is already made. As for the Alchemy Guild, I know for a fact that the only thing more valuable than the Guild's newest product is the land beneath us," he continued, "I'd surmise based upon the foot traffic in the markets today alone that it's only a matter of time before their supply runs dry."

She drew a breath and chuckled. "How productive. Was there anything else on your mind today, Xander?"

He rustled the dark patch of hairs on his chin. "Trifles." He of course did have a welcoming share of thoughts on his mind, yet was prudent enough to know that introducing new foods was a whole lot easier in minute servings.

At dusk, the young architect was flanked by a toil of lucid dreams.

In the first, he was transported to the innards of Tethia, to a colorful web of mycelial threads, where vivid streams of light wrapped around him in a blanket of hungry tendrils.

He emerged in a dank pool of water where a womp-beast's massive lips entered for a sloppy drink. He blinked, awakening inside the Nero Company Factory, where company men lay frozen in a haze of Lumina spores. He blinked again, finding himself behind the closed door of his office.

He twisted the doorknob to exit, only to be halted in place by an invisible entity—like a wall without a frame.

From the hallway, the overseer and lead builder stared inside, but his presence, however fast he waved his arms, was not recognized. Rather than sulk about it, he dwelled upon his prison dream, returning to his desk where he had begun to draft a new design: starting with a menacing trapezoid, oddly reminiscent.

Atop the fifth week of summer, his vigor pressed on anew. Perhaps it was the few sips of the Lumina Elixir Myleyn coerced him to try; or maybe the vision from his outlandish dream. Whatever the case may be, he felt invigorated like never before. Fresh blood and even fresher ideas surged through his veins.

Immediately upon entering his office that day, Marrin paid him a visit. The Alchemy Guild was in the market for a new base of operations—one with a requirement list as long as law.

Barron scratched his head. "*Really?* After breaking into their lab too?"

Marrin chuckled. "Guess they're short on alternatives."

Although aiding the guilds in any manner was a complete betrayal of his values, as fate would have it, he desperately needed a design and build project to sink his teeth into. He glossed over a few of the alchemists' requirements inattentively, meanwhile pondering a design. "I'll see what I can do."

Snatching some ink, a quill, and a straight measuring apparatus, an object no sooner leaked onto his page; a prodigious triad of mass, with thick, clean lines and high-reaching towers. Inspired by Maldinia's very own ensign, and perfected. He with veins throbbing erratically out the side of his head was but a conduit; unto his parchment, a vessel.

Later that same week he heard a slow patter upon his window.

Unlike his tiring quill, the fuzzy plain of Loarea welcomed the emergence of moisture with arms wide. Though like most summer rain bouts, it was incredibly short-lived—kind of like his focus was now, after hearing a knock at his door. Expecting additional requirements, he was slightly relieved to find not the overseer, but Remus, Steven, Darren, and Daemon. An adequate push, if anything, to find himself some lunch.

"What's that about?" averted Barron, crossing a mob of academy instructors and art peddlers on the main road.

The second builder taunted the art and historians as they passed by.

"You didn't hear? There's to be a demonstration today," chimed Remus. "The guilds are all up in arms about their new tax on goods."

"Why don't you join them, Remus? You haven't lived the full Maldinian experience until you have spent a full night in jail," joked Barron.

"At least someone didn't steal your boots," sighed Steven.

"They had holes in them, Steven. They were doing you a favor."

Back at the factory, inside his locked desk, he retrieved his schematic and picked up where he left off, a single vulture kebab heavier.

His first draft was now complete, and he was on to the next, topping off his triad of plateau-shaped towers with some elusive perches up high. And based upon the position of the sun's glow on his desk, it was nigh time to present.

"Have a seat at the war table, Barron. I'll be right over," said Marrin from behind dueling stacks of envelopes.

Distracted by the dizzying display of disarray, he redirected his attention to the overseer's walls, the longtime home of his banal "artwork." There were some accolades and other medals of his disseminated within the mix; though none so prominent as his old suit of armor, a massive piece of steelwork with a deadly gouge lodged into its left pauldron.

The overseer grunted up out of his chair with an endearing smile. "My apologies, Barron. Let's see what you got for me so far."

His saliva was already severely lacking as he prepared to slide over his latest schematic and speak. "It's a draft," he found himself repeating several times over again, before finally letting go.

"Hm," muttered the overseer, stroking his beard. "…Did you review the requirements list, Barron?"

"Of course. Why do you ask?"

The man pointed to the base of the center tower and squinted. "The alchemists are looking to triple their laboratory space. Just want to make sure we have enough room in here."

"This *is* spacious. Plenty spacious. Here," he said, pulling the schematic closer and tapping. "Have a look. Just over forty feet wide."

Marrin bobbed his head. "Why three heads? Did you bring the requirements list with you by any chance?"

Barron's lips had begun to curl as he pulled it out—even more so when the overseer listed some of the items off aloud. Humiliating. He resigned to the back of his chair with his arms folded, confident he had satisfied every single one of the guild's demands, yet he was still discouraged by the overseer's flaccid response.

"Sixty feet high? I'm not sure if we need something this excessive. The going rate of stone is quite steep right now. If the guild decides to get up and leave, we will have a lot of unused stones sitting on our books. We might be better off with something more matter-of-fact. Does that make sense?"

"Something cheap, right?"

"No," the overseer countered. "My advice would be to scale it back, though. We only need the essentials."

Barron sat there, rightfully fuming. It was a masterful piece of art; but this was Marrin's Nero, where dreams went to die. If his quivering scowl didn't express it, his cold departure surely did.

As he sat and stewed at his desk over the overseer's words, he pulled out a fresh sheet of parchment and started anew. And yet, even after a moon's passing, he had made little progress. He was appalled at himself for even trying.

Unable to stomach the sight of his painfully lacking revision-in-progress, he sent a knock on the lead engineer's door.

At least judging by the purple bags beneath his eyes, Lord DuSprite looked to have spent his day inside a dungeon. He fumbled forward to greet him, moving a rod with glass on its end to the floor.

Quite like Marrin's office, neither looked to be expecting women anytime soon.

"What *was* that thing?" curiously he inquired.

"New project. I call it a looking glass." He feigned interest as Devyn elaborated on his newest invention.

"Devyn, I did have a question for you. Unrelated to engineering…"

"Of course," he said with even flightier eye contact than Barron's.

Attempting to formulate his question in as few words as possible, he took a deep breath and smiled. "Do you ever give thought to the future of this company?"

"…Sometimes." He squinted. "Why do you ask?"

"Just curious."

Silence took precedence, forcing Devyn to fidget with another gizmo hidden in his lap.

"I am a bit concerned for our longevity, is all. I think the company lacks vision, Devyn. I fear in Marrin's absence our trajectory will regrettably remain much the same."

"How do you mean? Selvin?" he danced in thought, "maybe… though with this Lumina Elixir floating around now, I doubt leadership will change a whole lot anywhere."

The other sat there paralyzed in thought, raking his thumb aggressively against the prickers on his chin.

"*Barron?*"

Sweat dripped from his forehead, causing his hair to relax into bangs. "Hm? I should be going." Outside, he leaped off the front steps and sulked in the grass.

"He's never going to retire," he muttered in disbelief. "Never." As he stood there simmering on the lead engineer's words, he had found a surprising jolt of motivation; the cathartic sort one might find after shaking hands with their maker.

As he returned inside to retrieve his work, he even found himself smiling, wryly. "…I'm going to pay the alchemists a little visit, Marrin. Want to get some clarification on a few of their requirements."

"Very good," nodded the overseer.

To the upside-down thumb of the alchemists' headquarters, he sent a knock.

Following a lull, a blustery creak emitted from the hinges as a man in a leather vest, with the alchemists' ensign sewn upon his left breast pocket, peeked his head out for a look. "Yes?" asked the guild member.

"I am hoping to speak with Lord Vanic. I am Barron Alarie, the architect from Nero."

The man poked his head out some more, staring about suspiciously. "Just you?"

He nodded.

Several minutes passed without any word. Another five, maybe ten from there. As he remained there waiting beneath the Guild's holey portico, he considered how they'd react to his admission of his anonymous letter. *Perhaps then they'd find a little more pep in their step*, he thought.

Eventually, the man returned to greet him, introducing himself by name, before leading him inside. His name was Wendell, and he was the alchemists' official logistician (and official door greeter too apparently).

"Right this way," beckoned the man up a flight of stairs.

He felt like a leper in his unimaginative gray work uniform as the few unwelcoming faces stared at him from the floor above the common room. He wore a uniform suitable for in-office assemblies, and perhaps for supervising bridge repairs, but not here, not inside the Alchemy Guild's headquarters, where a nasty, brain-staving malodor skewed his judgment.

Through a doorway, up a coiling staircase into the master alchemist's study, a powerful waft of wet cedar invaded his senses, harkening him back to the Flying Fish Tavern. "It's the Nero architect," knocked Wendell onto a door in their path.

"Send him up, Wendell," responded a drowned-out voice, before returning to indistinguishable chatter.

"You may enter," he said, causing his adrenaline to peak.

He pinched his eyelids, providing a momentary lapse of reprieve as he took his first few steps into a dusty light towards the master alchemist. Within the fuzzy glare of a vial-shaped stained glass window, Lord Vanic's guest was difficult to discern. "Nero!" he waved him over, stepping out from a desk with nothing on it save for his fingerprints.

It was the closest he had ever been to him, the Alchemy Guild's second-in-command, his acid burn thrust clear in his view.

He had the look of a man in his early forties, who like his constituents scattered about in the common room beneath his floor, had seldom seen the *glow*. He was slender like himself; however, he too carried a great weight about his shoulders.

"Barron," nodded the architect, studying the sludge-green lining of his trench coat.

An uncomfortable feeling washed over him as he finally got an up-close look at the man's guest, now turned. It was General Jarcentinia, the last person he ever expected to see in the alchemist's tower, dressed down in a gold tunic with an ill-fitting smile fixed upon his face. "Lord Alarie," he stood, centering his ostentatious purple cape for a floppy handshake.

The outline of his whip had exposed within a bulge beneath his tunic, as he retracted his hand. Recalling his last encounter with the man, he couldn't help but skip the courtesy of a proper greeting, greeting him simply as "General." Though to be fair neither likely remembered one another's first name—an often unspoken, arguably underrated perk to the possession of titles.

"Best watch out for this one," he jested, allowing the other his spot at the master alchemist's desk.

Peculiarly enough to him, the general didn't seem at all disparaging like his last encounter with him. He wondered whether the absence of a certain overseer had kept him at ease. Whatever the case may have been, Lord Vanic did not seem at all rattled by the general's comment.

"So, have you come to tell me why I am still working in this derelict? Or are you here to condemn us?" he said stoically, before forcing a smile.

"Suppose it has its charm," he said, retrieving the alchemists' requirements list. "No, I have a few questions I want to clarify is all."

"Let's put it this way, the canyon dwellers were still kicking when it was first built," continued Lord Vanic, ignoring the sight of the requirements list like a plague. "Hard to tell by looking at it now but it used to be shaped like a vial…You have questions."

"I do."

"Well then, ask away. But first, before you bore me with Wendell's wish list, do you have a concept for me to peruse?"

"I do."

"Excellent. Let's have a look." Barron had a look of constipation as he reached into his bag to retrieve his last-minute revision, an unimaginative clone of the Nero Company's workshop. He took a long breath before setting it down and turning it the other way. "It's still a work in progress." He then paused in silence for a moment. "I just wanted to clarify a few of your requirements before applying more ink."

The master alchemist said nothing as he stared regrettably at the drawing.

He emitted a grunt as he leaned back in his chair, exhaling. "It's…" Getting ahead of the inevitable rejection, he swooped his hand into his bag and unfolded another piece of parchment. His original piece of work, the same one he had poured his heart and soul into only to be left standing in a pool of wilted entrails. "An alternative." He set it down and twisted the menacing, trilateral trapezoidal inception just beyond the man's grasp, before relaxing into the back of his chair.

"Now, now, what do we have here?" His subdued look twisted into one of eagerness, as he leaned forward for a closer look.

"If I'm being honest, a concept that I am particularly excited about."

He studied the fire in his eyes and smiled. "Why didn't you just show me this one from the beginning?"

His smile spread to himself, as he leaned forward to show him a preview of the specs.

CHAPTER 19

TIDINGS

"**W**as that Lord Vodgar I saw entering your office earlier?" Marrin held up a thick leather pouch in the air and winked.

It was not even yet noon and already the overseer was sporting dank pools of sweat underneath his arms. Of course, the sixth week of summer did start with a scorcher. "So, how's my lead architect faring?" was how he officially commenced their routine assembly that week.

"There was something I wanted to discuss with you today. It's about the meeting that I had with Lord Vanic last week."

"Make that two of us."

The man opened his mouth to speak, before suddenly shutting it. His eyebrows were fanning out every which way, edging closer his way. "Regarding *what*?"

"Couple of things. Firstly, I just wanted to commend you for your initiative on this project. You have your father's gumption. Based on the letter I had received, the Guild seemed very much enthralled with your design proposal. I believe I owe you an apology for my initial reluctance to your design."

Barron relaxed his arms by his side. "Thank you, Marrin."

"Unfortunately, and believe me it pains me to say this, but we can't move forward with the project."

He was in disbelief, waiting for a punchline that never came. "You're kidding, right?"

"The alchemists are relocating, son," Marrin said with a forced frown. "The whole lot of them are leaving—the merchants, the historians, the miners, all of 'em. No more tax immunity, no more guilds, I guess."

"And?"

"I know you worked hard on this, but we can't afford to leave the queen's good graces. Not now."

"Forget the queen. Who cares if it's here? Who cares if it's in the desert or overseas? Let the council stew over it, they'll get over it eventually. They need us more than we need them."

"This was not an easy decision," he replied. "Believe me, Barron. But I am confident we can remain neutral during this time of uncertainty, by treading carefully."

He sat there scattered, fumbling to arrange a few disparate words.

The overseer unfolded his rag and wiped his forehead, trembling. "I know it's not an easy elixir to swallow, Barron," he added, his focus visibly elsewhere. "But we're Nero, we'll come out of this mess stronger than ever. I know we will."

"Right."

"I got another job for you that I think you might like. The warden needs our knack on the river."

Later as he left the overseer's office, someone shouted his name from the lobby, where many men were gathered.

He raised an eyebrow and continued into his office.

It wasn't until hearing a sharp whistle that he had finally emerged to his doorway.

"What is this, a ponce party?!" shouted Selvin from the handrail, evoking the lead engineer and overseer to their doorways as well. "So, you've heard the news? The guilds are leaving!" He started nodding. "Yes! Is that what you want to hear? Now, unless I missed a rumor somewhere that states your jobs will be leaving for the desert—or wherever on Tethia is it the guilds are going—then I suggest you all find something to do." He shook his head, acknowledged by Marrin with a fond nod.

As for himself, unwilling to set aside his grievances over the overseer's thoughtless decision, he knew he had to do something. For one thing, even Myleyn had begun to take notice of his souring mood as the week went on. "Mopey," in actuality, is what she had called him. And mopey was not a good look on anyone, and anyone who says otherwise is either bitter, in denial, or both. What he needed was a good distraction.

He and his two underlings set their sights on the Pebblewood River later that week, not ten miles east of his winter estate. There they would lend their architectural expertise to a watchtower design.

To the Nero leader, it was clear that the warden was desperate for outside help. Likely, as the overseer had laid out helpfully for the disenfranchised company man, to avoid another "blunder." Curious, if nothing else, he had thought it as he left his office in the afternoon of yesterday. For starters if the warden couldn't handle a ragtag band of avarices from Taranchia, what could he handle?

"…What about iron? Steel?" suggested Third Architect Robert, drawing silence from his superiors.

Barron looked at him with an empty expression. The greenhorn talked more than a young man following his first ale. Not to mention, he carried a pompous weight around him wherever he went. And yet, in some way or another, he saw a bit of himself in him. Especially so at the present, on the receiving end of yet another serving of unsolicited advice.

Garvey was different, the red stripes' resident shipyard lackey. He was generally well-liked by all. Diligent and organized and, most especially, not afraid to get his hands dirty with documentation, he was Barron's favorite brand of logistician. "Too expensive," said the second architect. "And if I remember correctly, the warden's letter mentioned that this Taranchian stuff chews through metal."

Stumped, the two turned their gaze onto the ranking architect.

"Wood is fine. I don't see any problem with the design either. Why fix what's not broken?"

Robert sneered as he scanned about the two men's faces. "Well, they hired us for a reason…"

"No," he overheard Garvey whispering as he walked away, "they hired Nero. You're just here to learn." Barron pressed on beside the current, inching closer towards the only thing left of the guard post over the fall—a gaping hole.

The grass here did not just burn, it was purified. And still hissed, he came to learn, inching his ear close enough over the edge for a good listen.

"Careful there!" advised a group of penal drudges, extracting what's left of the watch tower's roost from the river's edge.

The warden approached him from behind, studying the crow sewn up his collar. "You're the lead architect, aren't you? Varus Alarie, if my memory serves me?"

He smirked. "My father *was* lead architect, for a time. I am Barron, his son."

The warden paced around the hissing ditch. "These Taranchian concoctions are lethal, the old marshlands are evidence of that. The Palasore family never knew what hit them."

"The Raknias were quite clever," chimed the man. "I can only imagine what sort of firepower we'd possess had Lord Raknia and the God King gotten along."

"Clever fools, gone like the rest of them," dismissed the man. "So, what do you make of our current design?" Garvey and Robert joined them around the divot to observe the exchange.

"It's fine," replied the man, "tall enough for our arbalists to hit their mark across the river, and thick enough to take a beating. Though, I do think it's missing a key component."

"What's that? A sprinkle of magic?" jested the warden.

"That would be nice. But no, I think a special balm will do. Something that can thwart the acid, chew it up, and wash it away. Then we add a special platform up top to apply the serum when needed."

"Whatever it is we tried it: the salts, water, you name it."

He bobbed his head, visibly unconvinced. The warden's attention meanwhile was elsewhere, whistling at a few eavesdropping drudges. "Get back to work!"

"Well, Master Alarie, I am always open to novel ideas."

"We'll see what we can do, Warden."

It had been about a half-hour since the lead architect disappeared inside of the Alchemy Guild's tower by his lonesome, in which the first twenty minutes had involved sharing his cover story, as per the warden's wishes—indeed the guilds' animosity to the warden was well known.

"…I may just have a solution to your problem. It worked for me. It may just work for your friend. That is if the site is contained."

"That's great news." Barron smiled, before awkwardly reeling into a frown.

"Tell you what," said Lord Vanic. "I will not only tell you where you can find this particular antidote, but before I will also pay you for your time."

"Pay *me*? How do you mean?"

"I need help with a new project, and I can't think of anyone better to help us. And when I say 'anyone' I do mean *you*. It won't be anywhere close in scale to our stymied construction...A real pity," he tutted.

"I thought you'd be relocating to the desert with the rest of them?"

"Is that what they are saying? Guess it must be true." He leaned forward with a dubious smile. "The tides are always changing, my friend... And not all tides leave lines in the sand. Some are like clouds, leaving nebulous shapes behind for one's construal."

"I do intend to run Nero someday, like my father before me. But perhaps I could loan my architectural expertise in my off-time—on my breaks and such. Does that work?"

"How about this, make your decision once you have all the information you need. Fair enough?" he arose, pressing his trench coat firmly against his body. "I suggest you pay a visit to the Sea Sprites. The East Sea holds an untapped trove of natural remedies not found on any shelves, ours included. There you will find Elder Aldabar."

The following morning, the three awoke early to a welcome breeze, setting off light with three mares, courtesy of the Nero Company. While a saddled horse was not the man's first or second choice, or third really, a full day's walk to the coves was not at all a good use of anyone's time. It was about noontime, on the cusp of Sprite's Forest, when the three had dismounted for a stretch, where Barron limped against a karnip tree for a "rest."

"You all right there, Barron?" The logistician chuckled. "We still have a way to go before we make it to the harbor."

"Sixty years since I've ridden a horse, Garvey," he groaned.

Southward they continued through the forest Sprite, eventually stopping at the only open establishment in Cilify Harbor, before continuing.

Far up the coast, winking caverns appeared, wrought within the side of the cliff. The home-place of the Sea Sprites. He felt goosebumps begin to form as they approached the great fall of Sprite's Drop, where winged denizens scooped the soon-to-be salted waters of the Pebblewood River with their pails. A first for tired eyes, the full span of the three hundred feet high micturating outlet—from this angle, cascading beautifully and brutally down the side of the cliff's many peaks.

"I'll do the talking," whispered Garvey, "the Sea Sprites aren't exactly fond of outsiders."

"Outsiders." Barron scoffed. "What do you think of that, Robert?"

Robert cupped his hand over his mouth, checking his breath. "I think that one's looking at me."

They searched, finding a young female with stubby wings tucked subtly behind her limber blue frame, grimacing back at them.

"No-no, I think she's looking at Garvey," remarked Barron facetiously.

Entering the cliff to the full breadth of stares, the men were watched by the Sea Sprites' spiritual leader, all five-foot-tall of him. While not olden per se, this Sprite was an elder, with a thin slit no longer than a key slot running down the side of his shrunken head. He was one of the few who possessed the gift, or *spiravis*, as the locals called this sixth sense into Tethia's very soul.

"You seek help, but with what?" he vetted them petulantly from afar, turning his ocean blue eyes onto the second architect, whose once uninspired hairdo had been swept into a patch of bald spots on their venture here. "I remember you. You're the one who brought the injured dock worker here; stepped on a poisonous barb, didn't he? You Neuvians are soft..."

"Yes, well—"

"Your clothes have no scent. You come from the capital city, do you not?"

"Lucky guess," Robert murmured under his breath.

"We could use your help Elder Aldabar," said Garvey, "a different kind of remedy this time."

"What are we dealing with?" asked the elder, evidently at a loss for the human's name.

"According to the warden, a concoction of deleterious components. Plants, mostly. It vaporizes matter on contact. We need something that can brave it. These men are risking their lives to defend our land and the capital has failed them."

The Sprite stared him up and down. "*And?*"

"Soldiers are dying," added Robert.

"Of course they're dying. That's what soldiers do."

Barron stepped forward impatiently. "We need something to shower our watch towers in so they won't disintegrate on contact. Name your price."

The Sprite rolled his eyes.

"The longer these watchtowers stand, the stronger our border holds," joined Garvey, "that's fewer Taranachians in our homes and yours."

He beckoned the men deeper into the torch-lit cavern, one filled with tide-swept shells that crunched like glass under the heels of their boots.

Amongst tiny, translucent pools of water, a corridor shaped by the tides revealed, at which point their host seemingly disappeared.

Robert stared about nervously. "It's empty."

"Not empty," replied Garvey, pointing upward onto a vast network of clever corridors. "They've placed their homes so very high that not even the worst of tides can reach them."

"Well, if they don't help us, I don't think it's the tides they'll need to worry about," added the man.

Elder Aldabar emerged with a bag in his hand. With the knot on its end loosened, the men took a peek inside. "A paste?" sniffed Barron.

"No better one than a lotus leaf. Bend any acid to its will."

"We'll take it..."

Later in the evening, the men had returned to the river to a watchtower in progress. Dismounted, Barron came upon the man with the bag wide open.

The warden snagged his chin for a stroke. "What is it?"

"Lotus vera," said Barron. "The best part is, the moisture from the rain will not affect it."

"Let me get this straight. I hire architects from Maldinia's premier build and design company to consult with me on the defense of our northern border, and you prescribe—what? Burn ointment?" he looked them over like they had two heads. "Let's give it a test then, shall we? Not that I don't trust you."

The warden signaled over one of his fellow soldiers, who fondled with a tear-inducing concoction. "Not quite as potent as the Taranchian stuff," said the warden, "but I think the idea will suffice. Last chance, Alarie..."

The nobleman nodded apprehensively, and the warden ordered, "Now!" triggering his soldiers to pour the liquid onto a shield. As the liquid fell upon its lathered wood surface, not a sizzle or a hiss could be heard; just a drip.

"You boys have done well," inspected the warden, "though I don't think one sack of it will be enough to cover the whole tower, much less the entire border."

"The entire border?" gaped Robert.

The man gleamed.

"Well then, should we go back for some more?" turned Robert.

The lead architect started breaking off towards the river bank with the warden at his side.

"*We?*" he heard the logistician whisper to the other.

CHAPTER 20

BRITTLE GROUND

The throne room hearths were disturbed briefly by a passing wind and a few determined footsteps.

Crownless as she emerged from her bedchamber, her hair tied up loosely in a bun, she had an inexplicable look of unease spelled upon her unblemished face.

There were hardly any shadows afoot, save for the blind spots around the white stone columns and the puffy ones that hugged her under eyes. An otherwise spectacular day for a steady amble through her garden. It is indeed why her lips were pressed when she opened her door, only to find her council members present, uninvited. Except for Lord Flumen, her entire council cast simulated smiles. Each appeared to restrain, waiting for the next to commence, staring at their shoes nervously as if their necks had been strained.

"We've been doing some thinking," spoke Lord Vodgar, opening his hand towards the assembly table. The man brandished a scroll which, aided by Lord Geldrin, was rolled from one end of the karnip table to the other.

The Law of Relinquishment, it read. *Relinquishment*—The word was inescapable from the naked eye, etched like a brand upon a thick sheet of wood fiber, pressed and dried. "Relinquishment," announced the woman aloud as if she were half reciting a spelling lesson.

Lord Geldrin cleared his throat, a shade of guilt tangible in his eyes. Lord Vodgar, on the other hand, welcomed the roll with an impassive frown.

"Well," said the woman, panning from face to face, "are you going to sign it? The law states that a majority vote is required for a relinquishment, so I take it this has been discussed beforehand?"

Lady Knish inched forward in her seat. "My Queen, if I may…we have thought long and hard about this." She exhaled, seemingly waiting for someone else to finish her thought.

"Of course, it's been discussed," chimed in the treasurer, "this is for the good of the economy." He tugged the curl of the nearest corner beneath his stubby elbow and signed.

"Very well, Ogden."

"I covet the same welfare for our people as you do," uttered Lady Knish, reaching for the wet feather, "your unspoken love for your people is admirable. However, I don't think it wise to destroy relationships that we have worked so hard to nurture." She averted her piercing glare as she quietly flicked her wrist.

A single vote was all that remained for the required majority.

"My queen." Lord Geldrin plucked his flabby legs apart. "I have been quite torn as of late. Ultimately, however, I believe it's the only viable option we have left to prevent any more merchants from leaving," he signed, his attention immediately averted to a stain on his slippers.

The queen's regent toiled in her seat as she prepared to speak the words into existence.

"Is that all?" The queen's words were answered by silence, as she began prematurely withdrawing towards her bedchamber.

"Where…are you *going*?" The treasurer stood. "You have been relinquished, per your father's law."

She stopped for a brief moment. "Forgot my sunhat."

Agitated, the treasurer summoned the attention of the ascendants adjacent. There were two of them guarding the door, and another beside her vacant throne, yet none seemed quite ready to make a move.

Before exiting outside, she stopped, placing her sunhat on her head. Positioning her toes toward the assembly table, she sauntered back over. They watched her tap the fourth paragraph with the gentle tip of her finger, drawing the intelligencer from his chair. Locking eyes, the two shared a subtle nod. "Please, Lord Flumen, if you will."

"It'd be my pleasure," he said, clearing the phlegm inside his throat. "In the event of a witnessed targeting…" He started nodding. "The affected party is thereby void of any present foray."

Flummoxed, the three sat in silence.

"Well then." The queen turned to her intelligencer followed by the rest of them. "Do any of you object to this?"

Realizing their last hold of power had been cast off the side of the plateau, their hearts sank. If you listened very carefully, an elusive, feral growl leaked from the pit of the treasurer's stomach.

"Guards." She turned. "Please escort these three conspirators from the premises at once, until I know what to do with them." Once they had gone, it was as if the clouds had lifted.

"Would you care to join me for a stroll through my garden? It'd be a shame to waste this beautiful afternoon inside." He obliged her offer, and the two descended the pathway into her rose garden. "Oleander, you look like you're going to hurl. What's troubling you?" She approached a pretty patch of roses at the head of her garden. There at the precipice of the butte, a collection of stunning purples stood out above the rest.

"They were Elaina's favorite." She wiped her eyes with her sleeve, turning to the intelligencer with a chuckle. "Do I have to extract it from you?"

"They will come for you, my lady."

"Of course they will."

"Does that not bother you?"

"What do you suggest I do?" She thrust her eyes off the ledge, into the courtyard, chasing them through the labyrinth of hedges. "They had every right to sign it."

"What now then, will you find replacements?"

"Well, I already have a spymaster," she smiled, "a bookkeeper, an emissary, a logistician."

"'I much preferred her in the role of troubled housewife,' I quote your emissary just this morning. How about your treasurer? 'The Luminas have diluted her mind,' I quote him." He found her eyes as she bent over to sniff a flower. "My lady, they will undermine you every step of the way. I assure you they will not stop until you are supplanted permanently. I might sound a little naive here, but I am quite certain their interests are compromised by the guilds."

She took a long hard look at the man and smiled. "Do you want to know why I stood by my husband's side all those years? Even after he decided to order our troops on our own people?"

Lord Flumen exhaled, dropping his present musings for a polite smile. "Ciguil was a great father to Elaina. She adored him, in fact. She didn't see the side of him that I did..." On the tip of her toes, she planted him a kiss. "...You taste of youth," she said, withdrawing her lips from the stubble of his left cheek.

He scoffed. "Coming from you, my lady. You are looking sprier than ever these days."

"I thank you. And yet somehow, I feel as if I am running out of time. I know there is more I must do for my people." He followed her to the podium. "I want you to get a pulse on the peoples of this great nation, Oleander. I want eyes in every street, in every tavern, everywhere; even in the woods on the cliffs afar. Figure out what the citizens of Maldinia truly yearn for and I shall do everything in my power to fulfill their wishes. If it is their wish to rid me of this crown, then so be it. I'll step down." She stepped closer into his vicinity. "I've asked the warden to keep a closer eye on the Alchemy Guild's doings. I would like you to do so as well. I feel their claws even as they retract."

CHAPTER 21

DARK IN A LIGHT PLACE

The overseer scanned about his warehouse, filled to the brim with curious eyes and calloused hands. Nero men; gray jackets of every color, shape, and size. "Is that everyone?" he looked now to his leads, standing timorously in his shadow.

Barron and Devyn were stuck somewhere between a shrug and a nod. Neither did either.

"All right, everyone!" shouted the lead builder. "Quiet now!"

"Men, I know it's about quitting time, but bear with me here just a few minutes of your time," he started, pausing for air. "Better yet, allow yourselves a few minutes of your time. You lot deserve it. In the last few months, I have seen engineers fill in as builders, architects as engineers, builders as foremen, and the list goes on. You lot should be proud. You are the backbone of this great nation, and likely the only thing preventing the realm from utter ruin."

He locked eyes with the many faces around the room, nodding and winking at them fondly like they were his sons. There was no mistaking it. He knew each of them by name, how many stripes they had, what color, most without even looking.

"Really, just try to imagine what this realm would look like today had it not been for our help…" He took another labored breath and stepped forward. "While there's still much more work to be done here in the capital, I am afraid my time as overseer will be coming to an end." Whilst his leads pretended to look surprised, whispers spread everywhere. Joy for some. Worry for most. For a man as entrenched with Nero as the bricks in these walls, can't just get up and leave without a few of them falling.

Against his chest came a battering ram. Finally. *Overseer Alarie.* It even sounded good.

He watched as the overseer removed his silver jacket and raised it in the air like a freshly sawed trophy head, quivering in his balance like the bloodied blade following its rigorous extraction. "As we look to see this chapter of Reconstruction through, I believe there is no one here more deserving to lead you men into the next…" he slowly creased his face into a smile. "…Selvin!" he revealed, "get over here! Remove your jacket!"

The architect bit his lip bloody and broke off, with fellow brown stripes swarming the man with felicitations. He did not stop in his office, nor did he turn his back once to witness the chosen man in his oversized jacket. He swung the front doors open and staggered outside into the grass, where he sent the tip of his leather boots, flinging soil indiscriminately overhead.

The noise inside had calmed some but his ears had not stopped repeating his name.

Selvin.

After fifty-seven long years at the top, Selvin, of all people, was his chosen man. He backtracked down the road with a senseless expression, descending into the vacant ditch of their former worksite. A bit of shade from the lip and a hollow marquee tent were all that remained there. The impression of the storage tents was discernible, and so too was the moat they had crudely constructed. Otherwise, silence.

He circled to the back of the old marquee tent, where the ground was wet with moss, unsheathing his blade. He then cocked his right elbow back and thrust it cleanly into its backside, and, with little effort, a crude gouge in the shape of a door had been made in the fabric.

He panted and stepped through, hugging the first tower of unfiled documents Marrin had not yet gotten to, tossing them carelessly out the tent's newest door like nut shells.

Outside he uprooted a large rock, one of the marquee tent's many anchors, and tossed it through, creating an awkward air vent. Then another.

His stomach turned as he struggled his way out of the tent's now collapsed remains. Meanwhile, his mouth had never felt so dry. As he found the alchemists' tower high up in the sky, he found himself biting his lip once more. Surely it was not the Guild's departure that had made him feel this way.

Then it came to him, revealed in a lucid mirage, what it would have looked like six months from now. It was mostly just a base, but that was irrelevant, it was *his* base. *A year from now?* he wondered, looking upon the greatness of his menacing trilateral trapezoidal creation with a smile.

He then recalled his vision from prison, in the process, realizing how crucially he had misinterpreted Xardrescu's message. He had the skills necessary, and no doubt the financial means, yet for whatever reason he still clung to the approval of an irrelevant dolt.

He lifted his jacket over his head, in the shade, reasoning.

No longer.

CHAPTER 22

MACHINATIONS

Myleyn knew it was unlike her betrothed to disappear without fair warning. A misanthrope, he was, though not a particularly rude or unreliable one. The truth: he had no memory of his evening plans with the girl, likely still waiting patiently in her den for the sound of his knock to resume wherever they last left off with their wedding preparations. As for his true whereabouts, they were a complete mystery. "Guild secrecy policy," the master alchemist regrettably informed him on the evening of their departure to observe a prospective job.

The only thing he could see was a weak glare and the few specks of fabric covering his eyes. The little chatter he could hear between Lord Vanic and Wendell was for the most part muffled by the sputtering of rocks in the spokes of the alchemists' upmarket carriage.

But it soon became apparent. The windows were closed, but he could smell the plums of Maldinax from a mile away, and taste the freshwater coursing through its veins.

"The old man is languid as ever," he heard Lord Vanic whisper to Wendell at one point on their ride, crumpling what he figured to be a letter in his hand. "Must I do everything, Wendell?" He whispered something again to Wendell as they came to a rolling stop. Words he could not get a read on.

"…they can watch all they want," he heard Wendell say, "we have been assured that no bother would come to us here. So far, our friend has kept his end of the bargain."

It was evening, or so he figured in the light's absence, the air still ripe with day's moisture, the crickets now out in full force.

He fumbled behind them like he had been teetering on the edge of a gangplank to his doom. He could not guess the exact vicinity, but he knew it was Maldinax. For despite all of the aimless detours their driver had thrown his way, the smell of plums had not yet evaded him.

Escorted into a footing of wilted shrubs, one of them sent a knock on a door. "Almost there, Barron," The master alchemist assured him. "Then we can get that silly blindfold off your face."

"Lord Vanic," greeted a man's voice he had not recognized. "Wendell," he added, whose voice had a hollow finish down the short flight of stairs he was soundly escorted down.

Save for a single lantern, which he could now see flickering on the other end of his blindfold, it was pitch black as if he had stepped into a hole. Like a heavy walk to the outhouse in the early hours of the night, he pressed on blindly with the remainder of his senses at the door. They led him down a ladder into yet more darkness, his brain doing its best to stave off the thought of the anonymous letter by focusing on his bitter breaths.

It was far colder here than a winter rain, though this no wine cellar, nor a body-drop, but a tunnel with hot flames on opposing ends of dirt walls compacted. He could tell by their echoes as the master alchemist and Wendell patted themselves free of cobwebs and dust and set forth. Long did they walk down a furnished tunnel, until a pale green glow had become so overtly apparent that it stayed, even after closing his eyes.

"You wait here." Wendell guided his legs into a chair in a room gone from the glowing light. "We'll be just a moment." He had little choice but to comply. Of course, this would not stop him from eavesdropping. It was the same pale glow that he had seen in their vat.

The first thing he could hear was a man walking past. He was carrying something, which jingled and clanked its way into the next cavity over.

"Your elixirs, my friend, as promised," he heard Lord Vanic say. "Just remember, not a word of this to anyone, or your fate too will be tied to this tunnel."

"You're forgetting whose tunnel this is," said another voice.

"You're right. But come to think of it, at the pace we're producing we should be able to build tunnels of our own. I am thinking of somewhere closer to the city. What do you think, Wendell?"

Wendell's voice was interrupted by the other. "You're sure these people knew what they were agreeing to when they volunteered for this experiment? What if they were impaired? Or worse, simple?" the stranger's voice was lost. However, something had just then occurred to him. This was no stranger conversing with the master alchemist. He had heard this voice before, somewhere. He wandered up at once out of his chair for a closer listen.

"I miss the Floating Lily," Lord Vanic said, as though musing to himself aloud. "If you and your father ever get around to cleaning up the Quincunx, do please let me know." *Duncan*, he just then realized. "...tell me, Lord Duncan, which poor sap wouldn't want a break from cleaning up weeds? Or dare I say, a few more elixirs to add to their collection?"

There was a tense silence that followed. In truth, it took a full ten seconds before Duncan had finally traded a response, allowing Barron just enough time to fumble his way back into his seat. "Trade one shackle for another, I guess."

When Lord Vanic had finally gotten around to removing his mask, he could see it; a glowing fog that rose like steam from the room just beyond him. "What do you see, Barron?"

He blinked for moisture and panned around one mess of a cavity, packed full of crates of unlabeled concoctions, coils, beakers, hoses, and the like.

"It's a mess here, isn't it?"

"Where's *here*?" Barron asked, half hoping.

"Underground." The master alchemist coyly smiled. "Now, can you guess what I am going to ask you next?"

"You want me to organize this mess for you? No. You want me to build you a space to put it, don't you?"

"Absolutely right!" Lord Vanic clapped. "Smart man. We have equipment wasting away, and even more alchemists with work that needs doing."

He smiled uncomfortably. "I am afraid I know very little about alchemy, much less the fundamentals of building a laboratory."

"It's less complicated than you think," replied the man. "We just need a space large enough, and, of course, sound enough to house it all. We have made several attempts of our own…" he trailed off to a cabinet, unlocking it with help from another. "…these of course are alchemists." Lord Vanic lay something cold in his hands which nearly slipped from his blood-fleeted grasp.

Next came a contract.

"There's one question on my mind."

"So long as it doesn't break Alchemy Guild protocol, ask away."

"I often wonder," he looked now to the glowing elixir in his hand, "how will you maintain your supply once your chief component fades into obscurity? It's not like vegetables, where you can just grow them again. Right?"

Lord Vanic chortled, triggering smiles from his logistician and the various other alchemists in their proximity. "I like this one," he said to Wendell.

With the sun's reappearance, he returned to the workshop like it was his last day, his hair unkempt, his shirt untucked. A scent of fresh sawdust in his nares as he sauntered his way through the lobby.

Marrin's transition plan was already in full swing, the overseer-to-be following the old man attentively around like he only had minutes left to learn.

Steven entered only moments after him. "…Did you not hear me shouting your name?"

"Not now, Steven," he replied. "I'm tired." Truthfully, he had his own transition plan in mind. A transition plan was conjured as he lay restless in his bed yesterevening, which not even a double dose of lazabloom sedative would cure (it's true, the Lumina Elixir was like lightning in the veins).

The first step in his transition plan, he would need to submit the necessary paperwork to legitimize his novel design and build company. This in itself would seem simple. But this was the land of bureaucracy, where dreams went to die. Thankfully, for all his debilitating guesswork blindly underway, he needn't look any further than his soon-to-be-wife, or rather, his soon-to-be-wife's father.

Whilst Myleyn and her mother bickered in one room about wedding-related minutia, in another, Barron and Landon readied his initial paperwork, a letter, and a bribe. According to Landon, the only way to expedite the process was to leave a generous donation to the realm's coffers. And indeed, he was right. Just four days later, on the afternoon of Thirdday, a sealed letter with the treasurer's seal had been slipped beneath his front gate. His newfangled architecture company had been approved. He was now an official founder. A founder of a nameless design and build company with a single contract, no base of operations and a nonexistent reputation.

It was a start.

That day he heard a brutish knock at his door, and so he crammed his short list of potential names for his newly vetted company into his drawer and quickly put on a smile. "What can I do for you, Marrin?" was how he received him.

"I just wanted to gauge how you and Devyn are feeling about the announcement," he said, entering, "I know it may seem like pandemonium around here right now, however, I'm optimistic that operations will return to normalcy soon enough."

He bit his cheek. "I admit, I was a bit surprised at your choice of successor."

"It was a tough decision, but as you know, Selvin's been with this company quite a long time, with more experience than any here."

He averted his gaze to his window, before reluctantly returning his attention back onto his supervisor. "Sure. As a builder."

"Yes, but even before that, I served with the man. He could marshal troops even better than I could."

Barron tilted his head to the side.

"Look, I'll need you and Devyn's help to ensure the birds are kept fed. Can I count on you?" He scanned for validation. There seemed none to be found. He was now pondering his archived design, and those lines, those sweet menacing lines.

Breaking from his daze, he forced a smile. "Lack of sleep, sir, my apologies. Of course. That's what I'm here for."

Marrin slapped his meaty hands on his desk and winked. "Good man."

The following morning, vagabonds traced the nobleman's path as he exited an elixir emporium, jeering him for a "little drop," as he wet his throat with yet another dose of the glowing stuff.

"...we don't have any money," groaned one. "Perhaps we could work for it!?"

"We can?" turned one of his friends.

As the beggars submitted back towards their usual loitering spot, Barron stopped and tapped his foot. "Are any of you good with your hands?"

They paused, panning to one another before advancing.

"Masonry? Carpentry?" pried the man, keeping them a comfortable distance away from his pockets. "Digging?"

Soon only a single slab had separated them from his pockets. He stared around for guards. With none to be found, he reached for his letter opener.

"We're farmhands," finally one of them answered. "Formerly."

As the vagabond clarified their employment situation, the man couldn't help but stare at their shoes—more like toes uninvited. If they were thieves, he reasoned, they weren't very good ones. "...Lord Stain-berry's wife blamed us for the raid. Got the old man to believe that we were the ones who invited the avarices inside," vented one. "Easier to blame the farmhands, I guess, than to address the gaps in their security."

"Listen, I really need to be going now, but if you men are looking for work, I may just have an opportunity for you in the weeks to come."

"Doing what?" they queried.

"Digging something," he replied, adding another slab between them.

The vagabonds stared at one another apprehensively. With another step between them, he rattled the elixir in his hand, causing their eyes to gleam.

Far below the queen's throne, in the annals of the keep, the intelligencer and warden convened for an amble through the crown's archives to review their progress with their latest work.

Expecting very little in the way of actionable insights, the warden thus far was pleasantly surprised by the young Lord Flumen's acumen. A whole decade between them, and without a single day served in the infantry. He was by all accounts a nobody outside of the queen's circle, with no discernable fidelity to anyone in the realm but the realm itself. Whether too naive to understand how the world works just yet or so very secretive that no one could think to guess his true loyalties, the warden could not yet discern.

"My informant spotted Lord Vanic's chauffeur in Maldinax," said the intelligencer, "conspicuously leaving, of all places, old Dardwick Plumscint's estate. The alchemists will deny it, I am sure of it. But it does make me wonder."

"Do we have the same informant?" chuckled the warden.

"You know of this? Don't you think we should get a closer look inside?"

"Tread carefully, my friend. Knowing and acting are two very different things. Knowing, for one thing, doesn't make enemies."

He began sifting through a dresser the length of his bed, filled with dreadfully gaudy overcoats and ruffs from a bygone age. "These were Ciguil's," he said, throwing on the tackiest of the collection, a floor-length dinner coat, a butter yellow color, with kitschy baubles for buttons. Intrepid in his posture, he inspected its roomy sleeves within a dusty mirror, with a childlike grin on his face.

"Do you remember in Gromula's Cave, that pit you and your men stumbled upon?"

"Yes," he said, throwing the overcoat back into the dresser without a second look. "How could I forget the investigation you had replaced me on."

"I couldn't have been the only one who found Lord Encore's cover story a bit strange."

"Well?"

"Well, for starters, I found no evidence to suggest that the Pyrithians buried their loved ones inside pits. The Pyrithians, on record, lay their kith and kin in the river, and beside. They believed their blood was hallowed, that it could replenish their precious Sol."

He leaned on one leg.

"Don't get me wrong, Gromula himself could have made that hole. I just find it odd that a studied historian would get a detail like this so very wrong."

Nodding, the warden stroked his chin. "Continue your recon in Maldinax. I'll poke around the cave some more. Perhaps finally we can put the mystery of the Gromula Day heist to rest. *Oh*, and one more thing, don't tell the queen." Later, he hung his head over the mysterious pit, tossing a pebble inside. It smacked around the bitter cylinder— much louder than he had envisioned, answered by a profound echo.

He panned about their sullen faces; nine of Victor's finest. Ones with the shadows, save for the few Luminas growing on the cavern walls, and the few lanterns they had brought along with them. "Normally I like to pick on you young guys first, but without you Lamb, we wouldn't have found this here hole. You've earned the right to call yourself spotter today." The man, shivering like a mangy, stray cat, opened his mouth for a long exhale.

He turned his attention next onto Rowan, the next youngest, who uncoincidentally found his attention seized by one of the Glowers.

"I'll do it," volunteered a grim voice.

The warden raised an eyebrow. "No Victor, you have one eye." He continued his search around the rim, panning the other probers' faces. Like lambs to a slaughter.

"Exactly, sight is out of the question."

"Your grave then, Victor." They began unfurling a heavy rope and hurled it over the side. The others, accoutering their leather gloves, grabbed a hold of the same rope Victor began his descent upon.

Before he went in after Rowan, the warden set his eyes on Lamb. "The emergency word is 'Grom.' Say it with me, 'Grom.' You will then reel us in like you've got the biggest fish you've ever seen on your line. Got it?"

Lamb nodded, and nodded again, reiterating the emergency phrase aloud.

Far detached from the humidity on the surface, it was only the raw chill left, their labored breaths, and the fleeing droplets from the little puddles in the cavity above. There were slots in the wall Victor had found, wrought down the side of the hole like a ladder, deep enough to fit their fingers and toes through, and even hold themselves up. To navigate the hidden ladder reliably, however…the limited light they had brought along with them had allotted them just enough range to observe their hands, and the oxygen leaving their lungs.

By the time they reached the ground, their arms were weary, and their gloves were wet. They could do little but tremble at the stretch ahead, a tunnel of bedrock, dirt, and clay, of inestimable length and age, to which round shape their minds could not even yet begin to grasp. One thing was for certain: no mortal instrument could ever have had any part in it. The unsettling thought on one's mind on the hollow highway to nowhere.

"I do hope the intelligencer was wrong about his theory," the warden whispered.

"Theory?" a few of them reacted.

Victor trailed ahead, stopping the rest with the click of his tongue. "These are footsteps. A man was here."

The warden knelt by his side. "How old?"

"Not long ago at the rate this water's seeping in here. This may yet be our missing assailant."

"I'll be damned. The old man slipped away right beneath our noses." He rubbed his hands together, looking over his investigators with a regretful expression. "I am going to see where these tracks lead. Anyone who wants to stay behind, be my guest. In fact, I encourage it. Just don't make any sound."

With Victor loose by his side, the light grew suddenly dim. And who could blame the other men? This was no ordinary investigation, but a test of will. And yet as he turned, there they were gaining, the solemn faces of his investigators, clasping their torches in one hand and blades in the other with flaccid certainty.

Beyond the range of their light, the footsteps led on, but the walls were melting in around them. There were no braces to be found either, nor supports of any kind.

"Up there." Xardwin pointed, revealing several holes above them—some the size of ripened pumpkins.

"The Imians' work?" asked Reginald.

"Not Imians," replied Victor, waving his torch at a hole, not eight feet over their heads where a ghostly-looking piece of skin hung crudely out of.

The warden's demeanor soured. He charged towards the lot of them with his sword out. "Should have stayed behind…"

"…do you hear that?" mumbled one of them, overhearing a rattle in the ceiling. Sediment had begun to rain upon their path. The warden pushed them back the same way they came. That was when an object came falling from the edge of their light's reach. "Other way," he said, "*quickly.*"

Their coifs, ones they had worn as if they were ten feet taller, were the only thing preventing their heads from caving in now. They rushed into the darkness blindly, on the face of it, in the opposite direction of the anomaly.

He was angry. Not specifically at the intelligencer, nor his men. For it was nothing he hadn't reasoned with himself, marching willingly into the belly of the beast for the slightest chance at finding their missing assailant. It was he who had made the mistake, him alone, coming here in the first place. A task he could have very well delegated to Victor, or another, like Anvel. But that was irrelevant now. The loose façade had begun to unravel in a shroud of fallen gravel, thwarting several of them from the forward assembly.

Even after regrouping, his investigators, and their dirtied, dented lanterns, could hardly find a way ahead. He heard one of them shout out Rowan's name as a shadow came vaulting down on top of his head. It was His children that came first, darting like hungry eels from the gaps in the ceiling and walls, their exuding forcipes locking indiscriminately onto their armor like flesh.

Two of them fell behind, parrying what little rubble their muscles could bear off a now-prone Rowan—and not just rubble, but the blood-hungry arthropods, too, stabbing their plated shells wherever their tips could catch.

Ahead, a great spawn of Gromula came bursting through a hole half its size, seizing Xardwin headfirst from the forward unit. Unto its offspring too young to absorb a healthy blow, a meal worthy of a prize.

With the clatter of a squillion pedes scampering, the men gripped their weapons and advanced, illuminating an area just large enough not to lose their step. The big one locked its unemotive, lidless eyes on the glare, just out of their formation's gaze, where the bristles of its many legs had come to a sudden halt.

As they awaited its charge, another monstrosity burst out from the ceiling right on top of their flimsy formation, sinking its lower teeth into Reginald's jerkin.

They began thrusting their swords at its pincers and the back of its head, but their blades were no match for its stalwart shell. At the very least, the shadow had lost its grip on Reginald, just as the big one came charging at them. They thrust their swords at the beast, the warden sending his short sword upward into the root of the other's face, sending the bloodied creature into a reeling screech. "Go!" he shouted.

Behind them, the men tossed their torches at Gromula's great spawn and sped on through a frenzy of disturbed soil. Hope was rekindled; a glimmer revealed within a toothy crevice ahead; but the window was closing fast. But not all would revel. Rowan tripped, causing his leg to be vacuumed into the mouth of the great beast, before being yanked into the ceiling where his helpless cries were stifled.

One after another, the rest rushed through the slit, flinging themselves unseeingly into the light, to a splash.

CHAPTER 23

AUTUMN'S EVE

Time moved quickly in the weeks that followed. As word of the warden's revelation in Gromula's Cave had reached the queen's ears, she and her council were rightfully enraged. How could the Imians have known about this passage? they now theorized.

Despite this, neither the families of the fallen Gromula Day volunteers nor the deceased probers, Xardwin and Rowan, whose bodies were unfortunately not found, would find solace in the queen's contrition. For events were unraveling in the realm like never before.

First went the Art and Historian's Guild, Guild Master Encore leading the charge. Next went the merchants and miners who, as sworn they would do if their tax on goods hadn't been reverted, relocated to the desert, where regulations were as soft as the dunes in which they and their families now inhabited.

In the absence of the guilds, inflation and emigration only intensified. With fewer abled bodies to go around, the farms were struggling to produce. Paired with a drying reserve, the queen had to do something to, at the minimum, make it through winter. Releasing a third of her military was the first difficult choice she had been forced to make. Her defenses had never been so bare. But she wasn't the only leader around to have made some difficult choices. With less and less resources being allocated to infrastructure maintenance, Overseer Selvin of the Nero Company had been forced to cut wages.

A week later, he released an eighth of his workforce.

As for the Alchemy Guild, their footsteps had all but dwindled from the public eye. In the markets, however, their influence was ubiquitous. Elixirs seemed the only commodity anywhere in surplus in the latter days of summer. Where abandoned storefronts once sat, elixir emporiums had taken their place, with lines out their doors for a taste of the Guild's newest product.

Desperate and downtrodden citizens—*fiends*, to which the few who have managed to keep their sanity called them—continue to forgo key provisions to obtain just a small taste of vitality. Thankfully for them, the Guild had sought to fill this crucial gap by introducing a new one-ounce alternative.

But the Alchemy Guild's consumers weren't the only ones blissfully indifferent to the trying times. While Barron Alarie's acquaintances scoured the open countryside on their days off for unrooted Luminas to barter, the now eighty-year-old crow had just purchased his second supply depot. Rather, Lotus Design had, Nero's first-ever competitor. Yet unlike Nero, to which the lead architect still gladly received a healthy stipend for his hollow appearance, Lotus would not be so easily burnt by the crown's failures.

He and the alchemists wore layers as they delved yet again into the underbelly of Maldinax.

It was the very first Seconday of Month Nine, Year One, Post Slumber, and here marked the first time in two weeks since he had found a cold so biting; since he had finished digging a space ample enough, and, of course, stable enough to hold all the alchemists' equipment. The best part was what might've taken a Nero foreman four months with a team of busy builders behind him, had taken him four full days with a band of eager elixir fiends. (Needless to say, as word got out of this "mysterious elixir spring," blindfolds fell in short supply.)

Initially, he figured Lord Vanic and Wendell had summoned him today to show him the finished product. But that would not explain the many extra miles of walking today. Nor would it explain why the ground was so damp, and riddled with soiled slabs of wood. Of course, he knew what they were. It only took five missteps to figure it out despite his eyeless vision. They were rails used for transporting goods, just like the ones he had found on his unplanned venture inside Loarea—older though, he conjectured, based upon the porosity of the wood and their width.

"Climb on," said Lord Vanic at one point, taking the architect and Wendell on one bumpy ride on a hand-cranked rail cart.

As their rickety path came to a screeching halt, a sour thought came to his mind, whether they had found out about his involvement in the anonymous letter. He was so far from home he couldn't help but think about it. However, after some deliberation, he figured even if the man did find out about his involvement in the uncovering of their former facility, it wouldn't change much of anything. Without proper help internally, the alchemists were beholden to him and his extensive breadth of structural knowledge.

Or so they believed.

Out from the annals of an ancient crypt, into the forgotten familiarity of light, his worries had faded. To his surprise, it was the smell of the sea, a nice warm sunlight on his neck, and a breathtaking view of the ocean that had welcomed his unfettered eyes.

"Welcome to Taranchia," the master alchemist said half-sarcastically.

He kept to his boots and the lime-tipped grass beneath him. For as beautiful as it was, it was far too bright for his tired eyes to bear. He followed the alchemists into the shell of a lordly castle, at the peak of a great hill, with his sleeve over his mouth.

Rock and stone, layered on a hill the size of Endurian, 'twas a beauteous Neuvian creation, left with but a few of its standing bones. Rested upon the edge of the ruined castle's peak, where evidence of a stone wall once proudly stood, its view emerged; the fierce waves of the East Sea matched only by the mystery of the Northern Waters. "I assure you, it's safe now to breathe," remarked Lord Vanic, slapping the surface of the ledge where he now sat.

"At least here it is," he inhaled.

As he looked below, reality had finally set in. They were hundreds of feet over a familiar tide, one he had seen more times than he could count, but in a place he had not trekked through once—the northeast peninsula of Taranchia that is, and so of the greater continent of Pelegra. Strategically speaking, a merchant's paradise, if not for a tide so violent.

"You're sure?" he winced, fretting about the damage he had already done to his body.

Lord Vanic chuckled, turning his gaze wide over the badlands afar. "The power of mushrooms, my friend. Or so they say…Now I am sure you are wondering why we brought you here."

"Initially," said the man, upright in his posture.

"Hard to tell now, but long ago, the most powerful of the old families once called this frightening corner of Taranchia home. The Raknias. The greatest of the Four, by virtue of location. But who am I to say." Just one look around, there was no denying it. Amidst war-torn walls and rain-sodden paintings, Raknia Castle was a lovely rarity. Like the petals of a wilted pekni flower, its magnificence had sustained even after life. The allure of what it once was, what it could have been, could never aptly be explored within the contents of a history book or fireside tale.

The three of them climbed up some stone steps, into a partially roofed-in section of the castle's second floor, where an impractical panoply still fiercely guarded its walls. There they found the chamberlain's room; a simple desk and one massive window melted halfway into the ravaged courtyard.

"Have you figured out why we have brought you here yet?" Lord Vanic smirked.

"My guess would be that you have come up with a way to circumvent your newest tax back home. Or maybe you have found some new friends across the sea to trade with."

"I am not at liberty—but we do need your help. Just know that no is an acceptable answer too. In fact, one sip from one of our special serums, and this whole venture will be rid of your memory."

"So, you have a title?" he asked, drawing immediate laughter from him and Wendell.

"I tried knocking," jested the man, his shoulders poised towards its doorless doorway. "It seems the municipality is ripe for the taking."

He forced a smile, however he looked to have stopped receiving oxygen. Until now, his newfound company had functioned just fine with the twenty or so vagabonds for hire. But that would end now. For a renovation project at a scale like this would require real builders, with skilled hands; a logistician too perhaps—someone who could oversee the monotony of the day-to-day operations. This would allow him to focus on the real work, plus prevent his hair from falling out.

There was much work to be had in the days, weeks, and months to come, however, he would not risk losing this great opportunity. It was time to free up his schedule. Already, as he sat there listening to Wendell drone on about the alchemists' wish list for the project, he visualized the look on Selvin's face when his letter of resignation eventually reached his door. And later too, when he finds out the identity of the mysterious poacher ridding him of his best talent.

Things were finally looking up.

CHAPTER 24

FALL

Amidst the licked foliage of an early autumn sunrise, nothing had felt more awry to him than an upriver wind.

There were Imian argots in the sky. Clever birds with great green wings of fur rustling like leather in the wind, traversing the river for reportable material. He had spotted one such exotic bird as he and his mother paced up and down the soggy fields of his riverside acre, discussing his latest work endeavors.

"I still can't believe you are working for the Alchemy Guild now," said Irina. "Not that there's anything inherently wrong with it. I suppose I just thought their presence was always a point of contention for you."

"Oh no. Not you too." He rolled his eyes. "I work for myself, but I will gladly take the alchemists' money."

She had a sorry look on her face, slightly disappointed. "It's just, Marrin was always good to you."

"...Not always."

"I'm sorry. I know you wanted the title, son."

"It's fine, mother. Let it go." He halted in place as if he had seen another. "Did you see that?" He held his finger up to the clouds.

She studied the trajectory of his stare.

"Up there," he pointed into a heavy glare. "There's another one."

She looked above again, then turned to him and sighed. "I do think Marrin always had a soft spot for you. He took a chance on you despite how young you were at the time."

"You think I was promoted somehow because of Father?" scoffed the man, "because he and Marrin got drunk in the same tavern every night?"

She looked positively struck, causing him to relax his facial muscles and veer away. "I was the best bloody architect at that middling company. Though who am I to say, all we ever did was fix bridges and dams. No longer."

With his schedule now clear, he came and went to that quiet corner of Taranchia every day in the weeks following.

Today was no different upon Raknia Hill, where he meticulously returned to work, surveying the bones of the old castle, taking in its limited inventory of salvageable material, whilst brainstorming a few miracle methods to breathe life back into it again.

By noontime, his rear was planted flat on the inside of a weathered shield, hanging his boots over the waves, while he sketched the many serrated shapes of the Taranchian coastline beneath him. In addition to a renovated castle, the daunting renovation he had yet to start, Wendell's requirements list included a dock. An even greater challenge at the epicenter of the dueling seas, with only but the tiniest sliver of land to build upon. Sturdy material alone would not be enough to withstand this force of nature. A special design would be required, one that could withstand the force of nature, and bend it to its will.

As he tapped his quill against a wanting sheet of paper, his thoughts went south, back home, where a great green flag appeared at sea—a gold I over a green backdrop—a stark contrast to the white-washed waves crashing against the behemoth of a ship beneath it.

He wasn't the only one that took notice. He was soon beckoned away from the ledge by one of the Guild's lackeys. The two watched as an armada with flags just like it amassed across the cheery horizon.

It didn't take but a few passing clouds before the Pebblewood River was beset by another bombardment. Yet unlike the futile defense of last, when war barrels were flung in the heart of day on an unsuspecting prey, this time the Maldinians were ready, despite being spread thin like never before. Within the frenzy of crashing war barrels and inaudible commands, the warden rang the bell of his newly erected watchtower and watched as a leviathan moth scurried off west to alert the others.

Boards no sooner crashed across the river.

Unto the Taranchian invaders came the Maldinian footmen, their towering shields repelling the invaders' swords and arrows like rain upon a tin roof. With little for protection, outside of the few salvaged wears scrounged from the weed-ridden wake of their ruined fortresses and battlefields, the arbalists at their rear made quick work of the Taranchians, filling the current with a helpful heaping of punctured souls. The luckier ones, the ones with limbs still serviceable, swam like mad for the last few jutting roots hanging off the side of the fall. The rest, the over-sodden ones, were now one with the chum.

"Warden!" he heard a voice call out, as he thrust his sword clean into an avarice's shoulder.

"Sir, I bring word from the vanguard," said a messenger upon his horse, "the enemy is landing on our shore as we speak."

"They would never." He scoffed at him.

"Sir," he said to a back now turned, "not Taranchians. Imians. A whole fleet of them."

As he backed away from the Taranchian's now overturned makeshift bridge, he had a grim look on. It was fear. For it had just then occurred to him that he had put his people in grave danger, more than any crack of any Imians' whip or cut from their scimitars could ever dream to inflict. "How many?" he asked, too busy readying his blue feathered bird to hear the other's reply.

He could visualize their plungers, and the sap-ridden rocks and gravel he and his men had dammed the secret entryway with following the failed recovery of their compatriots. A minor inconvenience for any future would-be thieves from entering the city unnoticed. As for a small army equipped with concoctions bred for destruction, activated by only a small drop of sweat, in the uncivilized hive of an insatiable beast, he could only speculate.

Atop the last leg of Sprite's Forest, he was met with an unsettling flood of muffled conchs, where he and his bird watched the Sea Sprites scramble to evacuate their women and young.

Aided by the forest vanguard, a unified force of three hundred winged spear-throwers strong, they watched the Tree Sprites bravely join the struggle against the amassing force of Imian invaders.

"You will get your people out of here, as far from here as possible," he said to an approaching figure.

"They'll never take Sprite's Forest," derided Elder Gray of Sprite's Forest. "How will they get up here without wings? They can't. The long walk around? By the time they make it to the harbor, Sapson will have more bodies than particles in the sand. What would you have me do? Our forest is our home, our way of life. If not here, then where else? To the city? Spare me."

"From where we now stand, Elder Gray, your forest and your loved ones might very well be fodder. Go south, go to the Screecher Hills. There, you will be safe, if not lonely."

The human stared yet again below, studying the whip-masters' foot-work. He could feel the quake of their tethered whips after every ruthless swing of theirs, seeking through the air for matter like a hungering tendril for light. For unlike the crowd control offered by their kinfolk's club whips, the Imian wet whip's lash struck hard as a hammer where it mattered most, with a handle as light as the cord in which it carries. A perfect tool for breaking armor, and lethal if met bare.

Outside of a stable footing on land, it seemed clear to him the Imians had little interest in entertaining such frivolous opposition. As they thwarted off the vexatious winged defenders with their slings and whips, a secondary unit cast their climbing hooks on the side of the cliff, onto a squinting ledge on the corner of the facing cliff—that same squinting ledge he and his men had leaped from during high tide.

Once the Tree Sprites had evacuated, the warden witnessed as a burst of wind, more powerful than any ocean tempest, came whirling out of the passage. The slit had shattered in the mere blink of an eye, as Imian and arthropod alike were ejected like bones, far from the cliff, some somersaulting through the air like tumbleweeds, out to sea.

His triumph in thwarting this incursion was a success. But elsewhere hope was fading fast. The Imian ships had all but left their shore, but his problem at the river had only worsened. News had reached him from the garrison at the Pebblewood River Crossing. There its defenders stood very little chance of holding back an unexpected storm. An unforeseen course, he thought, but not overlooked, for it remained the only standing bridge to accommodate a wide-scale invasion.

Outside of the arbalists, to whose understated image Maldinia's fleeting notoriety will forever be known, the stubborn descendants of the Imiandrian Empire were undaunted by the burden of plate armor, allowing for frictionless surges and over-the-head sweeps of the pale men's shells. Brutally effective in their efficiency for war, by midday the channel was theirs.

The storm came next for Plague's Keep.

Flanked by budding fields of little blue sprouts, the fort on the hillock sixty stone throws east of the Quincunx, poised little in the way of a challenge. Indeed, the mere sight of the Taranchian barrel lobbers was enough to strike fear in the hearts of its three dozen defenders.

With groundwork laid, Maldinax could do very little but prepare for the coming storm.

Conflicted in her thoughts and of those whose counsel she haphazardly considers, the queen had never felt so alone in her stone fortress.

"Plague's Keep has been captured," another flown message was read aloud by the queen. "Maldinax is within our enemy's reach."

"General Jarcentinia and his troops should be arriving there shortly." Lord Geldrin turned to the queen with an uncomfortable grimace. "Once Maldinax is secure, my lady, I assure you the general will return here."

She paced around the assembly table like an antsy bride trying to remember her vows. "What's *here*, Aloc? A rock? Your precious palace, your valley view? If I can't keep my borders and vassals safe, then what good am I? What good are any of us?"

"My queen. The enemy moves through our vineyards unchecked," added the spymaster. "Even if we do secure Maldinax, we are dreadfully outmaneuvered. I think we should heed the warden's call, and meet them head-on in Taranchia."

The woman wore a look of dread no sip of wine or affirmation alone could ease. She set her hand on the table and inhaled. "Then what are we doing holed up in here? Alert the Ascendency. We ride for Taranchia."

"But—" Lord Vodgar darted his eyes around. "As Lord Flumen has stated, we're still dreadfully outmaneuvered, my queen. And unlike us, the Imians have friends. Perhaps we can treat with them; maybe work out some terms."

"Terms?" She laughed. "I reward not one, but two acts of war with civility. King Marinus thinks me a fool. He won't expect my coming." The treasurer averted his gaze, though the kindle in her eyes was already ablaze. She started moving decisively through her marble floor towards her bedchamber. "Time to try on my wedding gown. I suggest you all do the same. And fast."

In the courtyard, amidst an assembly of readying souls, the queen met the tacit stare of her flaxen mare. A thoughtful face the creature possessed. One that cared very little for the elaborate steel casing held perfectly across her appendages, and even less for the elapsed red backdrop of the plateaus melted across her chest and shield.

She wandered off into the hedgerows, not for a distraction, but to the counsel of her late brother. Timorous and tearful as she greeted her late brother's eyes, she simmered upon end times, and whom, in victory or defeat, shall rule in the coming days.

With both eyes open, the enigmatic young soldier's crossbow was held as high as his prospects. She grazed her hand upon his plaque, reading, "Prince Maximillian Plateau III, 'The Heir-to-be,' lost his fight to lock-jaw at the hopeful age of twenty-two. "...I've never even swung a sword before," she overheard a voice say on the other side of the hedge.

"Careful there," she heard the intelligencer reply, aiding the regent with a basic, albeit misguided motion of her borrowed sword.

"Swing through your target," the queen emerged, swinging her sword with conviction. "My brother taught me that. You should have seen the look on my mother's face when she saw my brother teaching me that," she chuckled. "She was appalled by it."

"My father commanded alongside your late brother in the Desert War. The young prince was a great warrior, from what I hear."

"...He never had much of a choice."

"Are we ready, my queen?" entered the decorated ascendant supreme, Aer Paulvin Eldermore. He was only mortal, this great specimen of a human, yet upon the saddle of his great metal horse, Aer Paulvin Eldermore drew a presence greater than any living man could even dream to conjure.

She nodded. A heartening assurance trailed, for together, with her apprehensive counterparts of equally underused carapaces, all seemed, one way or another, okay.

"My ascendants," she started, inching herself from her inner circle in a gradual, forward-sweeping motion. By now, her posture was as stiff as the lateral cross across the faces of her fourscore guardians, and yet her crowned head of hair, tightened taut in a bun, exposed not a drip of sweat. "The time for diplomacy has long been severed. My naivety in wishing—waiting—for a state of peace and harmony is no longer a reality. These Imian reavers sue not for peace, but for the distinct resources of our land. But why? You might ask. While catching her breath in a gust of welcomed wind, she fished behind for approval. Together in their silence, her conviction, for a moment in time, wavered. But not enough to halt her coming thoughts.

"We are mere pawns in this veil of greed that has sulked our gardens for far too long. The guilds have nearly all but fled, but still, their grasp remains embedded within our soil like the stubborn root of an unrelenting weed. The Alchemy Guild, for one, continues to fleece our people and our neighbors with obscene, unsustainable costs for their elixirs; meanwhile, we suffer the ire. But that was then and this is now. Now, it is time that we sink these brigands' anchors. Nevermore will this ungrateful excuse of a king ravage our land unchallenged!"

A battle cry, her words induced. For others, contempt.

Barron stumbled upon Lord Vanic and three dozen alchemists just below the concealed entranceway into the Raknia Family Crypt, where he and his sitter sat hunkered in a damp cold. Although a welcomed relief, the master alchemist's demeanor was not at all welcoming. He immediately interrogated the man about his potential involvement in "the sacking of his new laboratory."

Despite a helpful reminder of his blind virtue, the master alchemist was not backing down. His operation was compromised, to say the very least, and he needed someone, anyone, to blame.

Whether a lapse of judgment or the much-needed reassurance in his trust in his partner, the master alchemist had finally allowed him in, if only a morsel, following a heated series of questions. According to Wendell, the gates of Maldinax were barred from the inside. The Imian king's chief lieutenant—"Lord Delmar," they called him—and his men had manned the ramparts on every wall, as its residents were wrangled into town square like cattle. On the back of an already waning number of peacekeepers and brave few militiamen, resistance had thus far been answered with swift retribution.

"Lord Vanic, there's a fleet out there," explained Barron's watcher. The rest of them quieted, as they awaited the master alchemist's command.

"We'll take our chances on the surface. You can come along with us, Barron."

"To where?"

"Dacmaster Castle," he sighed, "to visit my poor old ailing father."

As the disconcerted guild members rummaged through the sun-battered interior of Raknia Castle for blades not too far rusted to passably employ, Barron pondered whether remaining with this uncoordinated band of alchemists was worth the risk. Seeing these pasty lab rats and the rusty blades they had scrounged from Raknia's ruins, he was almost confident he would be safer trekking alone. But this was the coast, and out there was the savage plains.

For the sake of his flourishing business, he would comply. Of course, he gladly relished in the first opportunity he would get to slip away to the safety of his winter estate.

Low the orange horizon, down one of the many rocky knolls of the eastern coast of Taranchia, Lord Vanic scowled at the sight of the Imian king's sails, and above, where an argot flapped its glorious wings.

Later that afternoon, on a looming hill just south over the fence of Lord Stainberry's estate, the queen, joined by her council and the ascendant supreme, looked beyond to the neck of the northern river, to the scraggy canopy of the Pebblewoods; its reds and yellows and greens on the spine of its eleventh-hour preservation. However, this was no vista of anyone's dreams, but a gloomy autumn, with an unmistakable finish of burnt wood and flesh.

Her thoughts darkened, like any sane individual's would, simply imagining the horrors that awaited them at the watchtower on the world's end. And yet still she rode. Against the reservation of her council too, no doubt.

She aimed her troops towards the lonely banner waving, toward the sound of clashing blades, athwart the few abandoned, ransacked cottages left on the road unvoyaged. But no longer could the cadavers be ignored. Soldiers, and the few unlucky citizens taking their chances on the open road, were not to be ignored. Their bodies hacked up and stripped bare, lay beside their lifeless mules and carriages.

Notwithstanding the slowing interval of clashing swords heard beyond the thinning patch of trees, she kept her focus on the flag up high, synchronized in the rhythm of the beast beneath her as she gripped her longsword for a bloody match. It was far too much for her to bear, to seethe among the road, the soil, and the sprigs.

They spotted the tower first in a battle-weary sward, its braces dented, its rails chipped. It was a miracle that it was still standing. Beside it, a half-dozen soldiers were still fighting, infantry with standing shields and pikes, and arbalists, posted on the upper levels of the watch tower, readying their last few bolts of ammunition for another inbound wave of Taranchians.

But today was their lucky day. Unlike the Imian steeds' unseen, long ago plucked from these same mainland pastures, these were Maldinian warhorses, not so easily shaken by the sounds and sights of battle. Their heavy hooves jingled like bells in a cold winter, not to be mistaken by any friend or foe.

Following a fell swoop of the Taranchian invaders, the garrison had received their first real break. As for the souls of their lost brethren, they would not yet rest, for the pit was packed full of their vessels, and the fragments of the Taranchians' wet splintered barrels. "Where is he?" she exclaimed, eyeballing the warden's inimitable black armor in the pit.

"It must've been here before we even arrived," shared the ranking striper, gently acknowledging the soldiers as they uprooted the Taranchian's makeshift bridge.

Lord Vodgar sighed. "These are the reinforcements then..."

"My queen, we should keep moving," counseled the ascendant supreme, "it won't be long before we are spotted."

She held her breath, choking back the urge to cry. "Wait!" she halted the soldiers preparing to uproot the avarices' makeshift bridge. "Leave it be."

"I'm not so sure it will hold our weight," shivered Lord Geldrin from atop his kitschy yellow saddle, justly aware of his weight horseback in his comically outgrown suit of armor.

The intelligencer, who played a convincing soldier in another man's armor, approached the bridge, sending ahead his scouts. "I think it'll do." He leaped for a proper test of its flexibility (or lack thereof). "Single file, that is."

The metallic rattling of their fine fittings became quickly stifled over the whooshing wonder of Sprite's Drop, as they trotted, one by one, tell-eum teal and steel, in a last-ditch effort at a chance for a lasting survival.

Across the river, a faraway shore met the limits of their gaze, hundreds of feet below, separated by a daunting slope of weeds. There they would find a few stifled fires taunting them from afar. "So, they've gone," presumed Lord Vodgar, "we've allowed them to escape again."

"Gone? Without their ships?" commented Lord Flumen, returning with a scout from the precipice of the swishing drop. "I think not. Look, up north." Together they cupped their hands over their foreheads and watched the tail end of an absconding fleet. "They're only hiding."

"Trundles, my lord," approached another scout from the hill. "They are moving west, through Bastion."

"It's *him*. If we hurry, we can catch him," said the queen. "Lord Eldermore, send a unit to the ridge. Rain fire down upon their ships. The rest of us, we ride for war."

Aer Eldermore nodded, sending a sharp whistle through his ranks.

Lady Knish approached with a trepid look. "My lady, the air is toxic here."

"She's right," Lord Geldrin joined, sighing. "Even if we do come out of here alive...these effects, they are sure to remain."

Her eyes wandered about through the lime-tipped reeds and scraggly trees. "That I do not know, though I will not think less of any of you for turning back. Of course, if things take a turn for the worse here, I expect you to be of use elsewhere." A look of caution simmered on her council members' faces as she resituated her crown and proceeded into the tall grass.

The intelligencer clicked his tongue, collapsing in the moving line of solemn faces.

"Oleander, you're going?" remarked Lady Knish meekly, a tense inner struggle still brewing upon her pretty, powdered face.

"The grass looks green to me," he replied. "Greenish, rather." The intelligencer's parting words festered in the others' conscience, who, despite their uncomfortable disposition, had found the courage to press on. To the soldiers trotting midst their rear, it mattered very little their foundations of motivation, nor their skill in battle (or lack thereof). They were Maldinians, branded with the same plateaus on their chests and shields.

Several stone throws north, upon the second to last hill overlooking Bastion, Barron Alarie, alongside Lord Vanic and his band of wandering alchemists, came to a sudden halt.

"I count ten," whispered Wendell, prone on the other end of a prickly patch of shrubs with the rest of them.

"And us?" replied Lord Vanic.

"Thirty-four."

"Are you considering engaging?" whispered Barron aloud, rightly confused.

"I hope not," jested a guild member, raising his corroded cutlass like a last-place trophy.

"We do outnumber them," another voice said. "Look a bit small too, don't they? Like children. Why don't we send them for a little swim?" that same alchemist alluded to the cliff beside them.

"*The* Children," redacted Lord Vanic, glaring at his underling with disdain.

His many associates gave him a look as if he had two heads.

"Imian infiltrators, trained from birth," he clarified, "not some barefoot river rats from Trawl. Likely of the same sort that almost managed to infiltrate Lorea whilst we nattered the night away at the Gromula Ball.

King Marinus is here." He grimaced angrily. "That snake is probably on his way to claim his prize."

Wendell looked to him for a semblance of a plan.

"…We wait for now. Once his Children leave, we make our run. We conceal ourselves in the tall grass outside the derelict where we may properly hide our numbers." To the lightly guarded ramparts on the western wall of Bastion, he pointed, drawing many an eye. "Up the road some, on the hill, we sneak across the road unnoticed; we find something to lay across the river, then…" His thoughts were struck, earwigging a disturbance underfoot.

Tremors.

The waterside haven had soon grown heavy in a clamor, as citizens, with little in the way of belongings, piled out from the west gate, now closing, in a hurry.

"An earthquake," a few of them speculated.

"No," chimed Wendell, spotting a collection of archers inbound. "Friendlies."

"Look—the Children are getting away," an alchemist gawked. "Should we alert them?"

"No," snapped Lord Vanic. "This is not our fight."

"In peril, we ride!" they heard a voice shout outside the eastern gate amidst a commotion of heavy hooves.

The Imian king's ancillary force, whose short-lived stop had been halted by their mounted foe, altered for a last-minute defense. Using their light armor to their advantage, these descendants of the great Imiandrian Empire scaled the lesser slabs of scrap rock and wood where they prepared their slings with a prolific supply of rubble. On the ground, beneath the flimsy eastern gate, their whip-masters, their glowing blood teeming with untapped vigor, unwound their twines.

"It seems a bit dicey, sneaking about so closely to town with a battle afoot, don't you think?" questioned an alchemist.

Receiving a piercing stare from Wendell, he retracted his unsolicited thought back into his shell.

"Come now," whispered Lord Vanic.

Bereft of color and far beyond the fatigue of a hard day's work, the architect fell in line. Granted, he was likely not the only one who had recognized the implications of allowing the Imians free; least especially in the presence of his countrymen. And yet beyond the extent of his darkened thoughts enclosed, lay not the intent to speak out, but the equilibrium of a striving man's aspirations teetering.

In town, within the wake of a now felled eastern gate, a pall of sand billowed through the streets, obscuring friend from foe and horse from rider.

"Aid!" shouted the Ascendency's newest recruit, Alanthus Luca, whose cloddish frame had found an abrupt acquaintanceship with the surface.

The young ascendant's comrade-in-arms, Garris Lafitte, pinpointing his helpless cry, rushed over to slice the outstretched rope from his ankle, sending his foe onto the brunt of his spine. Assisted to his feet, the two fended off a rush of the foreigner's friends (as efficiently as one may through a few dirtied face-guards).

Her surprise attack was working, the Imians were staggering, yet she and her men, in their unwieldy suits of armor, were like sitting ducks out on the open streets of Bastion, coming quickly undone from their steeds within the amalgamating gale of ocean sands and badland dust.

Faith, not time, was an ally of theirs.

Faith, and a little upwind action. (The cough-inducing dirt that once filled the battlefield air was dissipating, a force not even the likes of the East Sea could bear.) The source of the Imians' power, the queen's men could not aptly infer, her and Aer Eldermore signaling what few soldiers they could scrounge in the epicenter of town, towards the great Trawl Tower.

In its closeness, stones were cast out from the holes in its foundation. But to no avail. The Maldinians' shields were held high, and approaching fast.

Aside from her evident lack of martial prowess, the queen's presence alone stirred even the most demoralized and downtrodden of her ascendants back into the fold. "This way!" shouted Aer Eldermore, creating a roof over a now concentrated line of fire on his queen.

The Imian king had little choice but to empty the old tower, the wet whips making quick work of their tight formation.

Aided to her feet by the intelligencer, the two deterred a violent attempt on her life, causing her to lose her left gauntlet. The rock throwers had finally found their mark, and soon her exposed flesh found serrated pieces of oxidized fragments, forcing her sword from her now bloodied hand.

Within the heat of battle, the argots had found their colors.

For the Imians, only moments from imminent defeat, they had found a glimmer of hope—the locals were returning.

Heeding their ally's call, the Taranchians' incentives had never seemed greater with the fertile valley now overwhelmed. And yet witnessing vivid windows into their town center now destroyed, they hesitated to engage. As for all the spoils that weighed down their bloated pockets and pouches, they may not have a home to return them to, nor a family to share them with.

"About time!" exhaled an Imian lasher.

"It's Skalk!" they shouted, beckoning the patchwork spearhead and his men towards the old tower. Just then a bald mortal with heavy shoulders and a sardonic grin exited the tower door alongside his avian handler. Garbed in a striking forest green and gold robe that glimmered in the setting sun, his soldiers created a quick ring around him.

He licked his lips, rolling his jewel-bogged fingers down the spine of one of the majestic birds, causing a shiver to run down its feathery spine. "Queen of the Pilfered Rocks," he spoke with a discernible accent, with a half grin fixed upon his sun-cooked face. "You have fought valiantly." He paced about. "Ill-advised of you, however, to sneak up on an Imian legion."

"You'll never take our land!" shouted a Maldinian soldier.

"The land?" he chuckled, "you can keep your farms! I now control Maldinax —yes, along with the production of your precious lifeblood. The same ones your alchemists have sought to clear our coffers for. But no longer! Me, my men, nor the young women of my isle, to whose swelling bellies harbor hope for a new tomorrow, shall no longer despair. Ascension upon us!"

"Aila Amadorus!" shouted his soldiers in their native tongue, throwing their arms in the air in the shape of an I.

Within the tail end of their short-lived moment of glory, he and his men were waylaid by a shock-wave, sending the lot of them onto their rears. "Drop your weapons!" commanded the great shadow of a man upon a flightless bird.

"Xander." She could hardly believe her eyes, his reappearance most unbecoming in an unflattering Imian array. His snatched helm, a tinge too tight for comfort, had the visible impression of his screecher's claw mark implanted within its frame. Victor and his elite probers, rushing quickly from the hole in the wall, bore similar scratches across their borrowed vests and leggings, their Imian scimitars now outstretched onto the king and his men.

"Xander, they've taken Maldinax," she meekly cried.

"Do it. Drop your weapons," called out King Marinus, whose men soundly complied.

"Why do you think I am here? Men, cage these birds." He hovered over the Imian king. "I hear your errand boy, Lord Delmar, likes to take hostages, so I thought to myself, why don't I?" One by one they snatched the Imians by their hands, binding them tautly with their own whips.

"Finish him, Warden!" shouted the treasurer, awakened from his stupor by the diligent pitter-patter of his steed.

The man's focus did not so much as falter. He set his focus westward, to the last standing gate in his way. "Get it open," he said to Lamb. "You and I are going for a little ride to Maldinax to put an end to this madness once and for all."

"Very well," conceded the Imian king, gliding on the belly of his robe through the sand and gravel. "I have been beaten."

As the warden and his hostage came upon his knelt bird, his grip wavered. The Imian king was rolling to his back, cackling, "It's time my Children!"

In the blasted gap of the eastern wall, a collection of tiny soldiers appeared—fledglings, no older than thirteen. One of them began to reach his hand into a pouch while another stepped beside him with a bladder. Victor's men, joined by the patchwork spearhead and his cohorts, sprinted for the rear wall to intercept.

"Aila Amadorus!" shouted King Marinus.

With the object's pewter shell activated, the Imian boy was soon beset by Maldinian and Taranchia alike.

Alas, not quick enough.

To the mortals caught within the proximity of its ghastly reach, the Imian plunger's unsettling emission detonated deep within their core. Their skin and wares yanked irrepressibly within its costly web, were ejected freely, toppling all and sundry in their path.

Bastion, and its flimsy walls and battered shacks, were no more. For the young ascendants, an affirming reminder of the often-overlooked wisdom of their elders before them. Yet no fireside tale or combat exercise could ever prepare any, impressionable or not, for this category of disaster.

Beyond the splintered carnage of the western gate, a stout breeze sent the last of the wrinkled banners sailing. Up the hill, Lord Vanic's company stood frozen, following the evocative release of a squillion cries.

"Come now," whispered the master alchemist, beckoning his men into the tall grass.

His men, deaf to the ebb and flow of the master's alchemist call, could do very little but witness. The architect among them, searching for a semblance of content, instead, stumbling a foot deeper, into the fringes of consideration, only to find its subjugated rhythm shattered by a familiar face.

"What are we waiting for?!" Vanic reiterated coldly from the safety of the tall grass.

The architect's attention was captured by the cry of a young ascendant, far too young to see another's pull unto the planet's roots. He shook his friend with all his might. "Wake up!" he shouted, "wake up, Alanthus!"

He stood there, hollow. "Alanthus, you fool…"

Far beyond the call to action, the young man had forfeited his life for a woman he had likely never met; for the relish of a meager wage he, nor his future family, would ever get to enjoy. *You fool*, he simmered. He stood motionless, his eyes refusing, before eventually absconding with the rest of them.

The red and splintered warden witnessed helplessly beyond at the last of the onlookers' lingering glares. He whose arm hung feebly by a thread, in another man's armor now ripped to shreds, could not so easily brook the eerie disregard, nor forget it. For now, sidetracked by the tainted coughs of a familiar tone, he had found a bit of strength left to crawl. As for the courage to meet a pair of pale eyes, he could not.

Supine amidst the pleated reeds, he witnessed firsthand the queen's gentle grace transcending beyond the physical realm.

"I am going to get you cleaned up," he said to her determinedly, frivolously sifting through dirt and blood. He gripped her waist and hoisted himself up to her face, where they both winced in pain.

She coughed. "You always were a thorn in my side."

He tightened his grip, and she began to sob in his firm embrace.

"I've failed you," he uttered. "I've failed us all. I should have killed him when I had the chance."

"You did what you deemed right, just as I have, marching here," she said, coughing up blood.

He ran his hand through her hair as the brown in his eyes darkened into a pool of mud. "...I won't allow it."

"Xander, there's no time for that. Listen...I need you to watch over them," she refocused, her eyes palpably transient. "...And watch over yourself..."

CHAPTER 25

CHANGE

Caskets of pretty petals under banners lowly waving: a memorial for the dead and a mere trifle in the greater cycle.

Uncertainty, beyond all certainty, had assumed its natural course.

As for the mislaid fallen, and their misfortunate family members, sprinkled high and low the bloodied vineyards and roads, fungi would thus serve as a last helpful set of hands. It did not have the familiar face of a family member or friend, nor one worthy of remembrance. And yet it'd be, forever and always, life's final gift of grace.

As for the waters of change, they were always free, though like the last fissure in the confines of a disregarded dam, following a great push, they were set free.

A whole season had gone since the Imian threat was dealt with, since the queen was laid to rest, and a new leader had been crowned. As another season passed, Barron and his growing team remained busy at work, completing the last finishing touches on Lord Vanic's newest trade port, far beneath a now-restored Raknia Castle.

But none such project would bring him greater joy than his once canceled project, now a reality soon to be underway.

In the musty den of the Alchemy Guild's headquarters, the mood was anything but bitter for most. For it was the eve of its demolition, and not a single tear would be wept for its demise. As for its smell, although a tinge less rancid than when he had last stepped forth through its warped halls, it was a soon-to-be afterthought.

In present company of this happy funeral were the guild heads, flirting with a climate more congenial to their malleable souls, every Maldinite worthy of matter, and of course, the mastermind behind the alchemists' newest headquarters-to-be, the Lumina Laboratory, Barron Alarie.

Save for a few choice words reserved in tribute for the late guild master, Lord Kregwick Dacmaster, purportedly killed during the Imian incursion, the otherwise lament of sorrow had been shied away at the door. "I would like to raise a vial to change," announced the master alchemist, fitted in his late father's old trench coat with a contagious smile.

He sent a reassuring nod to the realm's newest beneficiary, King Dandikauf Jarcentinia, wearing proudly his bloodstone crown, and to the residing council members who nearly unanimously nominated him: Lord Vodgar, Lady Knish, and Lord Geldrin.

Rerouted from the excitement, the architect downed his glowing beverage and looked upon his date with his arms folded. "...It's been well over a month since Duncan's last been seen. Andrea's just beside herself."

"He'll turn up," he replied, his attention overtly elsewhere.

"Barron!" called out the guild master, furtively dodging the inbound emissary and his niece. "I hope you aren't thinking of leaving before introducing me to this exquisite date of yours."

"Of course not. Vanic, this is Esca Vement," he replied, drumming up little in the way of excitement. "Esca, I would like you to meet my friend."

"Very pleased to meet you, Esca," he said, reaching out his hand.

Her face could not hide her repugnance. It was only after receiving a subtle glare from her date that she feigned a smile. "I am sorry to hear about your father's loss, Lord Dacmaster. I am sure this is a difficult time for you."

He frowned. "Ah yes, a real pity. It seems folks are just vanishing by the day. Though I should say he was not my real father. But enough about me. Lady Esca," he said, beckoning the two into his study. "I want you to look upon your date's fine work before it becomes a reality." He led them to his desk, where a familiar schematic was spread out. The towers, however, were not like those from before—they were now capped with great, big massive mushrooms. "Isn't it just perfect? Unlike this flimsy stack of wood, our new foundation will be of solid stone. Isn't that right, Barron?"

His face glowed with ambition. "Nothing seeps in or out."

"Barron worked very hard on it," she said, guided by every etiquette lesson she had ever been taught. "I hope the two of you can continue doing business together well into the future."

"Across Pelegra, Archon, and beyond."

"*Archon*?" questioned Esca aloud, turning to her date for clarity. "I thought the Luminas only grew here?"

He smirked, side-eyeing the architect. "My dear girl, who said anything about the Luminas?"

ABOUT THE AUTHOR

Jeffrey Pons is the creator of the *Returnity* fantasy series. With a passion for intricate world-building and character-driven stories, he aims to craft immersive tales that captivate readers from the first page to the last. When he's not writing, Jeffrey enjoys golf, exploring the mysteries of the cosmos, and dreaming of life by the water.

Returnitybooks.com

Instagram: @returnitybooks

THE JOURNEY CONTINUES

The sentient planet of Tethia holds secrets yet untold. As the shadows of a deeper threat emerge, alliances will be tested, and the true cost of ambition will be revealed.

Stay tuned for the next installment in the *Returnity* series.